CIRCLES MADE OR BROKEN

may channel *laran* power into whole new pathways. And in these all-new tales set on the world of the Bloody Sun, Marion Zimmer Bradley and the many talented writers who are an integral part of The Friends of Darkover lead us along such pathways to reveal many special moments in Darkover's past.

From the creation of the first Guild House to the story of a boy raised in a rebel Guild House, from the very beginning of *laran* circles to a Keeper's dangerous experimentation with *clingfire*—here are fascinating accounts drawn from the very start of the Domains through the era when they reigned supreme to the time when Terrans once again found their way to the planet and became the catalyst for changes in Darkovan society.

A Reader's Guide to DARKOVER

THE FOUNDING:

A "lost ship" of Terran origin, in the pre-empire colonizing days, lands on a planet with a dim red star, later to be called Darkover.
DARKOVER LANDFALL

THE AGES OF CHAOS:

1,000 years after the original landfall settlement, society has returned to the feudal level. The Darkovans, their Terran technology renounced or forgotten, have turned instead to free-wheeling, out-of-control matrix technology, psi powers and terrible psi weapons. The populace lives under the domination of the Towers, and a tyrannical breeding program to staff the Towers with unnaturally powerful, in-bred gifts of *laran*.
STORMQUEEN!
HAWKMISTRESS!

THE HUNDRED KINGDOMS:

An age of war and strife retaining many of the decimating and disastrous effects of the Ages of Chaos. The lands which are later to become the Seven Domains are divided by continuous border conflicts into a multitude of small, belligerent kingdoms, named for convenience "The Hundred Kingdoms." The close of this era is heralded by the adoption of the Compact, instituted by Varzil the Good. A landmark and turning point in the history of Darkover, the Compact bans all distance weapons, making it a matter of honor that one who seeks to kill must himself face equal risk of death.
TWO TO CONQUER
THE HEIRS OF HAMMERFELL

THE RENUNCIATES:

During the Ages of Chaos and the time of the Hundred Kingdoms, there were two orders of women who set themselves apart from the patriarchal nature of Darkovan feudal society: the priestesses of Avarra, and the warriors of the Sisterhood of the Sword. Eventually these two independent groups merged to form the powerful and legally chartered Order of Renunciates or Free Amazons, a guild of women bound only by oath as a sisterhood of mutual responsibility. Their primary allegiance is to each other rather than to family, clan, caste or any man save a temporary employer. Alone among Darkovan women, they are exempt from the usual legal restrictions and protections. Their reason for existence is to provide the women of Darkover an alternative to their socially restrictive lives.
THE SHATTERED CHAIN
THENDARA HOUSE
CITY OF SORCERY

AGAINST THE TERRANS
—THE FIRST AGE (Recontact):

After the Hastur Wars, the Hundred Kingdoms are consolidated into the Seven Domains, and ruled by a hereditary aristocracy of seven families, called the Comyn, allegedly descended from the legendary Hastur, Lord of Light. It is during this era that the Terran Empire, really a form of confederacy, rediscovers Darkover, which they know as the fourth planet of the Cottman star system. It is not apparent that Darkover is a lost colony of the Empire, until linguistic and sociological studies reveal that Darkovans are of Terran extraction—a concept not easily or readily acknowledged by Darkovans and their Comyn overlords.

    THE SPELL SWORD
    THE FORBIDDEN TOWER

AGAINST THE TERRANS
—THE SECOND AGE (After the Comyn):

With the initial shock of recontact beginning to wear off, and the Terran spaceport a permanent establishment on the outskirts of the city of Thendara, the younger and less traditional elements of Darkovan society begin the first real exchange of knowledge with the Terrans—learning Terran science and technology and teaching Darkovan matrix technology in turn. Eventually Regis Hastur, the young Comyn lord most active in these exchanges, becomes Regent in a provisional government allied to the Terrans. Darkover is once again reunited with its founding Empire.

    THE HERITAGE OF HASTUR
    SHARRA'S EXILE

THE DARKOVER ANTHOLOGIES:

These volumes of stories written by Marion Zimmer Bradley herself, and various members of the society called The Friends of Darkover, strive to "fill in the blanks" of Darkovan history, and elaborate on the eras, tales and characters which have captured their imagination.

    DOMAINS OF DARKOVER
    FOUR MOONS OF DARKOVER
    FREE AMAZONS OF DARKOVER
    THE KEEPER'S PRICE
    THE OTHER SIDE OF THE MIRROR
    RED SUN OF DARKOVER
    SWORD OF CHAOS

Marion Zimmer Bradley
Domains of Darkover

DAW BOOKS, INC.
DONALD A. WOLLHEIM, PUBLISHER

DAW Book Collectors No. 810.

First Printing, March 1990

2 3 4 5 6 7 8 9

PRINTED IN CANADA
COVER PRINTED IN THE U.S.A.

Contents

Introduction 9
  by Marion Zimmer Bradley

"Acurrhir Todo; Nada Perdonad" 13
  by Deborah Wheeler

An Object Lesson 29
  by Mercedes Lackey

Beginnings 40
  by Cynthia Drolet

Clingfire 53
  by Patricia Duffy Novak

Death in Thendara 63
  By Dorothy J. Heydt

Firetrap 84
  by Elisabeth Waters and Marion Zimmer Bradley

Friends 94
  by Judith K. Kobylecky

Manchild 108
  by L. D. Woeltjen

Just a Touch . . . 121
  by Lynne Armstrong-Jones

Mind-eater 127
  by Joan Marie Verba

Mists 140
  by Meg Mac Donald

Our Little Rabbit 154
  by Mary K. Frey

The Gift From Ardais 176
  by Barbara Denz

The Horse Race   191
   by Diann Partridge

The Plague   204
   by Janet R. Rhodes

The Tapestry   225
   by Micole Sudberg

To Serve Kihar   233
   by Judith Sampson

Introduction

And Contrariwise

In spite of my occasionally flippant approach to these introductions, I do sometimes take myself and others seriously; say, about three times a year. The other day I was in one of these moods, and it occurred to me to ask myself just what I think I am accomplishing—or what I want to accomplish—with a series of Darkover anthologies.

One thing that strikes me is that I have never stopped to ask myself much about what I am doing, or why. I usually know just what—on the ordinary surface level—I am doing; but it's either a fault or virtue of mine that I seldom know, very much ahead of time—or to put it more accurately, I never stop to think—about the deeper implications of what I am doing at any given moment.

Maybe that's a virtue; I don't know. For better or for worse, I tend to start things—whether it's knitting an afghan or driving across country, or a book—without any terribly clear idea of where I am going. A while ago someone asked me what I hoped to accomplish in the long run with Darkover. Hope to accomplish in the long run? I don't really know. When I start things, I am usually just going on with whatever seems like a good idea at the time. I began writing because I liked to write, and because it was the only profession I could get into, without an expensive college education, which would allow me to stay home and look after my kid—not to let him be raised by a woman whose market value was even less than mine. Also, I made it very clear to my first husband that I was not going to work eight hours at a job, then come home and wash and clean and cook while he worked eight hours and came home and put his feet up and read the newspaper. Since he didn't like the idea of sharing the housework, he let me have a go at it. And here I am.

In the same manner of taking a line of doing what seems a good idea at the time, I started a second kingdom of the Society for Creative Anachronism because I was lonely for my friends on the West Coast—and today the Society has I forget how many kingdoms, earldoms, shires, and provinces. I feel a little like Doctor Frankenstein.

And I have written elsewhere how the first few Darkover books were written because I was too indolent—or plain lazy—to invent a new world, and I found I hadn't said all I had to say about Darkover. Now there are something like twenty books, and here I am. At least one thing I am accomplishing with them is to get people thinking; for instance people are asking me what my serious artistic purpose is and where the series is ultimately going.

Well, I don't know that it's going anywhere. The one thing I've always said to myself is that the one thing I don't want is to write the same book over and over; the one kind of review I don't care for is to have a reviewer say, "Oh, just another Darkover book." If I want anything—and I probably do—it's to make some special new point with each new book. One thing I have accomplished is to get other people writing; is that good? Well, I think so, of course; and since these anthologies go on, the readers must think so, too. But serious artistic purpose? Who's kidding who? (Or do I mean whom?)

And yet, maybe this is too much to ask. Most readers of entertaining fiction—say, detective stories—are content to return time after time to the same setting, the same ideas; sometimes even the same characters. The London Post Office—fifty years after the death of Conan Doyle—still receives *hundreds* of letters every year addressed to Sherlock Holmes. The creators of Tarzan, Dr. Fu Manchu and Nero Wolfe have all approached the feeling of the Sorcerer's Apprentice—that it's easier to start something than to stop it or get rid of it again; and society richly rewards anyone who can entertain them this way. (Anyhow, it beats working.)

One idea that has somehow found lodgment in the public mind is that each story I select for the anthology is somehow official; that my approval of a story, or wanting to share it with other readers somehow gives it legitimacy in the Darkovan chronology. If it isn't apparent from internal evidence, let me state now that apart from the short stories I have written myself, no; the anthology stories are not official, or at least all of them are not. A few of them fall in so readily with my own feelings about Darkover that they might really—really in the context of the Darkovan universe—have "happened": that is, if I thought of it, I might have written them myself. But of these, there are only a sparse handful: Pat Floss' "The Other Side of the Mirror" seemed so near to what I had envisioned without bothering to write it down that now I think what happened between *HERITAGE* and *SWORD OF ALDONES* or, if you prefer, *SHARRA'S EXILE,* was probably what Pat envisioned. The stories written by Diana Paxson about early days on Darkover—say between *LANDFALL* and the Ages of Chaos—are very near to officialdom because Diana and I are dear friends, and her mind works much as mine does. The same can be said of the stories written by Elisabeth Waters, and a few other stories; as for the others, well, some of them are as near to my vision as—say—the fan fiction of Jacqueline Lichtenberg is like *STAR TREK.* Which may be much or little; perhaps a better analogy for me would be "As near to Sherlock Holmes as *THE CHRONICLES OF MARTIN HEWETT*—which I think very near indeed—or as near as the stories starring Nayland Smith and Dr. Petrie are to Holmes and Watson—namely, not very.

But getting back to this business of serious artistic purpose. I sometimes ask myself whether I have any; and the answer, to be honest, varies with my mood. Sometimes, I think; nope, no artistic purpose; I'm just having a hell of a good time—and it beats working—and I'm making a comfortable living at doing what I like best. Other times—when the wind blows from a different quarter or the stars have gone to other aspects—I tell myself that of course I am putting forth a series of very important social theories, and having a great effect upon the world wherein I live.

In fact, I can get very worked up about either of these views; which is why when some eager fan writes a letter stating either that I am a great guru of the New Age—don't laugh, I actually got introduced that way once at a convention—or contrariwise, that I am taking myself altogether too seriously, and hey, it's all just a game—sometimes I write them passionate letters three pages long—or thirteen—and sometimes I shrug, declare that it's a free country and the reader is after all entitled to his or her opinion, and file the whole thing in the wastebasket.

It's probably—I don't quite know—part of being a Gemini.

But then, I only believe in astrology about half the time. The rest of the time, I am as much of a materialist as Mark Twain, who—among other things—said of his own work something like: that anyone attempting to find a purpose or a meaning in it would be excommunicated, and anyone attempting to find a moral in it would be shot.

I feel that way, too.

But only half the time.

—*Marion Zimmer Bradley*

Acurrhir Todo; Nada Perdonad
A Tale of the Hundred
Kingdoms

by Deborah Wheeler

Deborah Wheeler is no stranger to these anthologies; I think she's been in every one of them since she made her debut in SWORD AND SORCERESS I with "Imperatrix" and followed it up with a story for FREE AMAZONS OF DARKOVER. She's been a valued contributor and friend ever since. As such, it's probably a work of supererogation—or, one might say, unnecessary, and far above and beyond the call of duty—to repeat, each time, that she holds a Martial Arts Black Belt in Kung Fu, that she has a houseful of hot and cold running cats and children.

This reminds me of a time when I was at a convention with the late Randall Garrett; he got the job of introducing me from the platform and said, "Marion needs no introduction to anybody here—" which precedes all introductions, of course—but he followed it up by saying, "so, I'm not going to introduce her," and sat down again, leaving me to introduce myself. Maybe that's what I ought to do with Deborah; there's really nothing I can say about her that hasn't been said often before in these spaces, except that she's the mother of my honorary grandchildren Sarah, nine, and Rose, who will be just about five when this book comes out; and that she has just finished a novel—I don't know when that will be out, but I don't have any doubts that it will happen sooner or later. Hopefully, sooner; I'm eager to read it again. (MZB)

The great hall of Avery stank of smoldering *clingfire*, dust, and sweat. Duncan Inverness stood in a corner with the junior officers and aides, watching the formal surren-

der and wondering, *Why did Father summon me from
Arilinn just to watch a few beaten men kiss his sword?
He was quick enough to send me there when he wanted
to get me out of the way.*

Many of the defending forces, including Lord Avery's
chief sorcerer, lay buried in the rubble of the once-
magnificent eastern tower, and more had fallen to the
swords of the Inverness troops. Duncan kept his face
carefully neutral as he watched his father, resplendent in
crimson and gold silk over his battered mail, take his seat
in the great carved throne.

Gherig, Lord of Inverness and half a dozen other kingdoms, lay his naked sword across his knees, stroked the
red-and-silver beard which was his sole personal vanity,
and ordered the prisoners to be brought before him. Behind one shoulder towered his elder son and heir, Rafael,
and behind the other, the foremost *laranzu* of his circle.
Rafael, his face streaked with smoke and dried blood
from his last berserker charge at the city gates, looked
out over the mass of prisoners with eyes as cold as a
hawk's.

Watching his older brother, Duncan shivered with
longing for Arilinn Tower and its people, who had taught
him useful work and valued him for it. Here he was nothing more than an encumbrance, with little knowledge and
less taste for warfare. The boys his own age stood in awe
of him because of the accident of his birth, while his
once-adored brother had become a blood-spattered
stranger, as quick to strangle an enemy with his bare
hands as spit at him. *I'm only here because Father thought
I was growing too soft in the Tower and a campaign might
make me more like Rafe,* Duncan realized. *Easier to put
a banshee chick back into its shell . . .*

Two burly Inverness men-at-arms dragged up Mikhail,
Lord Avery, reputed to be a ruthless administrator but
obviously no war-leader. With the death of his *laranzu*,
his effective resistance had evaporated, and now all that
remained of his psychic defenses were a few women of
minor talent huddled in the far corner with the ladies'
maids.

Avery himself was a lumpy potato of a man, his waxen

face marked by spots of hectic color on each round cheek, wearing a suit of ornamental armor a couple of sizes too small for him. He reminded Duncan of a boy he knew his first year at Arilinn, who bullied the smaller children until he learned to master his own fears.

"Always look beyond the obvious," his Keeper had repeated. *"Nothing, not physical appearance nor even* laran *is ever truly as we first assume it to be."* If Beral *was a coward underneath his boasting, what lies beneath Mikhail's mask of softness?*

Gherig adopted his sternest expression as he listened to the ritual words which completed the surrender. Leaning heavily on his guards, Mikhail knelt and kissed the hilt of the Inverness sword. Then the remainder of the Avery family—a pale wraith of a wife with a tight, resentful mouth, two tear-stained, pimple-faced daughters, and a boy well on his way to becoming a duplicate of his father—came forward one by one to swear fealty to their new lord. Gherig probably wouldn't even bother to execute them, Duncan thought, and remembered the stories of his father's first conquest, a gray wolf of a MacAldran who fought like Zandru's demons to the very last. Given half a chance, he'd have risen again, so there was no choice but to give him a quick and honorable death. As for the Averys, Gherig would only exile them, thinking them incapable of a serious threat.

The courtiers, minor nobles who'd stood by Avery from traditional loyalty, came forward next. Gherig arranged for hostages from their families and let them go with their lives and modest fines. Duncan sensed their relief, *Lord Avery would have executed us and confiscated our estates. All those stories about his hothead son slicing men to shreds for the sheer bloodlust were just soldier's tales. Inverness is a fair man . . .*

The *coridom* had been killed in the fall of the eastern tower, but his assistant waited with the rest of the household staff. Duncan was stunned by the sheer physical beauty of the young man who stepped forward to kneel at Gherig's feet. Slight but not girlish, he carried himself with a sword-dancer's grace. His red-tinted hair curled over his shoulders, just a trace long for a boy his age, and when he looked up, Duncan got a clear view of the wide, wine-dark eyes, the fine line of the beardless jaw, the full, sensitive lips. There was something both reserved and provocative about the way he stood before his new lord. Duncan considered this, together with the too-long curls—had he been Mikhail's catamite, and did that account for the perennial resentment engraved upon Lady Avery's prunelike mouth? *Too obvious, always question the obvious* . . .

Gherig gestured Duncan forward and ordered the boy, Anndra, to familiarize him with the records. Duncan remained on the dais, standing behind Rafael, bemused at this sudden turn of events. It hadn't occurred to him that his father had any actual use for him on this campaign.

Gherig dispensed with the Avery captains, again pardoning most of them with affordable fines, and sent Rafael down to supervise the cleansing of the dungeons. Rafael's men brought out the usual rabble, a handful of flea-ridden beggars squinting in the light. The first one cowered at Gherig's feet and confessed to stealing a pig to feed his family.

"Free him," Gherig commanded. Duncan smiled as a ripple of astonishment spread through the assembly. By morning, tales of the new lord's mercy would be all over the city, and he'd have a far easier time keeping order.

Gherig repeated this verdict for the other prisoners, pathetic creatures accused of relatively minor crimes. After they were gone, scuttling to whatever holes would take them, Rafael said, *"Vai dom*, there's one more prisoner, a special case."

Gherig raised one inquiring eyebrow. Rafael gestured to the far end of the hall where a slender, white-haired woman sagged between two guards. Her thin arms, scratched and filthy, shone through the tatters of her robes, and her feet were bare despite the chill. Beneath the tangle of her unbound hair, little of her face could be seen.

"We found her in a cell well away from the others. Heavily chained and guarded by this . . ." Rafael took a small box of wood and metal from one of his aides and handed it to Gherig. Duncan had never seen anything like it, nor felt anything like the disturbing vibration which left him nauseated and disoriented. Yet Gherig, turning the box over in his hands, showed no sign of discomfort.

"*Vai dom*," murmured the *laranzu* at Gherig's side.

"Yes, Aldric, what is it?"

The gray-eyed sorcerer took the box from Gherig. His usually impassive face, framed in a severely cut red beard, was ashen, almost shocky. He touched a panel on the side of the box, and Duncan's senses cleared abruptly. "This is a telepathic damper, and nothing to trifle with."

"A telepathic— What sort of prisoner needs that to guard her?"

Gravely Aldric approached the woman and stood for a long moment, scanning her for the depth and quality of her *laran*. "She has some talent, but it's deeply buried. I doubt she has more than rudimentary empathy, possibly some clairvoyance. Nothing that could constitute a military threat. You could have her tested to be sure. . . ."

"No, I trust your judgment, Aldric," Gherig replied. ". . . why would he waste this device to guard one harmless woman? *Avery!* What's the meaning of this?"

The conquered lord staggered forward, and this time there was no disguising the terror on his corpulent features. He fell to his knees before Gherig. "Lord Inverness! *Vai dom!* I beg of you, don't free her! You have no idea of the consequences—"

"What consequences? What did this poor old woman ever do to you?"

"She is an Aldaran Assassin, discovered by my circle—"

An Aldaran Assassin! Part myth, part conjecture, Duncan had heard them discussed in the Tower. Although outwardly ordinary, they were psychically implanted with suicidally fanatic killer conditioning, knowledge of their targets so deeply buried that no *laran* probe could uncover it. They behaved as law-abiding folk until the trigger code was given by their employer, when their conditioning went into operation. They were said to be infallible, a product of the most advanced *laran* technology, which is why they were attributed to the notorious Aldaran clan. Most of what was known was conjecture only, for no living Assassin had ever been interrogated. Duncan thought, *Mikhail must have kept her alive in the hope he could break her conditioning and force her to serve him, even against her own patron.*

"Aldaran Assassins are a myth, a bogey story invented to frighten wayward children," Gherig sneered. "We are not such cowards as to give credence to these tales. Yet she may not be so harmless after all. Give her a hot meal and put her back in her cell, well guarded. I'll decide what to do with her tomorrow morning. Here," Gherig tossed the damper box back to his *laranzu*. "Burn it, keep it, I don't care as long as I never see the thing again. Let's have some wine, and harpers to sing of how my son charged the Avery gates!"

But the victory feast was short, as if all savor had gone out of the rich stores. Gherig went to bed early, and alone.

And was found alone the next morning by his aides, stone cold. Careful examination of his room revealed a previously hidden passageway, its thick cobwebs recently disturbed. Rafael's first act upon assuming command was to personally hang the Averys from battlements, pimple-faced daughters and all.

They laid the body in the cold cellar until preparations could be made for a proper funeral. While the guards paced outside, Duncan sat alone in the ice-rimed chamber. Something niggled at the back of his senses, something which didn't taste right. He drew his thick black cloak around him and looked down at the stone butcher's slab on which his father lay. Aldric and the chief physician both agreed that he'd died from a single dagger thrust, the thin blade slipping between the ribs to pierce the heart.

"If the murderer wasn't actually one of the Averys," Rafael had insisted when Duncan pointed out that the family had been under lock and guard all night, "then it was one of their agents or sympathizers. Either way, the Averys were responsible for Father's death, and now I've put an end to them."

Duncan slipped off his gloves and opened the front of

Gherig's heavily embroidered tunic. The old man's face looked haggard, as if death had not yet brought him any respite from the stresses of his lifetime. Duncan parted the *linex* undershirt to expose the wound. The lips gaped a little, showing dark flesh beneath, but all traces of the bleeding had been washed away.

Shivering in the cold but unwilling to sacrifice the sensitivity of his bare hands, Duncan spread his fingers wide over the cut. Closing his eyes, searching with all his Tower-trained *laran*, he sensed the life-ashes of bone and muscle cells, the nerves lying like shriveled cords where once they sparked with energy. No hint of Gherig's spirit remained in the half-frozen husk. There was no trace of any misuse of *laran*, and after long moments of struggle, Duncan opened his eyes again. Why had he expected to find anything? Aldric, a potent *laranzu* skilled in matters of bloodshed, had declared the crime to be ordinary murder.

He gazed at his father's face, wondering why he felt so little grief. The grizzled veteran before him was a stranger. Duncan remembered a younger man, his red beard innocent of gray, who used to play with him by the fountain courtyard at Inverness, but never as long or as frequently as he craved, a man whose later visits were no more than a stormy voice brushing him aside and calling for Rafael's sword practice.

You gave me a place at Arilinn, even though you didn't know what it would mean to me. I owe you for this, at least, Duncan thought. *Rafe may think he's already caught and punished your killer, but I don't believe it.*

Duncan stepped into the street beyond the castle, his bodyguard at his heels. He paused for a moment, watching the Inverness captains organize repair crews and direct carts of hoarded grain for distribution to the townsfolk. Even here in the city, Duncan doubted there were many who'd want to bring back Mikhail's reign.

Unless, Duncan thought as he turned down a side street punctuated by entertainment establishments of the less proper sort, *unless that Assassin was involved.* Rafael had released her after the guards swore she'd been in her cell all night. An apple-cheeked scullery maid, perhaps hoping for a liaison with the younger son, told Duncan where she'd gone, an inn near the town gates. The innkeeper showed him to the private room where the white-haired woman known only as Mhari sat finishing her midday meal.

Duncan left his bodyguard at the door and sat down facing her. The woman glanced up, and he saw that she was not old. Her eyes were green like the sea, and she looked at him directly, like a *comynara* of the Towers or a bold Hellers girl. She wore traveling garb, full skirts and a wool-lined leather jacket. "I'm sorry about your father, *vai dom.*"

At her words, something broke inside Duncan, and his mouth flooded with bitterness. "Did you then repay him with a knife in his heart?"

He knew from the flicker of horror in Mhari's response that she had not. She'd been in the city well before the battle, and had spent most of it in Mikhail's dungeons. She must have been hired *before* Gherig's victory was certain. Duncan waved aside her denial, saying, "Lord Avery thought you were an Aldaran Assassin. Are you?"

Mhari sopped up the last of her thin soup with a hunk of hardbread. "If so, I have not killed anyone here," she said carefully, "so you cannot hold me accountable on that score. With both lords dead, the new and the old, all deals would be off, anyway."

"Who was your patron; can you at least tell me that?"

She shoved the empty wooden bowl and spoon across the table. "Even if I knew, which I don't, I wouldn't. What assurance could I offer if I let anybody know who hired me?"

"I'm not *anybody.* I'm Gherig's son, and he could've had your throat slit."

"I owe you for that, so I'll make a bargain, in exchange for safe passage out of the city." Duncan nodded, knowing he could easily arrange this. "The password was, 'Acurrhir todo, nada perdonad.' "

"Remember everything, forgive nothing," Duncan mentally translated the ancient words. *A rather vindictive choice of phrase.* He said, "Assuming Mikhail was right

and he was your target, who hated him enough to kill him?''

"Who didn't?" Mhari replied with some heat. "You saw his courtiers and how little love they bore him. Ask young Anndra Dell'Breya what happened to his family."

"Anndra? The *coridom's* assistant?"

"His people ruled here until about ten years ago. Mikhail took the castle in a sneak attack, put the old lord and lady and the two older sons to the sword, and took the daughter as *barragana*. She was only fourteen when she died in childbirth. What hold he's had over the boy is anyone's guess, but one look at him and you can imagine."

"How do you know all this?"

This time Mhari laughed in his face. "Liege lords come and go, but somebody's got to scrub the pots. Good luck to you, Gherig's-son. I don't envy you the scorpion-ant's nest you've stumbled into."

Mhari's words came back to Duncan several days later, as he sat in the *coridom's* office, going over the books with Anndra. The room was plain, well-lit, sparse in comfort but thick with years of leather-bound books. Anndra spread the current records out on the table, explaining everything in a dry, precise voice. The system was simple, but the required detail suggested an almost pathological preoccupation on Mikhail's part with every grain which was his, rightfully or not. Duncan glanced over the city ledgers, the records of fines levied and paid, momentarily stunned by their harshness.

"This will change," he muttered, "this pointless greed."

There was a firm tap on the door and the junior officer who served as Duncan's bodyguard stepped in. "Your pardon for the interruption, Lord Duncan, but I didn't think this should wait."

"What is it, Stefan?" Duncan got up and drew the man aside into a corner.

"You sent me with a packet of documents for the woman named Mhari, staying at the Salamander Inn, but when I got there, they told me she'd been found dead this

morning. A knife through the heart, much as the old
Lord died. I myself saw the body.''

*As the old Lord died . . . Had Gherig and Mhari been
killed by the same person?* Numbly Duncan replied, ''You
did right to tell me. Make sure Lord Inverness also hears
of this.''

As he turned back toward the table, Duncan caught a
glimpse of Anndra's momentarily unguarded expression.
Instead of the smooth mask of deference, the boy's face
flushed livid with some overwhelming, unreadable emotion. Anndra's eyes burned like two black flames, his lips
drawn tight across his teeth as if to throttle a scream, his
face first flushed, then deathly pale.

In compassion, Duncan brushed his fingers along the
boy's shoulder, an unusual touch for one Tower-trained.
Something inside the Dell'Breya boy exploded like a
clingfire missile and he cried aloud, his eyes no longer
human but miniature firestorms.

Images flooded through the widening cracks in Anndra's *laran* barriers, blotting out the quiet, sunlit room.
For a moment Duncan *was* Anndra as an exquisitely sensitive child, his talent just budding with adolescence, only
to be shredded by the dying agonies of his parents' fully
developed minds . . . *a girl's face—Lirelle!—dark-lashed
eyes the color of rainwater, a dimple at the corner of her
laughing mouth . . . his hands lashed behind his back so
tightly his shoulders almost dislocated, the flushed pudgy
face so close to his that he gagged on the wine-soaked
breath, soft hands patting him, lips pressed against his
teeth, the stinking tongue filling his mouth as Mikhail tore
his clothes away and he fled, fled into darkness lit only
by Lirelle's screams . . .*

Duncan scrambled backward, his heart pounding. His
breath came ragged, but no blast scorched his lungs or
crisped his skin. The illusion disappeared as quickly as
it had come. He took his seat, considering his next step.
The boy's traumatically-induced *laran* barriers were rapidly shredding, and he ought to have skilled Tower help
before he broke down entirely. The depth of his pain and
fury, still unhealed after all these years, dismayed Duncan.

The awkward silence had gone on overlong. Anndra, his eyes lowered under silky lashes, murmured, "Did you wish to see the household accounts now, Lord Duncan?"

"Thank you, no, you may return to your other duties. I want to review what you've already shown me."

As soon as Anndra gracefully bowed out of the room, Duncan jumped up and began pacing, as if he could walk off the questions that roiled within him. Anndra clearly hated Mikhail, but he was not the only one. Then why was it Gherig and not Mikhail who'd died with a dagger in his heart, Gherig who'd freed them? The *obvious* conclusion was that there was no relationship between the two facts, but Duncan could not escape the question. *What did Mikhail's death have to do with Gherig's murder?*

To distract his thoughts from this frustrating and unprofitable trend, Duncan scanned the neatly shelved ledgers, going back through the decade of Mikhail's reign. He took down a volume of tax rolls from eight years ago and opened it. The ink was still dark on the fine vellum, the handwriting meticulous, the contents very much the same as the record Anndra had shown him. Back toward the corner farthest from the windows the volumes were dusty, their leather spines showing age but not wear. From the time of the Dell'Breyas?

Duncan thought of how the records of Mikhail's reign revealed his personality. Perhaps there was something to be gained by learning more of the preceding lord. He picked a book from the top shelf and opened it, the pages crackling as he turned to the inscription. Dates, contents . . .

And there on the title page, a coat-of-arms in colors just beginning to muddy with time. He held it up to the window light to be sure of the motto in tiny, perfectly calligraphed letters across the family crest . . .

"*Accurhir todo; Nada perdonad.*"

The next day, Duncan sat alone in the *coridom's* office, the preliminary household inventories lying unread on the table before him. Anndra was already late, which was unlike him, but Duncan was just as glad to have a little time to sort out his thoughts. He knew now why Gherig had died, and who'd killed him, but he couldn't see a way to make Rafael listen to him, and if by some miracle he did, he'd never be free to return to the Tower again. He'd be chained to his brother's side as surely as if they were linked by living flesh. Already he pined for Arilinn, like an uprooted *kireseth* blossom withering on the stalk.

His thoughts came to an abrupt halt as he heard a faint knocking at the door, so timid, as if scarcely daring to be heard. He got up and opened the door. The girl standing outside was the same one who'd told him where Mhari had gone, and she'd clearly been crying.

"What's wrong, *chiya?*" Duncan asked, unexpectedly affected by her inflamed eyes and trembling mouth.

"Oh, Master Duncan, it's the new lord, he— he's taken Master Anndra, he'll— he says he'll *hang* him! Oh, please, can't you do something?"

"Where is he now?"

"South— south tower."

Duncan raced past her, pounding down the stone-floored corridor, up a flight of stairs, past several sets of astonished guards, up more steps. He burst on to the parapet, where Rafael had a hangman's noose around young Anndra's neck and was about to hurl him bodily over the battlement. Duncan had barely enough breath left to shout a warning.

Rafael paid him no heed, pausing only when Duncan grabbed one burly arm and yanked with all his might. Anndra, his hands bound behind him, was halfway over the slitted gray stones. Duncan pulled him back to the balcony.

"What're you *doing?*" growled the new Lord Inverness, his mouth distorted into a grimace.

"What are *you* doing?" Duncan retorted. "Hanging this—"

"This bloody-handed murderer, that's what! He's the one who slaughtered Gherig. My man found the dagger in his possession—Aldric swears it's the right one. Let *go* of me, you young pup!"

"You brainless *cralmac!*" Duncan screamed with

enough genuine outrage to penetrate his brother's killing haze. "You've already killed Mikhail Avery without stopping to think if you had the right man! Are you going to make the same mistake all over again?"

The flush on Rafael's face cleared a little. He loosened his grip, and Anndra dropped to the floor. Duncan caught the expression on the boy's face before his head fell forward, a look of such agony that it tore at his heart. "Rafe," he said, "Anndra *hated* Mikhail."

"So Father thought—trusted him—let him loose in the castle—free to come and go—to sneak around wherever he pleased."

"Won't you at least listen before you hang another man for all the wrong reasons? Rafe, you've got to hear his story before you judge him."

Finally Rafael nodded and signaled the guards at the end of the balcony to follow them to his private chambers. Gherig had originally selected this suite of simply furnished rooms instead of Mikhail's opulent quarters. Rafael took the central seat, a plain piece ample enough for his bulk. Duncan removed the ropes from Anndra and pushed him into one of the other chairs. The boy sat like a waxen image, his dark eyes lifeless, no trace of his powerful *laran* flickering past his desperately tight barriers.

"You'd better have a good explanation for this," Rafael muttered. "I'll grant you this cub hated Mikhail, but why would he kill Gherig, who freed him?"

"I didn't say he killed him."

"I told you we found the dagger in his things, and damned careless he was with hiding it, too. Aldric says it was the one used to kill Father as well as that woman from the dungeons."

"I know."

"If Anndra didn't kill Father, who did?"

Duncan took a deep breath. This was the moment when all might be lost. He kept his voice calm, using every scrap of Tower discipline, forcing the ring of truth into his words.

"You did."

"*I?*" Rafael leapt to his feet, shouting, "*I?* I loved

Gherig more than I love my own life! How dare you accuse *me,* you treacherous—"

It took all of Duncan's Tower training to stand immobile as Rafael encircled his throat with his hands, hands that had run with hot blood on countless battlefields. *I cannot fight him strength against strength. Either he will remember the love we shared as brothers, or I will die.*

After an agonizing moment when Duncan's vision swam red and then gray, Rafael released him with a savage jerk and threw himself back in his chair, obviously shaken. "Give me one good reason why I should not hang you at the side of this traitor."

"You were right, Rafe. Anndra did hate Mikhail, hated him so much he even managed to raise the price of an Aldaran Assassin. Mikhail guessed correctly; he *was* the target, although he wasn't sure who hired her. But consider this," Duncan began pacing, moving between his brother and Anndra Dell'Breya. The boy sat hunched over, his downcast eyes unreadable.

"Consider this," he repeated, praying for strength, "the Assassin was somehow discovered by Mikhail, imprisoned, even guarded by a telepathic damper lest her trigger phrase be delivered psychically. Anndra must have been desperate, having come so close only to be blocked. Then Avery fell, and he saw his new lord—just, merciful. So merciful he would not even execute Mikhail, only exile him beyond Anndra's reach. What was he to do then—allow the monster who had slaughtered his family to go on living? The monster who turned his sister into a prostitute when she was still a child, who—"

Anndra was weeping silently now. His dark hair hid his face, but his agony shrieked like a banshee through Duncan's mind.

Duncan went on. "He couldn't get past our guards to kill Mikhail himself, and he couldn't reach the Assassin, so he had to get someone else to do it for him."

"*I* killed Mikhail."

"Exactly."

Rafael ran his big hands over his face, his cheeks gone suddenly bloodless. "He killed Father so that I would

blame Mikhail— *I* would be his Assassin. I never stopped
to think . . .''

Duncan leaned over his brother's shoulder, hating what
he must do, knowing that he had no choice. "Even here,
everyone knew your reputation—berserk in battle, hot-
tempered. The harpers sang of it that first night for the
victory feast, don't you remember? You used to boast that
you were like a blade in Father's hands, that he did the
thinking for both of you."

"What of it?''Rafael shot back. "I was not the one to
creep into Father's bedchamber, *I* did not slip a dagger
into his heart—this *bre'suin* did, and he will hang for it!''
He lurched forward as if to throttle the boy then and
there. Anndra's shoulders sagged a little farther, and
Duncan knew that he would do nothing to defend himself, not even a single word of explanation.

Quickly he continued, "Had you been a man who
thinks before he kills, a man who considers and questions
the obvious—*a leader like Gherig*—then he could never
have used you, and Gherig would not have had to die for
his vengeance.''

"That's true enough," Rafael admitted, subsiding,
"and I will be the one to pay for it. But I can't let Father's
murder go unavenged.''

"Don't you think he's been punished enough—'' Duncan began, but Anndra cut him off.

"How *dare* you offer me compassion? When I was
innocent and had done no wrong, Mikhail destroyed
everyone I loved, and then would not let me follow them.
He kept me alive, at his side, in his bed, telling me how
merciful he was!'' His voice came in ragged gasps as the
fire raging behind his eyes threatened to engulf his fragile
sanity. "Now that I have blood-guilt on my hands, I don't
deserve to live!''

"The real blame for Gherig's murder lies with Mikhail, not this tormented child," Duncan said quietly. "I
wondered at first why Mhari was killed when she hadn't
fulfilled her mission. Anndra couldn't take the chance
she'd told me something vital, just as he couldn't wait
until Mikhail was in exile to track him down. So he used
the password to get close enough to kill her, and that

started me thinking of the connection between Mikhail's
death and Father's.''

Rafael nodded. ''All he had to do was nothing, and
his place here would have been secure. No one would
question him going about his duties. The way the dagger
fell out of his cloak, he *wanted* to be caught. But I still
don't know what I should do with him. Even if he did
have good cause, I can't turn him loose.''

''Send him to Arilinn for healing and training. He has
laran of great power, which he has not used against us,
not even in his own defense. He may yet learn to use it
for good. I think he at least deserves a chance to make
up for the wrong he's done.''

Rafael ran one hand through his thick red hair as his
face slowly regained its normal color. *He's not a stupid
man,* Duncan thought, *or a cruel one, but only one who
has stood too long in his father's shadow.* ''Arilinn, then,
but you'd better get him out of my sight before I change
my mind. I suppose you'll want to scuttle back there with
him.''

Duncan drew a surprised breath. He'd assumed he'd
have to stay on at Avery, acting as *coridom* and helping
his brother make the right choices from now on. He saw
how close he'd come to making a terrible mistake in of-
fering to be his brother's counselor. ''Would you really
want me here, looking over your shoulder? Even if you
didn't come to resent me, you'd never feel free to make
your own decisions, as you must.''

Rafael got up and drew Duncan into a brother's embrace. Only Duncan's *laran* senses told him how close
the big man was to tears. *''Bare is brotherless back . . .''*
His mouth muffled against the crimson leather of Rafael's
tunic, he said, ''Keep Inverness and Avery, rule them
well.'' *And let me return to my own place, my own inheritance . . .*

Gripping Duncan's shoulders in fingers of steel, Rafael
drew back. ''Where did you learn wisdom so young? Is
this what they taught you at Arilinn Tower?''

''Only to look beyond the obvious, even in the human
heart . . .''

An Object Lesson

by Mercedes Lackey

Mercedes Lackey lives somewhere in the southwest; Tulsa, I think. She is a computer programmer for an airline, with access to airline tickets, which is how I happened to meet her at so many conventions. No doubt she'll be going to them professionally now; she's written a very nice series of books, in spite of their being about sentient horses—having been brought up on a farm I have no sentimental feelings about horses. She has also written several stories in Sword and Sorceress about a pair of female adventurers, beginning with "Sword-Sworn" in S&S III and continuing with their adventures; after which she wrote two excellent books called THE OATHBOUND and OATHBREAKERS, also about Tarma and Kethry.

Now, writing again about female adventurers, she tells a story about—what else? Free Amazons. I still get more stories about Free Amazons than all other stories put together. Maybe the next of these anthologies ought to be another Free Amazon anthology. The fact that so many people continue to write about them ought to indicate that you think it's worth doing; and I'd be happy to put one together. Meanwhile, this one should hold you. (MZB)

Alina n'ha Kindra, Guildmother of the tiny Singing Waters Guild House, waited for the rest of her new sisters to settle on mats about her. Tonight's Training Session would be a little different; tonight—because of a question one of the two new girls had asked today—*she* would be speaking, rather than questioning.

There were only five expectant faces turned toward her in the twilight gloom of the Music Room. This House

trained mostly guides, and all but two of the older sisters
were out on trails tonight. Alina was one; Maia, down
in the kitchen cleaning up after dinner, was the other.

The five girls finally settled, and Alina turned to the
youngest among them. "Sabrina, you asked me an odd
question today; would you repeat it for the rest of your
sisters?"

Sabrina hung her dark head and blushed, her normally
pale face going crimson. "Guildmother, I didn't think it
was that odd—it just—I mean, I just couldn't understand—" She took a deep breath and composed herself,
raking a hand through her untidy curls. "I just wanted
to know *why,* if the Dry Town men hate us so much as
Rafaelle says, why they leave us alone? It doesn't seem
logical."

Rafaelle giggled, and Sabrina glared. Alina couldn't
much blame the little blonde for her outburst; Sabrina
was such an *earnest* child, that it sometimes seemed she
lived her life by "logical" and "Not logical."

"That is a perfectly good question, Sabrina—and as it
happens, I know the answer. It is an answer that goes
right back to the days of Varzil the Good, and to the
Sister who deeded this very land to the Guild, Tayksa
n'ha Elayna. Listen. . . ."

"Zandru's hells, I still can't believe it," Tayksa said, for
what must have been at least the twentieth time. "Peace!
I *never* thought we'd see peace!" She wriggled a bit, hoping to get the rock digging into her backside shoved over.

Deena, who was a good bit drunker than her longtime
sword-sister, laughed and reached past the fire for the
wineskin between them. Her straight brown hair stood
up all over her head like a chervine's winter coat. "I wish
some of those fools from *Dom* Andra's levy could hear
you. They think you'd fade away to nothing without
something to fight."

Tayksa snorted with contempt, and leaned back against
her pack, looking up at the stars. "That's because they
haven't got any more imagination than a rabbithorn. It
took us—what?—*three damned years* to convince them
that the Sisterhood fighters knew what they were doing;

and now that they believe *that*, they're convinced we can't do anything else!''

"Well," Deena replied, her words slurring just a little, "It wasn't one of *them* that got singled out by old Varzil for—what'd he call it? 'Conspicuous Service,' wasn't it?''

Tayksa snorted again, and grabbed the wineskin back. "Damn right, conspicuous! Pretty *damned* conspicuous, bein' the only Redshirt stuck behind the rebel lines when the rest of you pulled back! My kind isn't supposed to be conspicuous—and that's *one* time I wished I *wasn't* so damned conspicuous!''

Deena blinked at her across the fire. "Good thing you stuck beside old Varzil, or we wouldn't be *seeing* peace.''

"Well, I *was* his bodyguard and he'd gone into one of those trances of his, and I could hardly leave him, now, could I? At least old Copper-Top gave me back the family farm. I dunno what I'm gonna *do* with it, but it's nice to have it back.''

"What *are* you going to do?" Deena wanted to know. "You just hailed out of there without saying anything when they gave us leave; just wanted to know if I wanted to come with you.''

"First, I—''

"We.''

"Good enough. *We're* going to make sure nobody's 'borrowed' any of the land, and make sure my neighbors know *who* owns it again, and *who* gave it to her. *Then* we're heading down into Thendara and help put the Guild together. I've got a feeling there's gonna be some opposition. . . .''

"You, too?" Deena shook her head so hard her brown thatch trembled. "I thought you didn't put any stock in premonitions.''

"Not a premonition; it's logic. Most men aren't gonna be happy about us *or* our charter. When we were just crazed women with nobody protecting us but Avarra or our own steel, nobody cared. But with the Charter—we got *legal* protection. Man comes lookin' for his wayward wife now, we got the law on *our* side." Tayksa sat up, and her dark hair fell into her eyes; she shook it away. "No, they aren't gonna be happy. 'Specially if *comynara*

ladies take a look at us and decide they like what they
see.''

"Some peace."

"Yeah, it won't be real peaceful for us. I guess there'll
be about one *bad* incident; Varzil'll stand for us, an' it'll
all simmer down to resentment. But there's gonna have
to be an object lesson, seems like there *always* has to be
an object lesson.''

Deena ruminated over this for some time, blinking
sleepily at the fire. "I hate to bring this down out of
philosophy,'' she said finally, "but this wine is going
right through me.''

Tayksa snickered. "Teach you to drink that much.''

"I'll be right back.'' She levered herself to her feet
and slid quietly out into the darkness. Even though she
wasn't making any special effort not to be heard, she
made no more noise than a rabbithorn. That was one
reason why they'd partnered so long; Deena's woods-wise
ways, and expertise with blade and bow—Tayksa's equal
expertise with blade, and with other things—many not so
obviously weapons.

*Not much longer for bow, not if old Copper-Top gets
his way,* she mused. *Everything that strikes at a distance
is going to be banned.* She yawned hugely. *I'll give up
my bow if that'll rid us of* clingfire *any time.*

But Deena wasn't "right back''—she didn't come back
at all—and as the moments passed and Tayksa's alarm
grew, she finally figured out why.

Zandru's hells!

She called herself every name in the litany of stupidity
for not *thinking*. *Peace, oh sure, we're at peace—somebody
tell the damned* Dry Towners *that. Numb-brained city-
brat! Forgot all* about *the Dry Towners! How could I be
so stupid?* She didn't move; took care not to change her
expression or her position. *And neither of us is old or
ugly. Avarra bless, you'd* think *that after too-damned-
many years Dee would at* least *stop to take a look around
before she drops her britches! Zandru's bloody hells!*

The wine cleared out of her head far faster than she'd
hoped, and she began to *think*. Finally she had a plan;
moving lazily, carelessly—but without making a single

movement that *wasn't* screened by her body—she extracted certain very small tools from her pack and slipped them into seam-pockets in her boots. Then she yawned again, hugely, stretched, and wrapping herself in her cloak, curled up beside the fire and pretended to doze.

She'd *hoped* to get off without them hitting her in the head—but her luck didn't stretch quite that far.

She came to with a lump under her left ear, a splitting headache, and a most unhappy stomach. *They must've tied me facedown over a packbeast. If they did that to Dee—I* don't *want to be the one that's there when she wakes up.*

She took a quick inventory without opening her eyes. She was lying on her side, and from the metal burdening her wrists they'd already put the shackles on her that Dry Towners always loaded their women with. *Oh, stupid move, lads. Very stupid. You don't realize how stupid. But I do.*

She still had her boots—which was the second stupid move. All they'd done was to take her knife-belt and her *obvious* weapons.

That was even stupider.

Male voices, speaking harsh gutturals, babbled off to her right. Three of them. One spoke in tones of authority; that one paced. The other two wheedled, one nauseatingly subservient.

Pacer must be the head man. Whiner talks more than the other; he's probably the one that caught us.

A clink of metal. And a handful of words spoken in a dismissing tone.

"*Well done, my good and faithful servant. Go get drunk, and I'll have a bit of fun.*" *You think. Lady Avarra, grant Dee hasn't woken up yet, she'll get herself killed.*

Pacer's footsteps came close, stopped just out of arm's reach of Tayksa. She moaned realistically, and stirred a little. A toe prodded her in the side. She moaned again, and fluttered her eyes open.

And shrank back in what looked like very genuine fear from the bearded face leering down at hers.

Meanwhile she was taking a quick inventory of everything she could see. Which was mostly just an enormous bed, decked with costly stuffs and made of precious—to Dry Towners—wood. With no one in range of sight or hearing but Pacer. She contained her fierce joy. *Fool, oh, vauntingly male fool—you have no notion of what you let into your bedroom this night.*

For Tayksa was not just *any* women, not just *any* member of the Sisterhood.

Tayksa was—or had been—an assassin.

When her brother ran the family farm into the ground, he had sold five-year-old Tayksa away to what he *thought* was a Thendara whoremonger. But the man was no pimp; he was a thiefmaster, and he had bought the tiny, agile child with the express purpose of training her to climb into otherwise inaccessible places. And when she grew too old to fit, she had begun to take on a prettiness that had another value. That was when he trained her to kill.

You men, you fools, you never learn. You look at a pretty, big-eyed, frightened woman, and you think— helpless.

She whimpered a little, and tried to wriggle away from her captor. He snickered, sure of easy prey.

The thiefmaster had *never* been unkind—never taken advantage of his purchase. Partly that was because his taste ran to his own sex; partly because while Tayksa had been his tame thief, it would have been too easy for her to escape him, and partly because when she became his tame killer, *unkindness* could have gotten him a taste of her new-won skills. So she never had any reason to leave him.

"Now, little one, little rabbithorn," the Dry Towner said in bad *cahuenga*, "you have no reason to be afraid. I only wish to make a true woman of you."

Then came the day that her master set her to kill the wrong person—a scholar and *comyn* lord more open-minded than many, who had been guarded by the hired blades of the Sisterhood. *They* intercepted her long before she ever reached him—but instead of turning her over to their lord, they turned her world inside-out, then made her one of them.

A true woman, hmm? So what am I now, a boy?

That was why it was Tayksa who had been Varzil's bodyguard—for no assassin could ever hope to pass another assassin. The powers that great lord commanded were formidable—but not proof against treachery, poison, the knife in the dark.

She allowed him to grab her chain and haul her to her feet with it; permitted him to paw her as much as he wanted, all the time making the little moans of fear he expected. And she waited, waited while he dragged her across the harsh stone floor of the room a step at a time, waited while he pushed her down onto the softness of the bed, waited until he was at *just* the right angle—

And pulled her left hand hard against the loop through the front of her belt, whipping the length of chain—*just* long enough—around his neck and pulling it tight as she shoved her knee into the small of his back.

His neck broke with the *snap* of a dry branch. She got herself free and scrambled to her feet, standing back from the thrashing body that voided itself in death and made a real mess of the expensive bed coverings.

When he finally stopped kicking, and she was certain the noise wasn't going to bring anyone, she turned her attention to her bonds. Maybe those chains gave other women trouble—they hardly hampered Tayksa's movements at all. But then, how many farmgirls or pampered *Comyn* ladies could scratch the back of their necks with their toes?

Her boots yielded a lockpick, which made very short work of the manacles, and a thin, keen-bladed knife, which dealt with the belt. She spent just enough time to free the chain from the belt-leather; a length of chain was a useful weapon, even against a sword.

Now—what do I remember of Great Houses? Her mentor had made her study common plans of all house-types, even Towers, on the grounds that you never knew where you might find yourself held. . . . *Where are they likely to have put Deena?*

There were little cells, she remembered now, where new captives could be held pending the whim of the chief of the Great House. Tayksa didn't often have reason to be glad that she was considerably prettier than her sword-sister. *Now* she was. Given choice between her and Deena—

The fool chose me. Thank you, Lady Avarra.

There would be guards in the anteroom outside the bedchamber. Not necessarily even human guards; Dry Towners were known to have made treaty with *cralmacs* before this. No matter. Tayksa didn't intend to leave by the door, anyway.

Deena was *quite* awake, and glaring with red-eyed rage at the barred door to her cell when Tayksa opened it. They'd shortened her chains right down to a few links, so that her hands were pinioned against her belly, and they'd shackled her ankles as well. Small wonder the Dry Towns bandit chief had chosen the—apparently—fragile Tayksa; if Deena had done what Tayksa *thought* she might—

Her expression went from purest rage to purest joy when she saw *who* had opened the door. Her whispered exclamation had all the fervor of a shout. *"Tay!"*

"Shush. I got the guard to these cells, but there may be more within hearing." The cell was nothing more than a plain stone cube, not even a pallet to cushion the floor. Tayksa knelt beside her partner and began working on the locks. "What'd you *do* to them? Zandru's hells, you could have gotten yourself killed!"

"What?" Deena looked bewildered. "I woke up and found myself—oh, the short leashes. I gave them a little trouble when they jumped me; I guess they figured prevention was better than singing soprano. How did you—"

"Later." The lock of the right manacle clicked open; Deena held still until the left did as well. "Bastards are a lot bolder than they used to be—properly speaking, we weren't on Dry Towns lands at all."

"That's because the Domains have been busy fighting each other instead of keeping this scum where they belong," Deena snarled. "Seems like as long as it's only a couple of peasant women or one of those bitch Sisters that gets taken each year, the lords don't give a hang.

Idiots, fools, and cretins! *One* of these days it's going to be a Lady of the Comyn that's kidnapped out of her own Domain, and *then* what will they do?''

"Profess great sorrow and write her off," Tayksa replied cynically. "*No* woman is worth that much fuss. *You* know that; that's why we're forming the Renunciates." She sat back on her heels and stared at the stone wall over Deena's shoulder. "Remember what I said about object lessons? Feel like delivering one?"

"Huh?" Deena rubbed her wrists and looked at her quizzically. "Like what?"

"Like teaching these sons of *cralmacs* that you don't take action against a Renunciate, and do it *now;* write the lesson in such bloody letters that they'll *never* forget it." She shuffled over a bit and began working on the irons pinioning Deena's ankles.

She felt a shudder run through her partner's limbs, and looked back over her shoulder at her. Being raised as an assassin had given her a rather peculiar outlook—and there were times, she knew, when she frightened even her long-time partner.

"Do you mean what I think you mean?"

Tayksa nodded curtly. "Kill 'em all, and let the gods sort 'em out." The lock on the ankle-bar popped, and Deena shook her legs free. "Well?"

Deena sighed. "I'm in."

The armory had been right next to the holding-cells; both women had supplied themselves with bows and several quivers of arrows. Deena had gone to unlock the doors of the women's quarters; and to place balls of oil-soaked rags in all the windows she could reach. Tayksa went off on her own quiet little hunt.

The guards were *not* expecting arrows to come flicking down the corridors at them; nor thrown knives, nor someone swinging down from above with a garrotte. In a way, this was reminiscent of her last big job before she'd been caught. She'd employed the same tactics there, too. And with the same success.

Haven't lost my edge.

She jimmied the locks on all the doors she could find,

jamming them *shut*. This was going to be a most interesting evening for the inhabitants of *this* Great House
when the fire-arrows flew. She wondered how many of
them would have the wit to go out the windows.

She met Deena in the hall just outside the women's
quarters; pried the window open, and took a quick look
around. Two of the moons were up; which, she couldn't
have said. Their light showed that this window let onto
the back of the Great House, and the open space between
the House and the stables. There was no betraying flicker
of movement to show that this area was patrolled.

"Looks clear. Think you can still remember how to
get to a roof if I lead?"

Deena groaned, but nodded.

"Give me a breath, then follow."

She slipped out the window; found easy finger- and
toe-holds on the rough sandstone blocks of the face, and
began the climb upward. In a moment she heard the hiss
of cloth against stone, a faint rattling of arrows in their
quiver, and Deena's nervous panting.

And this is an easy *climb. Oh, well, I'm lost in a forest.*

They made the flat roof in good time; Tayksa slipped
over the edge and huddled against the low parapet for a
moment, checking for guards on the roof. There were
none, and she chuckled a little under her breath at the
chief's laxness.

Or pride. It might be counter to his kihar *to admit he
needed guards on his roof. The gods know.*

Deena sprawled over the edge of the parapet a moment
later; Tayksa steadied her, then led her in a bent-over
scramble across the rough stone of the roof to the farther
edge. The L-shaped stable was just within jumping distance.

She made the leap without thinking; heard Deena's
muffled yelp, felt the other land sprawling beside her.

"Next time *warn* me—"

"Get out your firestarter," Tayksa replied, peering
through the moon-cast shadows. Let's give them a warm
night."

First to go up were the piled bales of fodder just outside the stable. Next were the balls of rags Deena had

wedged in the windows. By the time they ran out of fire-arrows, half the Great House was ablaze, and the din was enough to wake the gods.

And the running figures—*easily* identified as men by dress and lack of chains—were *so* easy to pick off with the light provided by all the fires.

At some point, just before they ran out of arrows, someone let the panicked horses out of the stables. The two on the roof exchanged a single look when it became obvious that the frightened beasts were going to pass directly below their perch in a few moments. "Never argue with a gift from the gods," Tayksa said philosophically. "And besides, my arm is getting tired."

"It's a good thing these Dry Towners never heard of the Compact," Deena observed, slinging her bow.

Tayksa laughed—and then the herd of horses came blundering around the corner and it was time to pick one and drop. . . .

"It *is* a good thing the Dry Towners hadn't heard of the Compact," Sabrina observed soberly. "But, Guild-mother—Tayksa was not a very nice person."

"Which is why you will not hear of her very often," Alina replied. "And yet the Guild has much to thank her for. She took on tasks that many of her sisters were too—fastidious—to deal with; and this very Guild House is built upon the farmland she deeded to the Guild at her death. She is buried beneath the armory; that is why the plaque is on the wall there."

"The one that says 'Let those with clean hands recall that they owe this to those whose hands are dirty'?"

Alina nodded. "Indeed. And that is the lesson for you all tonight—the lesson that the Dry Towners learned so well that even today they shudder when they speak of Tayksa's Shainsa Massacre."

Beginnings

by Cynthia Drolet

Cynthia Drolet made her first appearance in one of the funniest stories to appear in SWORD & SORCERESS V; *the very funny "Dragon Lovers." This time she brings up a matter which has been neglected in the tales of the Comyn: "the great gulf which is beginning to separate those with* laran *from those without it." Yet that is one of the basic problems laid out on Darkover since the very beginning. And therefore, with good reason, Cynthia Drolet has called her story "Beginnings." And so we see that she can be as good in writing a serious story as a comic one. (MZB)*

"No, *leronis,* you are wrong!"

Though I was half the room away I could feel each one of the boy's muscles trembling and I knew it was only his fear—and his sorrow—which spoke so boldly.

"I am sorry," I told him with a sigh. It was that awkward moment that I always dread so, for I have never found the right words to say. What words are there, after all, that a half-grown child will truly listen to, truly understand? No matter what words I use, they all seem to hear the same thing.

That they have failed.

That not only I, but society, has rejected them. That they have been found unworthy, inferior.

And most disappointing of all, that they are not special.

How does one explain to a child about latent or recessive genes that may well be passed along to their children, or even their children's children? How does one explain the importance of every individual on a world where the human population numbers only in the thousands? How does one explain that all children carry within themselves their own special abilities, without which the fabric of society would be thin indeed? Children eight, nine, or ten don't want to be told such things. They want to be told that they, too, have those powers of sorcery—*laran* they call it now—that they've heard about since the time they were suckled at their foster-mothers' breasts.

It is not the children's fault, of course. From birth children are now being conditioned to believe that *laran* is the greatest of all gifts that can be had. Relatives, friends, or even strangers inquiring after a new mother will ask first what sex the child is and next, their voices falling to a near whisper, "Is the child thought to have *laran?*"

So they are brought to me—young boys whose voices will start to crack within the year, young girls whose cycles will be upon them before their next birth days.

Eager and anxious, trembling with the need to be different, they stand before me. Eyes big with the question so often thought about, so often dreamed: Do *I* have *laran?*

I look. I test. I evaluate. I judge. And then I pass sentence.

The young boy gazed at me with defiant eyes, his little fist clenched tight around the dull blue stone in which not a flicker of light had shown. Another head-blind child without *laran*. Another disappointment. Another failure.

"It comes to some later, I've heard."

The boy's voice was tight and full of unshed tears. I heard the question behind his words, the desperation, the hope that there was still hope.

Of the hundreds of children I had turned away, perhaps a handful of them, with smug shining faces, had returned to me after puberty, and the stones I handed them had lit with the living glow. Only a handful.

"To some, but only a very, very few." I saw the determination in the young face that said '*I* will be one of those very few,' and I closed my eyes in pain, wondering not for the first time, nor very likely the last time either, why I had chosen to give myself so much pain.

But, of course, it had not really been my choice at all.

I was eleven when Rafe found the cave. It was high summer and the threat of the Ghost Wind loomed over us daily. My foster-mother had warned us not to venture too far away from home, but the all-too-seldom-felt warmth of the sun tempted us past the limits of our earlier explorations.

We were to the base of the northern hills when Rafe shouted in excitement. The cave was not deep—in fact, the stray red rays of sunlight that angled in touched the far wall, faintly illuminating it. Ordinarily such a find would have not rated more than a quick look into the cave and then on to more interesting discoveries.

But this cave was far from ordinary.

The far wall sparkled like a starlit night. Tiny blue crystals gathered the feeble red light and flung it back at the sun. And in the upper right quadrant, shimmering palely because the sunlight barely reached that high up, was a small moon in the starry sky.

"Merciful heavens." Rafe swore softly as he advanced on the crystal moon. But even as he approached it, his body came between it and the sunlight and the little moon darkened. He retreated to the mouth where I was and we both just stood there, spellbound, for several heartbeats. Then Rafe started to inch forward again.

"Do we dare?" I asked.

"If we don't, someone else will. A cache like this won't remain long hidden." That was Rafe, always practical. But I could see that even he was a little fearful. He went up to where the moonstone was lodged and I held my breath as he put his hands to it. The sunlight on his back exaggerated the red highlights in his coppery hair and for a moment I imagined I saw flames dancing there. The muscles in his back and shoulders tightened as he tried to move the stone, then relaxed when he gave up the effort.

"It's no good. I can't budge it. We'll need tools. Metal ones if we're not to damage the crystal."

"Metal? Who's got metal to lend?"

Rafe grinned. "Did I say anything about *asking* for a loan?"

"Rafe!" I was appalled. We had all been taught that, next to murder, stealing was the most serious of all crimes. People here had little enough without others trying to take what they did have.

But Rafe just smiled. "I only plan on borrowing some for a little while. And besides, who would think to punish us after we bring the crystals to town?"

I knew a number of people in New Skye who would, but I held my tongue. Rafe was older than I.

The next day I met Rafe as planned in a small field just outside of town, where the ripening grain stalks swayed and nodded in the brisk breeze that was blowing down from the mountains. Rafe had with him a carefully wrapped bundle, and the MacAran twins, Camilla and Lew, were tagging along behind him. I grinned. Nothing could be kept secret from the twins for long.

Rafe noticed my grin and scowled. "They caught me in their father's barn—with these tools," he admitted. "I had to tell them what we were up to."

"I'm glad," I told him. I liked the twins and knew we could use the company. And the extra hands. Like me, Rafe and the twins had also thought to bring along small sacks to carry the crystals back in. I wondered how much we'd get for them in trade. Enough, I hoped, for the stag pony I'd always wanted.

"Did you get the candles, Margoli?" Rafe asked.

I showed him the two slender tapers I had managed to smuggle from the kitchen.

"Then let's go." He swung the bundle of tools to his shoulder and we were off, Rafe in the lead, myself second, and the twins bringing up the rear. The warm air drew sweat from our skins which the steady wind kept sucking dry, cooling us off. It was a perfect summer day.

When we got to the cave, the sun was not yet high and the cave, still in shadow, was dark. I lit one of the candles and we entered. The tiny candle flame reflected from a hundred jeweled faces. Light seemed to shimmer off the walls of the cave like sunlight off of snow. A dozen such candles burning in that small cave would surely blind us, I thought.

"Come on." Rafe urged us into action. "Wick and wax won't last long."

"What do you want us to do?" Camilla asked. Like me, she and Lew were only eleven, so leadership naturally fell to Rafe, the oldest.

"Start gathering the smaller crystals. Margoli and I will work on getting the big one loose."

For the better part of the morning we worked, Rafe gently coaxing the crystal from the wall with a small chisel and awl. The first candle burned down to nothing and the second was half gone when, with Rafe's triumphant cry, the huge crystal came loose at last.

The twins tugged Rafe out into the light to get a better look. I followed more slowly, something prickling the hairs at the nape of my neck now that my attention wasn't absorbed in candles and crystals. Rafe knelt with the crystal in his lap and Camilla and Lew bent over it, their sun-red hair blowing across their eyes. The crystal seemed to mesmerize them, and when I glanced over, I saw why. Deep within the stone a pale fire was stirring.

"No!" I cried, throwing my cloth sack over the stone. The three faces contorted as though I had physically wrenched the crystal from them.

I met their angry stares. "We shouldn't try the big one until we can get the smaller ones to work for us first. It might be dangerous." How I knew that, though, I could not say. Like the others, what little I knew about the blue stones came from watching a few of the adults handle them. The stones were forbidden to the children since they held a power that had yet to be fully explored.

Nevertheless, by instinct or by an awakening of something within me by handling the stones, I knew that we were not yet ready to try to master the big moonstone. I took four small tear-drop shaped jewels from the number that Lew and Camilla had gathered and handed them around. Rafe scowled when I gave him his. Whether he was upset because I had usurped his power over our little group or because he was impatient to begin work with the large stone I didn't know. I suspected it was because he was angry with me—Rafe had always liked power and the position of authority. Throughout his childhood he had kept company almost exclusively with children either his age or younger; children he could exert control over. Not that he was ever cruel or hard or forced any of us to follow him. He simply expected us to support him and we did—his was that kind of personality.

"Now, look into your stones," I told the others. "Try to make them—" I searched for words I didn't have, "—come alive."

"How?" Camilla asked.

Again I didn't have the words. "By concentrating. By *wanting* to make them glow." I stared into my stone and almost immediately blue light flared within it and the jewel grew comfortably warm in my hand. The light within waned and flared, waned and flared, pulsing with my own life rhythm. I lost myself in the bright jewel while the wind blew on around me.

I don't know how long it was before I tore my eyes away from my stone and saw that Rafe had only managed to produce a faint flicker in his, and that the twins' stones held no sparks at all. Lew and Camilla were staring wistfully at me and Rafe. Not knowing why I did it, I reached out and touched first Camilla who was closest to me and then Lew. As my fingertips touched them, I felt a shock run through us and a spark of blue seemed to dance along the line where flesh met flesh.

They cried aloud, first with surprise and then with joy, for a tiny blue light appeared in each of their crystals. I heard them laughing and realized with a shock that neither of them were laughing out loud. Their eyes reflected their laughter, but the emotion came from *within*. Somehow I was sharing their thoughts. Curious, I shifted myself so that I could put an arm around each of them, hugging them close. There was a sensation of warmth, security, and love. I felt Camilla there in my mind like a fire-tailed comet and Lew was there like a huge granite wall, stolid and unmoving. I could feel their excitement and I could feel them reaching out tentatively with their minds and touching me back.

Then Lew put out his arm and drew Rafe to him. Camilla moved around so that she, too, could touch Rafe and we held to each other in a small, unbroken circle. At our touch I saw the fire in Rafe's jewel flare up from a mere spark and I eased into Rafe's mind, finding that he was like an elusive shadow, almost insubstantial.

Camilla's own arm had found my shoulder and so when I reached down to draw the cloth sacking away from the moonstone, we were still in contact. I lifted the jewel and placed it in the center of our circle and watched the light within it grow. There was a curious tugging sensation in my chest that spread outward through my body and I realized belatedly that my crystal and my pulse had changed to match the pulsing of the fire within the moonstone. The other three jewels resonated in perfect cadence with the moonstone as well. I felt myself drifting, thinning, twining, no longer an individual—no longer Margoli—but a part of a greater whole. I was not scared— the feeling was far too pleasurable for fear, but something pricked at the back of my—our—subconscious. Some care. Some threat. Something to be attended to.

But nothing seemed more important at the moment than the sharing we were experiencing. The dissolution of self into self was a pleasure beyond anything we had ever experienced. Like disinterested observers we watched our bodies begin to move, shrugging out of their cumbersome clothes. Our bodies clung together, touching in ways that we'd seen adults touch. Moving in ways that we were only beginning to dream of in the night. We saw blood, but there was no pain. Only pulsating warmth and pleasure that built and built, sustaining and sustaining, until all awareness focused on that intolerable pleasure and it burst at last, thrilling us through in its aftermath.

We disengaged then, bodies and minds, slowly gaining back separate identity. My first awareness as Margoli, single and unique once more, was that it was deep twilight, the sky already well purpled over the mountains. The next thing I noticed, even in the failing light, were scattered blue petals and a faint dusting of gold in the creases of my body.

"The Ghost Wind!" Rafe had recognized the signs as

well. "Hurry! We have to get back to the settlement quickly."

He was right, of course. To be in the open like this, far from the protection of our homes, when the Ghost Wind blew was almost certain death. I glanced up at the sky. No clouds. This, then, was only a lull in the Wind. It would blow again tonight. And if the Wind blew the *kireseth* pollen as strongly in New Skye as it blew here, then the others there, parents and foster-parents alike, might not even realize we were gone. And even if they did, they might not be able to withstand the effects long enough to search us out. We were four frightened children on our own in the night.

Lew heard the shrill cry first.

"Ya-men!"

We all froze, straining to hear, too, and on the breath of wind that blew over us we all heard that flesh-prickling cry.

"They're coming this way."

Somehow I knew it wasn't fright that made Camilla speak so. There was a—knowledge—in her voice that I had never heard before. I had always thought of Camilla as a shy, uncertain girl-child who would be happy sitting in her home birthing babies all her life. Then I remembered the impression of her I had gotten in our rapport: the fire-tailed comet. Had contact with her crystal changed her so much so quickly? Or was that simply a secret part of her which had always longed for release?

"How could they know we're here?" Lew asked.

Camilla shrugged. "They smell the power I think. They know we have the crystals."

"How do you know that?" I heard the anger in Rafe's voice, sensed the thought beneath the words: *another one trying to undermine my authority?*

I shook my head to clear it. Surely I was just imagining things. The Ghost Wind did things to the mind better left forgotten.

"I don't know how I know. I just do." I could feel the distress in Camilla. But I could sense, too, that she was telling the truth. For whatever reason it had happened, she *did* know.

"How far away are they?" Lew apparently believed her, too. After all, they were twins, sharing that special telepathy that most twins, identical or otherwise, have. I wondered if maybe I had picked up some of that ability from them.

"Not far. They'll be here soon."

"What should we do?" Lew asked.

Camilla looked stunned. "How should *I* know. I only know they're coming, that's all."

"They'll be armed," Rafe said quietly. "They always are when they attack the settlements."

I bit my lower lip. The seed of an idea was forming itself in my mind, but it seemed too crazy to be worth pursuing. No one else, though, seemed to have any other suggestions to offer, crazy or otherwise.

"Maybe we can use the crystals to help us."

"That's been tried," Rafe reminded me. "Remember *Dom* Beltran? He did something to their minds when they attacked his home, but they killed him anyway. There were too many of them for him to handle."

"There are four of us," Camilla reminded him.

Rafe turned to Camilla. "And how many of *them* are there?"

She seemed to sink inside herself as she considered his question. "Eighteen certainly. Maybe nineteen."

Rafe paled and I knew he hadn't really expected Camilla to be able to answer him. But the certainty of her voice was beyond question. "We can't stand against that many."

"Not alone," I agreed. "But what if we tried standing together? Didn't you feel the power when we were connected with the moonstone?"

"She's right," Lew said. "It could work. Besides," he gestured toward the sound of the approaching Ya-men, "what other real choice do we have—aside from dying?"

So maybe the idea wasn't so crazy after all. One other saw sense in it. And again I caught a flash of Lew-as-granite-wall, stolid and unwavering.

Rafe sighed. "When the possible is no longer possible—"

"—do the impossible," Camilla finished. She reached out and took Rafe's hand. Then Lew's joined hers.

With a sinking heart I saw that there was no recognition of the physical contact as there had been before—no shock or blue light coursed between the flesh this time. Slowly, without much hope, my own hands joined Lew's and Rafe's.

I gasped.

Whether it was me or simply the fact that I completed the circle, we all felt the shock of contact once more. A little more surely than before, I reached out and collected our minds into a single focus and the moonstone in the center of our circle glowed with an incandescence that lit the darkened sky for several paces around.

"They're here." It was Camilla's voice, but I knew she didn't speak the words aloud.

"What are we going to do?" That was Lew's question and when I heard it, I nearly panicked. I guess I had thought that somehow the moonstone would provide the answer.

It was Rafe instead who did. "Think fire. It's the one thing the Ya-men are afraid of."

We thought fire. Camilla thinking of a hundred burning candles, Lew of pit-tamed flames, and I of torches. It was Rafe who got through to us and caught us up in his thoughts of fire running wild, eating the land as it ran. Fire, uncontrolled, terrified me, but I knew the Ya-men terrified me even more. With a cry I gave my thoughts up to the thoughts of the circle, feeling Camilla and Lew join in until we were meshed in the circle as closely as when the Ghost Wind had brought us together.

Only this time pleasure was replaced with pain.

It began slowly, a few sparks blazing in the brown grass at the Ya-men's feet. Sparks which were joined by more sparks as the Ya-men rushed in on us. A hot blast of air drove them back to where the sparks had become flames and the flames merged into a wall of fire. The smell of burnt flesh sizzled in the air, a fragment from Lew's heightened senses.

The Ya-men, screaming, began to run from the flames, moving upwind to escape. But the fire was no natural one and it raced after the Ya-men, spreading around them, overtaking them, burning them alive.

The screams were deafening. A hundred Ya-men could not have screamed so loudly. Then I felt the air hot in my throat and my own skin was suddenly burning, my own flesh melting from my bones. Fear tore at my heart and the pain was so intense that I longed for death to take me quickly. Near me, in my mind and in my ears, I could hear Camilla screaming and screaming and screaming.

_"We_ aren't burning!'' Lew's thought was ragged, almost lost in the screams, but I forced myself to listen, forced myself to look out over my body and see that I sat upright, unmoving, hands clenched to the others' hands. The pain and the burning were the Ya-men's, focused through Camilla and passed along to us.

I pictured myself mentally slapping Camilla and was a little startled to find that it had some effect. Camilla stopped screaming and the Ya-men's thoughts blurred.

"We have to break contact!'' I shouted, though I couldn't tell if anyone heard. I focused on Camilla, not sure what I was doing, moving purely out of instinct. Gently I eased her out of the circle and the pain left with her. Next I nudged Lew out of contact and the fearful taint of burning flesh dissolved.

I turned to Rafe and tried to reach him, to disengage him from the lure of the moonstone.

"Rafe!'' I cried, but all I found was flames. Everywhere I looked I saw flames, and out where the Ya-men all lay burning, I saw a fire out of control.

"Rafe, it's over!'' I tried again to break his contact, but he was far beyond my untrained powers.

So I broke contact from him and from the moonstone. Lew and Camilla were leaning over him, slapping his face, trying to get him to open his eyes, to respond. I could think of only one thing to do and I did it, without thought as to consequences, not knowing what the consequences could bring.

With Lew's help, I tore the stone out of Rafe's hand.

If I had thought the screaming of the Ya-men was terrible to hear, I soon learned that there was something even more terrible. The screams of a friend in torment.

And more terrible than that was when they stopped—abruptly, as if his vocal cords had been severed.

Then Rafe's body spasmed—his back arched, his legs and arms went rigid. The spasm lasted maybe fifty heartbeats, then his whole body relaxed like a rag doll suddenly dropped to the ground.

It happened twice more, the spasming and the relaxing, but the third time was the last.

It was Lew who refused to let me cry, who pressed me to gather him and Camilla back into the circle and control the raging fire. With just our small stones we would never have been able to stop it, but with the moonstone it was the work of only a few minutes before the fire had been reduced to ashes and the ashes to dust.

Then we held to one another and cried.

We learned many things that day—that it was possible to combine our powers and focus them through a single matrix. And that there were matrixes on the planet that could amplify those powers dangerously.

Most importantly, though, we learned that children with *laran* should be taught to control their gifts before they could damage themselves or others. My gift, it appeared, was to bring out the *laran* in others. A catalyst telepath they call me now.

So Camilla and Lew and I used the moonstone one last time to erect a tower to the west of New Skye where we could teach those with *laran* how best to use it and how best to avoid it using them. With matrix power we laid pale blue stones one atop another, interconnecting their electrical fields to hold them together.

The tower is everything we hoped it would be—a training ground for those who have the talent. An experimental site where new powers are tested and new techniques are perfected. Where half-remembered technologies are resurrected.

But there is still much to learn.

What I fear most, though, is not the *laran* itself, but the gulf that is beginning to separate those with *laran* from those without. But mine is not the *laran* that can see into the future and so my misgivings may only be the muddled thoughts of an old woman.

Still, things are changing and it takes no powers of farseeing to observe that. Already people are beginning to move into the hills near where we've built the tower. New Skye Tower we named it in our language, the language of the first settlers. But language is a living, changing thing, and already those who are moving into the area are corrupting the name, running the words together, and adding a lilt to it so that it takes on a whole new sound.

Neskaya.

"Perhaps all this is for the best," I tell the angry, head-blind boy that has no trace of *laran* and never will. "Yours can be a normal life."

But my heart is breaking as I send the boy away.

There is no such thing as normal anymore.

Clingfire

by Patricia Duffy Novak

Coryn Hastur, Keeper of Hali Tower, and Arielle appeared as characters in my STORMQUEEN (1978) and "Clingfire" tells me more about them. This is the kind of story which isn't nearly as frequent as it might be, but exemplifies the kind of story which I like to read. All too many stories, especially those laid on Darkover, tell me nothing I didn't know before. In this story there is a serious moral dilemma; and I feel strongly that a story should be about something. This one is.

Born in Boston, Patricia Novak spent several years in Zaire, as a vocational agriculture teacher for the Peace Corps. After spending a year in Washington, DC as an aide to a Representative, she returned to school and presently holds a position as an assistant professor of agricultural economics. She is still in the "trying to figure out what I'm doing" stage of fiction writing and says "Clingfire" is her first fiction sale, though she has had research articles published in academic outlets. She is married to another professor of agriculture and has three cats and two dogs. She should keep it up; this is a good start.

The six were linked in telepathic communication, minds conjoined, pouring their energy toward the Keeper whose hands extended into the circle, toward the matrix, directing the flow of the force. They were narrow hands, delicately bonded like a woman's, but no one, looking at those hands, would fail to see their strength. Coryn Hastur, Keeper of Hali Tower, was one of the most powerful

53

telepaths in the Domains. He knew this and accepted it with neither pride nor humility; it was all he had.

Coryn's angular face furrowed in concentration and drops of sweat beaded on his brow as, one by one, he pulled the molecules of precious copper up through the stubborn rock. Hard work and he hated it, but had the circle been holding properly, he would have been almost unaware of it. Something was wrong, his control was slipping. There was a cramp in his leg, he realized with the outer shell of his mind, a bad one, one that must have been building for some time. With the barest flicker of consciousness, he directed an irritated message to Aliciane, the young monitor, *Can't you do your job? Pay attention!* Instead of responding as he wished by easing his leg muscles, the monitor grew flustered, and he felt her agitation flow along the link, snapping his hold on the circle.

While the others of the circle blinked in confusion, Coryn turned to the monitor, his face white beneath flame-bright hair. "Stupid girl," he spat.

The girl looked frightened. "I'm sorry," she said meekly.

"Sorry!" he mocked, flushing with anger. "If you cannot monitor properly, then go back home and be put out to breed with the rest of the cattle." His voice was ugly and hard and he saw the girl cringe, but he didn't stop; he couldn't. "All that work wasted!" He flung out his hands in disgust.

"Coryn, don't." Mira, an older woman with whom he'd worked for years, had recovered enough to speak.

He glared at her without speaking, sent her a mental slap with his *laran,* and then stormed out of the room.

Still shaking with rage, he rushed along the corridors of the Tower, hardly knowing where he went. He found himself at ground level, stepped through the protective force-field, and walked out onto the grounds. He hated mining metals. It was exhausting, boring work, a waste of his abilities, and now, a whole night's work had been lost because that cow of a girl did not know how to ease a cramp.

He walked along the lake shore, allowing his jangled

nerves to be soothed by the whispering of the cloud-waves. He wanted Mira back as monitor, did not want to suffer through the training of that half head-blind girl, but Mira had to work in the circle now that Arielle had been called home.

Gods, how he wanted Arielle! He had known all along that her father would not let her stay in Hali indefinitely and had thought he was prepared to let her go. But he missed her. Zandru's hells, how he missed her.

He sat down on the damp ground by the lake and pulled up handfuls of marsh grass, only to toss them angrily aside. *Bare be back without brother,* he thought, repeating the old adage to himself with grim irony. His back was watched all right, but with suspicion, not protective fidelity. He had been sent to Hali Tower when the first throes of threshold sickness came on him and as far as he knew would never be allowed to leave. No hold, no hall, no wife. All the things a Comyn lord was raised to desire, his brother had denied him.

He dreamed for a moment of being master of his own hall, wondered how it would be to father children for his own pleasure rather than at the command of the *leroni* who ran the breeding program. For a second, he saw in his mind a pretty tableau, himself and Arielle, their children before them, warm and contented at a cheery hearth.

A random thought, like a stone thrown in a pool, shattered the pleasant image of his dream. *A Keeper holds power,* he thought, and he loved that power, was exhilarated by putting his will to trial in the matrix circles. There was the clean satisfaction from devising something new that no one else had yet envisioned. The Keeper's life had been thrust upon him; he had never chosen it, but it had its compensations.

He felt himself growing calmer, the terrible flare of his temper dying back into ashes, and as his rage deserted him, he became aware of other sensations. His stomach growled and he felt suddenly light-headed. He needed something to eat; it was always so after working in the circles, and he had been too angry to stop and take something before leaving the Tower.

He stood up slowly, brushing the dirt from himself.

Well, there was nothing for it, he had to go back and make his peace with the others. Then with one of the sudden mood changes that both exasperated and delighted his friends, he burst out laughing. *Holy Bearer of Burdens,* he thought remembering the things he'd said, *there'll be hell to pay this time.*

When Coryn had left the Tower hall, Mira moved to comfort Aliciane, the young monitor, who seemed on the verge of tears. "Take something to eat, child," the older woman said. "Come." She led the girl to a table at the back of the room where refreshments had been laid. "Do not mind Coryn. He did not mean it."

The girl snuffled, allowed Mira to feed her some dried fruit, but didn't say anything. Mira put an arm about her. "He is irritable lately, *chiya,* more so than usual."

The girl wiped at her eyes with the back of her hand. "Surely, child, it is not so bad as that," Mira said. "We have all been the objects of his rages. He misses Arielle. That is all."

They ate in silence for a while and then Barak, the circle's technician, came up beside them and poured himself some wine. "Coryn should not have spoken to you so," the big man said to Aliciane, shaking his head. "He is worse than ever lately. It is a pity his brother will not allow him to marry."

"It would not much matter," Mira said, giving Alciane a pat and turning to Barak. "Even if his brother allowed him to wed, it would surely not be to a dowerless *nedestro* daughter of a Di Asturien."

"Aye," Barak agreed. "It has been hard on Coryn, but still I wish he would exercise more control of that temper."

Coryn, appearing in the doorway in time to hear this last, laughed and said good-naturedly, "It would be well if I could, Barak. I am detestable, a banshee," he grinned, "or at least as hungry as one in a feeding frenzy." He moved with catlike grace to the table, helping himself to juice and sweet cakes.

Mira let him eat and then sent him a thought. *You hurt*

Aliciane's feelings badly, Coryn. How can you be so un-kind?

I did not mean it, Mira, he answered. *You know I did not.*

But she is not used to you, as we are.

Coryn put down his cup, went humbly to Aliciane. "Will you forgive me, cousin?" he asked. "It has ever been so with me. My mouth opens of its own volition and words pour out before I can even think them." Aliciane smiled a little, and he took her hand. "There, now say we are friends, *chiya,* and I will get us both some wine."

Alciane accepted his apology and he talked with her for a while, bantering and teasing, until she was laughing with him and good humor was restored all around.

Coryn settled himself comfortably into a chair beside Mira. "You can be charming when you have a mind to," she observed dryly. He laughed.

The next night, Coryn worked alone. He was supposed to be resting, but he had come so close, during the last war, to understanding the nature of *clingfire* that he could not let it go. He took out a beaker, one he had bound with the matrix so it would not shatter, that held just a bit of the dark red substance which would, he knew, if it touched his flesh, burn and burn, all the way to the bone.

He had little concern for his own safety, but he hated working like this, alone, whenever he could find the time, instead of in the circle where he would be able to try things he did not dare do by himself. With the Domain now at peace, there seemed little opportunity to exercise the full range of his considerable talents. *Another war,* he thought idly, *would be nice.*

With skill born of long practice, he focused into his matrix, felt his mind's power sharpen into a penetrating knife. With eyes closed, he saw the *clingfire,* magnified it, magnified it again, and again, until he was staring at the very structure of its atoms.

Here and here, he thought, *are the points of instability. If it could only be made to explode by itself, what a weapon it would make!* He studied it, touched it with *laran,* as he had so many nights, and then he saw how he might use the instabilities one against the other to make it combust from within.

He saw it, and he could not stop himself from doing it. Carried away by the rush of his discovery, he pushed against the bonds of the atoms and felt them yield.

Coryn saw an explosive flash of light, brighter than a hundred suns, heard a roar louder than thunder in the Hellers, and then he saw and heard no more.

She stood at the open door of his room, not knowing how best to approach him. *He must hate this,* she thought, *being forced to sit quietly in bed, eyes bandaged, as the long days slipped by unheeded.* It could have been so much worse, she knew it, and feeling a sudden chill, she pulled her shawl tighter about her shoulders. The matrix-bound beaker had not quite held against the force of the explosion but only the fragile lip had given way. His wounds had been caused by the flying glass fragments; no *clingfire* had reached him.

She felt him touch her with his *laran*. "Arielle?" he asked, turning his bandaged eyes toward her. "Can it truly be you or am I dreaming?"

"I am here, Coryn," she entered the room, carefully closing the door, and sat down beside him on the bed. "I came as soon as I could."

"And are you glad to see me, *chiya?*" His voice betrayed an uncharacteristic uncertainty.

"Very, very glad," she answered.

"But my eyes?"

"Your eyes will be fine. Mira told me."

"And my face." He indicated the hash of red welts on his cheeks.

"You were never so terribly handsome, Coryn Hastur, that a few scars will make that much difference."

"Not so terribly handsome?" He pulled her to him. "What a blow to my vanity! I thought I was the most beautiful Comyn lord you'd ever seen." His breath was hot against her throat and his hands fumbled at her clothing laces as he whispered, "How much I've missed you, *preciosa.*"

Gently, she pushed him away. "Coryn, you should not. You are not yet well."

"Well enough," he laughed. "And it has been well over a tenday since I've worked the matrix. I'm full of energy. You'll see." He pulled her back toward him more insistently.

Arielle laughed. "You are incorrigible. But first let me tell you the good news." She pulled away from him again and this time she kept his hands locked in her own.

"I have just come from Allart and Cassandra. They send their wishes for a speedy recovery, and, oh, Coryn!" she squeezed his hands. "Allart has persuaded your brother Regnald to allow you to marry whomever you wish."

"How did he do that?" Coryn asked, dropping her hands and sitting up with interest. "For I swore it was my brother's intention to keep me forever in Hali Tower."

"And so it was," Arielle agreed, "but Allart has offered to wed one of his Elhalyn cousins to your brother's *nedestro* heir if he will concede this favor. The alliance with Elhalyn will assure his *nedestro* son inherits and he no longer fears your claims."

"How good of Allart!" Coryn said. "But why would he do this for me?"

"Apparently the girl was already much taken with Regnald's son and threatened to throw herself from a Tower if she could not have him, so it was not too difficult a bargain. And you know that Allart and Cassandra remain fond of you even if you did send *clingfire* against them and try to pull a mountain down on their heads."

Coryn laughed. "Those were good times," he said, then quickly added, "No, *chiya,* I don't mean that I wanted to hurt Allart or Cassandra, I was sorry they were caught in Damon-Rafael's web, but it was such interesting work!" He smiled and patted her hand. "And you were with me then, *preciosa.* "

"There's more," she said with rising excitement. "Allart has offered to dower me if I will guide a fosterling through threshold sickness. I need not come to you a poor woman. That is," she hesitated, "if you want me."

"Want you? Want you, *preciosa?* Let me show you

how much I want you." She leaned into the proffered circle of his arm and he ran a hand along her shoulders, took the silver butterfly clasp from her hair, and then turned her toward him with urgency.

"Gently, Coryn, your eyes," she whispered.

A little later, Arielle sat before the glass, carefully rearranging her hair. Out of the corner of her eye, she watched Coryn who was lying back on the bed, hands behind his head, face turned in her direction.

Arielle gave him her sweetest smile, although she knew he could not see it. "I cannot stay long," she said, regret evident in her voice. "The Elhalyn fosterling is fast upon the threshold and I must earn my dower. Shall I tell Allart and Cassandra to expect you as soon as the bandages are removed?"

"How's that?" he asked, coming alert. "Why so soon? It will be some time before you finish your duty to the fosterling, will it not?"

"That is so," she said answering his last question, and then explained, "but Allart's cousin is already handfasted to Regnald's son and Regnald is eager that the *di catenas* ceremony take place. If that is accomplished before we are properly wed, then Regnald may decide not to honor his end of the bargain. There is no reason why we cannot marry while I earn my dower. Allart has no objections. He himself has offered to perform the ceremony for us if we wish."

Coryn didn't say anything, but Arielle, long attuned to him, felt him struggle with doubts. "Coryn?" Tears blurred her eyes and her voice broke. How many times had he sworn to her that his dearest dream was to be lord in his own hall with her as wife? Why now these doubts? She forced control of her emotions, as she had been trained to do, and when she spoke again it was with an even cadence. "What is wrong, Coryn? I sense some struggle in you."

He hesitated. Arielle could feel him trying to give order to his thoughts. *"Chiya,"* he finally began. "I do want to marry you *di catenas* and become a fat and lazy landholder. It's just that," he paused searching for words, then shrugged and continued. "I just don't want to leave Hali yet. The *clingfire,"* he said and his voice grew enthusiastic, "I have almost discovered how to make a weapon from it that will be ten times more powerful than any we have! And then, I have discovered something else in the earth, another mineral that might be made to explode. I don't want to stop just yet, Arielle. Not before I finish this. Couldn't we wait a little while? Or couldn't you come back here after your duty to the fosterling is over?''

Arielle heard few of his actual words, but with her sensitive inner awareness, she caught and held their meaning. She felt, for a moment, as if she were seeing him from across a vast distance, but with clarity, and he was, in that moment, like a towering mountain that she perceived for the first time in its entirety instead of stone by stone.

Then the moment passed and her control shattered and words she hardly knew she spoke burst from her lips in sharp gasps. "Coryn, no!" she cried and all the color drained from her face. "These weapons, your *laran*. It is an obsession. It is a sickness. It is just like *clingfire*. It will eat you to the bone." She stopped, unable to continue, and ran from the room.

"Arielle, come back," she heard him call, but she would not, not now, not ever.

A few hours after Arielle had swept out of his room, Mira came to see him. She found the young man sitting on the floor, casting stones into a cup, using *laran* to aim. *Does he have no idea how badly he hurt her?* Mira wondered. Aloud she said, "I thought you might need some company, Coryn, but I see you are not upset after all."

He put down the stones. "Arielle told you?" he asked, but it was not a question and he did not wait for an answer. "I don't know what to do, Mira. I don't want to lose her. I'm delighted my brother has agreed to our marriage. But I don't want to leave yet. Surely, we can wait a bit or else she can stay here. I don't much care about the dowry. I want to finish this work I started."

"That work nearly blinded you and may kill you yet." Mira's voice was stern.

"Oh, that was just carelessness, *breda*. I won't be so foolish again. I must get Allart's permission to work with the *clingfire* in a twelfth-level matrix so we can harness that force. What a weapon it will make!"

"I can see you are far more interested in the *clingfire* than in Arielle," Mira said with acerbity, "so I will leave without giving you her message."

"No, no, *breda,*" he protested. "Of course, I want Arielle's message, but why won't she bring it herself? Surely, she is not still angry?"

Mira felt herself more irritated with Coryn than she had ever been before. He could be so thoughtless, so unaware of how he hurt people. Although she had planned to deliver Arielle's message gently, she spoke bluntly instead. "Arielle is gone."

"Gone?" Coryn looked stricken and spread his hands before him in a gesture of supplication. "Gods, where did she go?"

"She's gone back to Allart and Cassandra and has said she will wait three tendays to hear from you, no longer. At the end of that time, she will let her father arrange a marriage for her. Now that she will have a dowry, a suitable match can be found."

"Three tendays?" Coryn seemed stunned. "Will she not come back?"

"She swore she would not."

"Oh, *breda,*" he whispered. "What am I to do?"

"It's your life, Coryn. You must decide." And then, sensing his pain, she added more gently. "You are a talented *laranzu* and I will be sorry to see you go, but here is your chance to attain the things you say you desire."

Aliciane was monitor. She had gained mastery over her *laran* and could now adjust the circle easily. The six were locked together in concentration, and energy flowed along the links toward the Keeper who, with a thin, determined hand, directed the flow to a row of batteries. Except for the scars that burned like lines of force across the Keeper's narrow face, it seemed on the surface that nothing had changed. But on a deeper level, nothing would ever be the same. Coryn Hastur, Keeper of Hali Tower, no longer deceived himself about what it was in life he wanted.

Death In Thendara

by Dorothy J. Heydt

*There is a constant controversy in the world of sf and
fantasy whether the Darkover stories should be called
fantasy—or science fiction. My answer, in congruity with
what I said in the introduction, tends to vary with my
mood. I think, for instance, that DARKOVER LAND-
FALL is very definitely science fiction, though it deals
more with the sociological problems of colonizing a new
planet than with spaceships per se; as for the others, it's
hard to tell, though I am equally sure that
STORMQUEEN, though based, I think, on solid science
is fantasy.*

*But I have never been surer of anything that the stories
Dorothy Heydt has written about that odd couple, Donald, Terran, and Marguerida, Keeper, are science fiction—unless you could call them detective stories? At
least this one is a whodunit.*

*Dorothy Heydt lives in Berkeley and is married to a
computer wizard; which makes it possibly easier to think
in terms of fantasy. Her kids, who seem to be growing
every time I see them—kids do—one of each kind, are
almost frighteningly articulate; it comes from having parents like this.*

*Dorothy, too, is working on a novel; so I'd better enjoy
her short stories while she's still writing them; some day
a novel editor will grab up this major talent, and then
what's a poor anthology editor to do? (MZB)*

The man had not been dead long. The heat of his blood
still rose like smoke from his body, making the dust

motes dance. The little flies were only beginning to descend to see what they could find.

A single blade of sunlight slanted over Marguerida's shoulder, splitting the darkened room in half, lighting up the dust and the flies. *Laran* showed her more: a shabby table with a dust-smeared top, a shabby chair thrown sideways to a filthy floor, a family of crawling things slipping through cracks in the walls to fight the flies for their dinner. It was not a likely place to find a man, even a dead man, so well-fed and so richly dressed. The silken folds of a scarlet cloak rippled about the mound of the dead man's belly. Marguerida took a step forward, and the sunbeam slipped over the glimmering silk to strike green fire out of the dagger hilt that rose out of his chest.

Someone has saved me the trouble.

Marguerida took a deep breath and let it out again. There was a fragrance in the air, pungent, medicinal, and almost strong enough to drown out the stench from the street. The building against which this shabby little hut leaned looked like a warehouse; there might be hay in it, or resinwood—but it didn't smell quite like resinwood. She might have put a name on it, if her mind weren't so dulled with fatigue; and she might have put a name to that other thing as well—

There were voices behind her, down at the end of the twisted alley, voices in the spaceport dialect and the sound of footsteps. "Are you sure? I never heard a damned thing." The flat inflections of a Terran's voice; Marguerida had heard a dozen like it already.

Three men came into view as she turned in the doorway; a Darkovan wearing the tunic of the Guard, and a pair of Terran city police in their drab uniforms. *"Vai leronis,"* the Guardsman said, shock in his voice. "What in the world are you doing here?"

"I heard a scream," she said.

"So did we," the Guardsman said. He was a short, mouse-colored man, perhaps twenty or twenty-two, handsome but for a scar that ran down one side of his face. "Did you kill him, *vai domna?*"

The two Terrans glanced at each other. Plainly they had been about to ask the same question—and in no such respectful tone. One of them was tall and beefy, almost fat, with skin like curdled milk and hair as red as Marguerida's own. The other was little and slight, with delicate features and skin the color of a Terran chocolate bar; she had never seen anyone like him before.

"I did not," she said.

"Did you see anyone?"

"No." Then her senses sharpened a little, and she said, "But there is someone near here—in that warehouse, perhaps—who is badly frightened and trying to hide. Anyone who lives around here might feel like that at the approach of the Guard. I would still suggest, if I may, that you go and look for him."

"We'll do that," the big Terran said after a moment. To the Guardsman he said, "Rafael, why don't you see the lady home—"

But Marguerida had gone into the hut and was bending over the body. "Don't touch anything," the Terran said sharply.

"I shan't," she answered. "A Terran of my acquaintance told me how you can tell who's been handling a thing from the patterns of his skin. I don't want to disturb them. He hasn't been dead very long; but long enough, I fear. His personality is dead. There's nothing left but a whiff of basic identity, like the smoke from a burnt-out candle."

"Do you know who he was?"

"Oh, yes; a petty criminal named Tamiano, no job too low, no reasonable offer refused." She bent lower. "Now, this is interesting—"

"*Rafael,*" the Terran said.

"He's right, *vai domna,*" the Guardsman said. "This is no place for one of your station. Please let me take you away."

I've been living off the barren side of a winter mountain, and last night I helped to kill eleven men, Marguerida thought, *and will you now offer to shield my sweet innocence from the harsher things of life?* But she rose in apparent meekness and let the Guardsman lead her away. The man's offense had been wiped out in his blood; if not by her own hand, then by any hand whatever that the gods had chosen for their instrument. She was not inclined to be finicky about it.

"Well, I can't say I'm sorry," Donald said, and began to cough. The breathfire he had been keeping at bay this tenday was making another attempt on his weakened defenses, and the Terran physicians had put him to bed as soon as they had their hands on him. The black of his hair stood out like ink against the pallor of his skin and the unnatural whiteness of the Terran bed linen. "Not that I bore any personal grudge, not really; but this planet will be better off without him."

"He tried to kill you. I resent any man's attempt to interrupt the life of my sworn paxman."

Donald smiled, for she had only sworn him to her service the night before. "Even retroactively? You lend me grace, *domna,* but please don't take the trouble. As you say, the gods took care of it."

". . . She was using *what?*"

"Thornleaf. It grows up in the mountains." The door had opened and a pair of Terrans had walked in; Marguerida brushed her veil back over her face, though she knew at least one of them. Jason Allison had received them when they came to Thendara that morning and had some kind of liaison office with Lord Regis Hastur. The other man Marguerida didn't recognize: some tall thin Terran wearing sterile Terran white and looking out of cold Terran eyes.

"On the third day after the crash—*s'dia shaya, Domna Marguerida,* good morning, Mr. Stewart—the patient developed an inflammation of the lower respiratory tract, locally known as "breathfire" and resembling pneumonia in most respects, but the infectious agent is fungal. By the evening of the fourth day the patient was febrile and comatose; at which point, fortunately, this lady appeared on the scene." Jason turned to Marguerida again and bowed. *"Vai domna,* may I present Dr. Ronald Curtis, who has just arrived from Terra. Dr. Curtis, Lady Marguerida Elhalyn, of Alba Tower."

The Terran raised one pale eyebrow and extended his hand. Jason made a jittery motion as if to try and stop him; but Donald had explained this Terran custom and Marguerida was long enough Keeper to touch whom she would. The thin hand in hers was warm and moist. *I suppose the reverse of the old saw may hold as well: warm hands, cold heart.*

"Thornleaf . . ." Curtis mused, as he looked at the panel of strange-colored shapes at the foot of Donald's bed. "Well, you could easily have done worse." (He sounded as though the admission hurt him.) "This white count is a lot higher than I'd like, but with the infection he had that's hardly surprising. Yes, you did the best you could."

"Thank you," Marguerida said. Her voice was mild, and perhaps the Terran could not see the glint in her eye through the red mist of the Keeper's veil.

The door opened again. "Mizz Elhalyn? Oh, there you are." These were two more Terrans in uniform, wearing insignia of a spaceship crossed in saltire with a sword. "Come with us, please; we've got some questions."

"Now, just a minute," Jason Allison began.

"It's just routine," the other Terran answered, and indeed he sounded bored and indifferent. "We've got the body of a murder victim down in the morgue, and we need Ms. Elhalyn to make the identification."

"Surely the city police who brought him in can do that."

"Probably they could, but we can't find them."

"Can't *find* them?" Marguerida murmured. She and Donald exchanged glances. "Why don't I go and look at this dead corpse, Donald, and I shall bring you word." Donald inclined his head, and Marguerida walked between the pairs of Terrans like a queen reviewing the troops, and out the door. The uniformed men hurried to catch up with her.

They fell into step on her right and left side, an action designed to make her feel like a prisoner under guard, but Marguerida's bearing kept them from bringing it off. It is possible for one person dressed in green, among a thousand dressed in red, so to walk and stand and hold herself as to make *them* feel out of place. Marguerida, her head high beneath her tattered veil and her frayed robe flowing behind her, made her Terran escort look like stable boys pressed into service as honor guard, and more than one Terran office clerk dressed in sensible shorts or jumpsuit felt uneasily that she had too little on.

The dead man was cold now, lying in a cold room under a cone of blue light that made him even colder. A servitor dressed in deep red turned back the cloth that covered his face. "This is the man," Marguerida said. "At least, I can tell you that's the man I found dead this morning. When the doctors allow my paxman Donald Stewart to get up, he will identify him for you as Tamiano, all-purpose middleman in that unpleasant quarter where we found him."

"That won't be necessary," Jason Allison told her. "The Thendara police know all about him."

"But that's not the knife that killed him," Marguerida went on. "Did you find it in the body like this?"

The guards exchanged glances. "The autopsy hasn't been done yet," said the man in red. "He's just as he was brought in. What do you mean, it's not the knife?"

"The knife I saw in his body was old," she said. "It was well-made and the stones in it were real. It was Tamiano's own knife and had been with him for a very long time; I think his family must have come down in the world."

"How did you know that?" said one of the guards.

"When an object has been with a man for a long time, when he has used it often and is familiar with it, then it takes on an image of his nature. I don't know how to say it in Terran."

"Psychic resonance," Jason put in.

"Resonance, thank you, that's a good word. That knife had resonance with Tamiano's life, and also with his death, because it was the knife that killed him. The shock of the death lay over the pattern like a film of dirt. This knife—" she moved closer and held her hand near it.

"Don't touch it," Jason said. "Not till they've checked it."

"I don't need to. This knife is new; no one can have owned it for more than a few days. It hasn't even any trace of its maker, because it was made quickly and impersonally and without care.''

"Yes, it looks like standard Terran Zone trade goods,'' Jason said. "Take home a souvenir of scenic Darkover. Who's doing the autopsy? Dr. Ching? I'll leave him a note.'' He touched a panel on the wall. "To Dr. Ching from Dr. Allison. When you do this Tamiano autopsy, I'd like to sit in; there's some indication the knife in the wound was substituted after death. I can get hold of an endonanoscope if you like, to look at it in situ. See you then.''

He turned round and smiled blandly at the scowling guards. "Will that be all, officers? Thank you very much. *Domna* Marguerida, I'll take you to lunch and explain what parts of the menu you'll want to avoid.''

"She's not to leave the Complex!'' one of the guards said.

"Really?'' Jason said, still with that smile. "Is she under arrest?''

The guard glared at him.

"By your leave, *vai domna,*'' Jason said, and led Marguerida away.

"Why should I not leave the Complex?'' she asked when they were out of earshot.

"Because they suspect you of having killed him,'' Jason said.

"Is that all? What would they do if I had killed him, as I intended to?''

"Attempt to arrest you, get overruled by the Legate once Lord Regis had spoken to him, grumble a lot, and close the case officially unsolved,'' Jason said. "I am surprised, frankly, that they're putting as much diligence into this case as they are. Like most of us, they're overworked these days, and they don't really *care* who did in a petty hoodlum from a Thendara slum.''

"But what about the knife?'' Marguerida said. "I can understand someone stealing the old one, which was valuable, but why put that piece of trash in its place?''

Jason shrugged. "Maybe someday we'll find out. This is the cafeteria.''

A jumble of sights, sounds, and smells, stuck through

at odd angles with the random thought-fragments of people who had never had to learn to keep their minds in order. It was like a bowl of poacher's stew with all the claws and spines left in, and Marguerida clamped down her thoughts as hard as she could. "I'm sorry," Jason said. "It is rather confusing, isn't it? One learns to shield against it. I can get you a telepathic damper to help you over the hard parts. Would you rather do that before lunch?"

"No. I can cope with this, and I'm hungry."

He led her to a wall full of Terran machinery and showed her how to push the buttons. They carried their own trays with their own hands (*get used to it,* Marguerida told herself, *the Terrans have thousands of machines and no servants at all*) to a cluster of tables by a window looking out over the spaceport. Two men were rising from a table as they came to it, trays full of wrappers and trash in their hands. One smiled at them and said, "Hi, Jason. We're done here;" but the other dropped his tray, scattering his little shreds of plastic all over the floor, and knelt down to pick them up.

Jason and Marguerida set their own trays on the table and bent down to help. As they both reached for the same shred, the man's hand brushed against Marguerida's and jerked back as if her fingers had been red-hot. But when they all got to their feet again, his face was bland. " 'Scuse me," he said, and carried his tray away to dump it in a trash bin.

"What's the matter with him?" Marguerida said.

"Well, it could be your Keeper's robe, and the color of your hair," Jason said. "That's Robinson, the Trade Commissioner; he's been on Darkover long enough to acquire a certain respect for the Comyn, even if it's mostly based on legends and street talk. In addition to that—forgive me if I speak frankly—you are not an unattractive woman. I know, I know, you spent years being trained never to notice things of that kind, but if you spend much time in Thendara, let alone in the Terran Zone, you will have to take them into account. Robinson would have seen you first as a pretty woman, and then the tales would flash into his mind about how a Keeper can burn a man to death with a touch. . . .''

"But not in an ordinary social gathering," Marguerida said. "He would have had to do something threatening. Step on my toe, at the very least." And they laughed, and Jason asked how Marguerida had come to acquire a Terran paxman, and they sat down and ate their lunch.

They put their own trays into the trash can, to be recycled (as Jason explained it) back into more plastic. The two guards met them at the cafeteria door, standing shoulder to shoulder like a barricade. "We've found Kevin Price," one said.

"Congratulations," said Jason politely. "And who is Kevin Price?"

"He's the police officer who brought in the body of Tamiano," the guard said.

"And did he explain how or why the knives were exchanged?"

The guard grimaced. "Price will never explain anything again. We found him in a supply closet with an oxygen tube around his neck."

"Dead?"

"You bet, dead. So now we need to ask Ms. Elhalyn: Where were you around 1300?"

"Twenty minutes ago? We were both right here, eating lunch," Jason said. "You can have your pick of five or six hundred witnesses."

The guard said a Terran word Marguerida did not know. "Then it's the man."

"What man?" Marguerida asked.

"Stewart. He was right down the hall."

Marguerida took a silent breath, and tucked her hands safely into the depths of her sleeves. "And where is Donald Stewart now?"

Donald was still in his bed, with a guard outside the door. Another man in a guard's uniform was inside, tall and narrow-eyed, pale from years under Darkover's cool sun. *"Mierda,"* Jason muttered when he saw him. "That's Commissioner Grey, Security."

"There you are, Dr. Allison," the Commissioner said. "I've just been explaining to your—uh—patient here, ordinarily there would be difficulties in deporting him before he's released from the hospital, but as I understand it his condition is stable and he can be transferred directly into the sickbay of the *Crown Imperial,* which lifts off at sunset. They'll continue the treatment you've outlined.''

"Do you think you'll get my cooperation on this?'' Jason asked quietly.

"I think I'll do it with your cooperation or without it, Doctor. Perhaps you'd rather discuss it in the privacy of your office?''

"I'll stall them for a couple of hours,'' Jason told Marguerida in *casta.* "I can't promise more. You'd better see Lord Regis, and quick.'' He followed the Commissioner out the door.

"All right,'' Donald said. He was lying back against his pillows, and his expression was almost cheerful. "Now it all makes perfect sense. It's a frame.''

"A what?''

"Somebody is working to make it look as if you or I killed these people, in order to cover up who *really* did it. And Security believes it, so they won't investigate any further. Which means we're going to have to find the real murderer ourselves. Blast it, why has it been so many years since I read any murder mysteries? I've forgotten a lot of the techniques. However, I've got a couple of hours to think about it.''

"*I've* got a couple of hours to get up to Comyn Castle.'' She put her veil down and turned to the door.

"There are aircabs at the spaceport gate,'' Donald called after her. "Most of the drivers are Darkovans; they'll take you for free.'' The door closed sharply behind her. "Because you lend them grace,'' he added softly, and settled down into his bedding and stared up at the ceiling.

"He left orders not to be disturbed,'' the young man said as he led Marguerida through the hallways of the Castle. "But this is important. You can't let those good-for-nothings lay hands on your sworn paxman, can you? I'd like to think Lord Regis would do as much for me, if there were need." He smiled, and opened a heavy wooden door into a dark-paneled room where Lord Regis sat with a tall, thin woman whose hair was fading from the sunset color into twilight.

The Regent looked up as the door opened. He was a young man still, under his mane of white hair, but his eyes were tired. "Dani, I thought I said—" he began, and broke off. "Marguerida Elhalyn, I believe," he said. "Welcome to Comyn Castle. You honor us with this visit, but I understand it isn't merely a social call?"

Marguerida explained in a few sentences how matters stood. "That's strange," Lord Regis said. "I know the Commissioner of Security, and this kind of action isn't typical of him. He's a decent and conscientious man—in his public life, at any rate. It feels as though someone had been putting pressure on him. Very well, as the Terrans say, 'fight fire with fire.' I understand it actually works on Terra." He rose and went to a Terran communicator on a side table, its slick plastic in garish contrast with the age-darkened wood and the faded tapestries of the deeds of Varzil the Good. "The Legate had this installed a few days ago, when things were so unquiet in the streets. Now, if I can only remember how it works—"

"Let me," the woman said. Her fingers flickered over the controls, and a face appeared in the viewscreen; she backed away quickly so that the Terran could not see her. "Don't worry," she said softly to Marguerida. "If by any chance Lord Regis can't win over the Legate, there are other steps that can be taken. If need be, I can keep the *Crown Imperial* from taking off."

"Thank you, Legate; I wish you a quiet day," said Lord Regis, and touched the control that blanked the viewscreen. *"Domna,* your paxman is safe for the next few days at least. At least till your doctors pronounce him healed. In the long run, though, what he said is right; you need to find out who really killed those men."

"Donald suggested it might be the person who had hired him," Marguerida said. "To keep him from talking, just like Price."

"Tamiano did a number of jobs for me," the woman

said, but I didn't kill him. I've been here with Lord Regis since dawn.''

"Who else might have killed him?"

"Anybody," she said. "I'm not the only person he worked for."

"Domna Marguerida,'' Regis said, "I hope we'll see you here again as you get your threads untangled. We have a few of our own here. Thank you, Dani, that'll be all. Andrea, what do you suggest for—'' and the door closed behind them.

The aircab, in defiance of spaceport regulations, sailed in through the gate to deposit Marguerida at the door of the Terran hospital. As she stepped into range of its sensors, the door swung open and the tall figure of the Security Commissioner blocked it.

"You were told not to leave this base," he said.

"Really?" Marguerida asked, remembering Jason's words. "Am I under arrest?"

"It could be arranged," the Terran said. "You set foot off this base again and I'll personally arrange to put you in a cell with guards outside it. And then I'll put more guards on the guards.''

He's afraid, Marguerida realized. *Lord Regis is right, someone has put pressure on him. He fears disgrace, he fears . . . disclosure, maybe. What has he in his past that's so dark, this decent and conscientious man?*

"And that's all I've got," she told Donald. At least I've bought us some time.''

"Well, I've thought as hard as I could," Donald said. "Classically, murder—I mean the business of solving and proving it, not committing it—rests on three legs. There's motive, means, and opportunity. Two murders, that's six possible leads. But most of them don't seem to go anywhere.

"In both cases—Tamiano and Price—anybody could have had the opportunity that didn't have an alibi.''

"A what?"

"Proof of having been somewhere else at the time. I have one for Tamiano, you have one for Price; but that doesn't help, because they think we've been conspiring, each to cover the other. It doesn't help, of course, that you went there *intending* to kill him; and if you had told me, *vai domna,* I would have felt it my duty to advise against it." They both smiled. "You didn't file an intent-to-murder on him, did you?"

"On that piece of street garbage? Of course not. Though if my suspicions are right, that he came originally of good family, perhaps I should have."

"I thank any God who may happen to be listening that you didn't. Anyway, opportunity doesn't get us anywhere. The means, in both cases, were right to hand. The oxygen tube that throttled Price was there in the supply room, and we can assume Tamiano had his dagger on him."

"Day and night," Marguerida said. "And have you any idea why the knife was taken, and that piece of pot metal left in its place?"

"If you hadn't been around to interfere, they would have assumed that was the murder weapon—and not go looking for any other, that might have the murderer's prints in it. In the old days they checked for fingerprints that could be wiped off, but now they go for skin cells that get into the crevices of whatever you touch.

"We're left with motive, traditionally the weakest leg to rest a murder case on. Especially for Tamiano: anybody who knew him, and quite a few who didn't, could have had a motive to murder him. As for Price, it's likely he was killed to shut him up before he told what he knew about Tamiano. (This is assuming they were killed by the same person, and that somebody else didn't kill Price for a different reason altogether.)

"Somebody must be running fairly scared at this point. The Security Commissioner, for example?"

"I don't know," Marguerida said. "He's done something, I'm sure of that, but it doesn't feel like murder. Taken bribes, maybe, or some kind of unauthorized woman."

Donald blushed under his dark beard. "Well, I trust your judgment. Who else do we know of that's scared?"

Before she could answer, the door opened again. It was

the Terran doctor—what was his name? Carter—with a clipboard in his hand and an unexpected light in his eye. "Have you seen Dr. Allison? I wanted to tell him— Maybe he mentioned it to you, about the Pantophage?"

"It probably slipped his mind," Marguerida said. "He's been having problems with—" she looked at Donald.

"Administrative jurisdiction," Donald supplied. "What's Pantophage?"

"It's what we're giving you now," the Terran said. "Dr. Allison suggested it because its effects on fungal infections of this sort are remarkably like the results you got out of your thornleaf, Ms. Elhalyn. He thought there might be a possibility of exporting thornleaf for medical use—I gather Darkover could use a lucrative trade item or two. I was curious enough to go over to the analytical laboratory and look them over."

He held up his clipboard and waved it a little, like a small flag of victory. All his Terran standoffishness had vanished. "The active agent in thornleaf is the same molecule that Solar Spices and Pharmaceuticals sells as Pantophage. They've been testing it over the last couple of years, and just brought it out before I left Terra. Interesting, isn't it, how different life forms on different planets can use the same basic chemistry. How do you prepare thornleaf for consumption?"

"Pick it when it's young," Marguerida said, "and steep it in water. It's best fresh, but the dried leaves will serve, too. You have to pick it before it flowers, or it's no good; all the virtue draws out of the leaves and goes into the seeds."

"Can't you process the seeds as well?"

Marguerida shook her head. "There's something else in them that's poisonous. The hill people do make pillows of the seeds sometimes, for children who have chest trouble, or old people. You sleep on it all night and inhale the fragrance, and—" Her voice trailed off.

"Are those the little pillows you used to be able to buy in the bazaars," Donald asked, "with the leaves embroidered all over them in red thread? I remember those. When I first came to Darkover they were in every stall;

in fact, they were a drug on the market. Nowadays you don't see them any more."

"Pity," Dr. Curtis said. "I'd like to see one, analyze the seeds." A soft chiming filled the air, seeming to come from nowhere, but Dr. Curtis stopped it by touching a band on his wrist. "Sorry. That's my pager. I'll see you later." And he was gone.

"That's what I smelled in the hut," Marguerida said slowly. "Thornleaf seeds. They must have been in the warehouse next door. I suppose we could get some for you— Oh, has he gone? Dr. Curtis?" She opened the door again, and Donald heard her draw in her breath. "Wait! You, sir. What's your name? Come here, please."

She led a man into the room, a small Terran in the uniform of the city police, with skin the color of a Terran chocolate bar. "Sousa," he was saying. "Fernando Sousa. I remember you; you're the lady who found the body."

"And you and Price delivered it to the hospital, yes? What did you do after that?"

"I don't know what he did; I went to bed in my quarters. We were working watch and watch putting down riots over Festival Night; I've been running short on sleep. I just got up half an hour ago to visit a friend who's in here with a cracked head. Why?"

"Do you remember someone changing the knife that was stuck into the body? Substituting one for the other and taking the first knife away?"

"Not while I was there. But I wasn't there all the time, you know. That little alley isn't on the maps, so I went up to the street to guide the groundcar in. You'd better ask Kevin Price."

"Some other time," Marguerida temporized. "Tell me one other thing. Do you know where the Commissioner was all morning?"

"You mean Robinson?"

"No, no, Commissioner Grey," Donald said. "Your boss."

"My god, you want an alibi for the Commissioner? He was in the Ops Room from 0700 onward, and I suppose he's still there. He was there when I called in to get the groundcar."

"All right," Donald said. "Why'd you mention Robinson?"

"Well, I saw him coming in late. He's a fussy old bird and keeps very regular hours, but this morning I saw him coming in the gate just ahead of Price and me and the body."

Donald and Marguerida exchanged glances. "But there's no motive," Donald said.

"None that we know of," Marguerida said. "Anyway, you said motive was the weakest of your three legs."

"That may be, but you'll find Security will still want to find one before they try to bring it before a court. Mr. Sousa, what do you know about Commissioner Robinson? Any skeletons in his closet?"

"There must be one someplace," Sousa said wryly. "He got assigned to Darkover, after all; you usually do that by screwing up somewhere else. But he seems to like it here; he finished his term, and went back to Terra for a year, and then came back here. That was about a year and a half ago Standard. That's all I know about him."

"Thank you," Marguerida said in an abstracted voice. "Mr. Sousa, you'd probably go and check in with your superiors; I have a feeling they have been looking for you. Thank you for your time." She opened the door for him and closed it behind him.

"The timing it right," she said.

"You still don't have a motive."

"I know where I might find one," she began, and broke off. "Zandru's hells—if it's still there! He's had all day!" and she ran out of the room.

Donald sat bolt upright, and with some effort of will made himself lie back again. It was her planet after all, and she was well able to take care of herself. He, on the other hand, was under doctor's orders to stay in bed. She would be all right. Even though it was getting late—why, the sky outside his window was practically dark. He touched the controls at his bedside that closed the curtains and brought up the room lights. He lay back and took a deep breath, and coughed, and breathed again. And the door opened.

Three men walked into the room, not in uniform but in civilian clothes that did not seem quite to fit. They were all wearing Darkovan-made boots, but they had Terran blasters in their hands. "All right, Mr. Stewart," said the tallest of the three. "Get up and get dressed; you got a ship to catch. I know you don't feel so good, so if you can't walk that far we'll carry you."

"I believe Lord Regis Hastur spoke to the Legate about this—"

"That may be," said the other, "but once you're off-planet, Lord Regis has got nothing to say about it. Come on." He made an upward gesture with the muzzle of his blaster. The hand that held it wore a cuff of heavy leather, studded with brass.

Donald got up in silence, put on the nondescript space-man's coveralls they handed him. Off-planet, back into space where he belonged: the thought was bittersweet. For a man who called no world home, Darkover was as fair as any planet might be. *Maybe it won't matter,* he thought. *The breathfire will probably solve all my problems at once.* "Is it cold outside?"

"Not too bad. The sun's just gone down."

"I'd better get my jacket." He found it in the small locker behind the bed, and struggled into it with an effort that made him cough again. He stumbled, and brushed against the bed's controls—and the light went out.

The curtains kept out the meager twilight. Their eyes adjusted to the bright artificial lights, none of them could see. But Donald knew where things were in that room, and the others didn't. He heard two of them stumble against each other, and curse. Something brushed against his arm, hard and knobbly, and at some level he realized it was the leader's wrist cuff and that meant his gun was not pointing at *him*. He reached out, grabbed the weapon and twisted it free, and ran for the door. He knew where that was, too.

Out in the corridor he nearly stumbled over the body of the guard that lay before the door; righted himself, and plunged onward. Adrenaline shot through his blood;

he would worry about breathing later. *I'm coming, Marguerida*. He heard stumblings and cursings behind him, ducked into the lift, and drew one long gasping breath as the door slid safely closed behind him.

It was almost totally dark in the street, dark as Zandru's cellar in the alley. Marguerida found her way by feel, *laran*, and scent. The hut where Tamiano had died was dark and empty, but a thin line of light showed under the next door down, that opened into the warehouse. Cold emptiness inside, and one Terran atom lantern, and one man. The door opened inward.

The first thing she saw was a small shape like a half-emptied sack, embroidered with leaf-shapes all over one side. A seam had ripped and spilled its filling across the floor. Even in the cold air, there was a faint smell of thornleaf.

The man had a blaster, and its muzzle was pointed at her head. "Get inside," he whispered in the spaceport dialect. Marguerida smiled.

"Thank you, Mr. Robinson," she said. "Once again, you've saved me the trouble."

"Get *inside!*" he hissed. "What do you mean, saved you the trouble? What do you mean, *again?*"

"Why, you killed Tamiano for me," she said. "He owed me blood for attempting the life of my paxman. Then again, I wasn't certain why you felt a need to kill him, so it's good of you to tell me."

"I'm not going to tell you anything!"

"You're telling me right now. I'm not much of a telepath, you must understand, but fear screams like a banshee in rut. You're shouting it into my ears."

Robinson clutched at his mouth with his free hand, as if to stifle the silent voice. His blaster hand was trembling, but its focus never went very far from Marguerida's head. *He is searching for the strength to pull the trigger.*

The door behind her pushed open, and sent her staggering almost into Robinson's arms. The man made a little whining sound, and steadied his blaster with both hands, but he didn't fire. A tall figure filled the doorway.

"Elhalyn, you're under arrest. I warned you, if you left the Complex again—" Then he caught sight of Robinson, and the blaster.

"Move, and she dies," Robinson whispered. Grey didn't move. The blaster lay so still in his hand that a star in the sky behind him could be seen mirrored on its surface.

"Let me tell you quickly what's been happening," Marguerida said. Robinson's fear still shrilled like a banshee in her mind, chilling her blood, but she forced her voice into steadiness. "He's been sending thornleaf seeds to Terra, selling them to Solar Spices and Pharmaceuticals, who can steep the virtue out of them without the poison. Tamiano was doing the day-to-day work of collecting and shipping. Why he bothered to have them sewn into pillows I don't know, unless the Empire charges a tax on medicines."

"They do," Grey said. "Solar would have had to pay it, not Robinson; they probably paid him a cut of what they saved."

"So. And Tamiano wanted a cut, too—or a larger cut than he was already getting—or maybe just silence money. So Robinson killed him with his own knife, then changed it for another that hadn't his handprints on it. But Price saw him. Perhaps he wanted silence money, too; perhaps he wouldn't *take* it and promised to report him. Where does Terra send men who have failed on Darkover, too?"

"You don't want to know," Grey said. "What about it, Robinson? Are you ready to come along quietly?"

"If you move, I'll kill her," Robinson said again.

"If you fire, I fire," Grey said. The star reflected in his blaster was perfectly steady. "If you shoot me first, *then* her, you might get us both. But I've got eight men out here, Robinson, at every door and on the roof. I didn't come here just to arrest one unarmed woman, not after the autopsy report came in. You can't escape all of us."

"You're bluffing," Robinson whispered. "And we're leaving." And he took another sidewise step toward Marguerida, and flung his arm around her throat.

It was his last conscious act. The sounds that he made,

as the flames raced across his body, were not the speech of any creature that still had its mind. Marguerida backed slowly away from him as the flames crackled and whispered, beating out the sparks that had caught her sleeve. The blaster fell from the remnant of his hand and skittered across the floor into a corner. He was ashes and cinders before he hit the ground.

Donald appeared out of the dim shadows into the pool of light that poured out of the doorway, and skidded to a stop. He looked at Marguerida, and at Grey, and at the pile of ashes on the floor. "You didn't need me after all, did you," he said, and laughed, and coughed, and sat down on the ground. Marguerida steadied herself against the doorpost, and sat beside him.

"This is just as well," Grey commented, and put his blaster away. "Because I *was* bluffing." He folded his long legs and sat down beside them.

The sky was very dark now, and a double handful of stars had come out. The four moons made a loose cluster above a wash of purple-red where the sun had set. "Except about the autopsy findings," Grey said. "They showed that a narrow blade had been substituted for a wider one. So I began to think you might have something there."

The sky outside lit up for a moment, and through the open door they could see a long streak of green rising against the stars.

"That's the *Crown Imperial* taking off," Grey said. "Maybe I should call in, have her held in orbit. There's I don't know how many tons of thornleaf seed on board, on its way to Terra."

"Let it go," Marguerida said. "Send them a few more shipments, even. Let them build up a market."

"They don't need to know Robinson's dead," Donald said. "We'll collect his share of the proceeds in his name. We'll need the funds, for a good Earthside lawyer."

"Let them build up a market," Marguerida repeated. "Then we'll make an honest company of them. Donald, here." She reached behind her and held up the half-emptied pillow, torn seam upward, like a sack. "You can breathe this till we get you back to the hospital."

Donald took it obediently, and got to his feet. "That was Robinson, wasn't it?" he said. "Look, he had the dagger on him all the time." The green stone glinted among the ashes, and a little wisp of smoke rose through the lantern light till it vanished among the shadows in the rafters.

Firetrap

by Elisabeth Waters and Marion Zimmer Bradley

One of the lines which has stirred up the most curiosity—at least in me—is in THE FORBIDDEN TOWER, *where Damon, returning from timesearch, wonders if he has frostbite. Callista takes off his shoes to see, and Damon reassures her that he was joking. "I wasn't," Callista says, "Hilary got into a level where there was fire, and her feet were so badly blistered that she couldn't walk for a tenday."*

When Lisa and I decided to collaborate on a story for this anthology (we began with "The Keeper's Price," title story of the first of these anthologies), we looked up this episode, discussed it for a good long time; then I did a first draft and Lisa went over it. How else does one collaborate?

Who are we? Well, if you don't know who I am, you may have picked up this book by accident; welcome, and have fun here. Lisa has been living in my household for several years—since 1979, in fact—and manages successfully, with her orderly mind, to battle the chaos and stave off entropy. All the stories about Hilary I have written have been written with Lisa's input, whether or not they bear her name.

As for me, I started this whole thing. Darkover, I mean. (MZB)

". . . and while the season is slack, and there is so little to do," commented Leonie, "it will be good practice for all of you to look everywhere you can think of for abandoned matrixes. Some of them have been forgotten from the Ages of Chaos. I have also heard rumor that Kermiac of Aldaran is trying to train matrix workers in his own way. That sort of thing should not be allowed, but the Council says that if I intervene, I will be recognizing that Domain; and so for the time being I can do nothing. In time to come—well, enough of speechmaking,'' she concluded. ''It should be enough to know that in this you serve our people.''

She went away, and the little group of younger workers in training gathered to look after her, each one secretly hoping that he or she would be the one to reclaim one of the lost matrixes from the Ages of Chaos; perhaps one of the old, forbidden matrix weapons from that Age.

''There is rumored to be an ancient one in our family since the early days,'' said Ronal Delleray. ''I did not realize how important it could be. I do not think it is a dangerous one; I could lay my hands upon it at any moment.''

''Then you should do so. Leonie will be pleased,'' said young Hilary, the Under-Keeper. Hilary Castamir was about fifteen; slender to the point of emaciation, her dark-copper curls lusterless, her spare-boned face bearing the insignia of longstanding poor health. She would have been pretty if she had not been so sickly-looking; even so, she had grace and fine features, the mark of the Comyn strong in them. ''And if Leonie is pleased enough—''

She broke off, but Ronal knew what she did not say, though like all Keepers Hilary had learned early to barricade her thoughts even from her fellow workers in the Tower. *If Leonie is pleased enough with me, she will not speak again of sending me away.* They all knew that Hilary was a telepath of surpassing skill, but that her health was not robust enough for the demanding work of the Tower, especially that of a Keeper.

The new young apprentice, Callista Lanart-Alton, looked even more frail, but she managed somehow to avoid the devastating attacks of pain and even convulsions which again and again confined Hilary to bed, or kept her out of the relay screens for ten days or so of every moon. And as Callista grew older, nearer to the time when she could take on in full all of a Keeper's responsibilities, the day grew nearer when Hilary, for her very life, must be released and sent away.

Ronal was fond of Hilary, with a little more than the bond which bound Tower worker to Tower worker. Though he was not at all the kind of man who would ever have pressed his attentions upon this sick girl, who was also a Keeper, the discipline of concealing this fondness from her, even in thought, would be, he sometimes thought, the destruction of him. But he told himself grimly that it was good discipline—for if Leonie had caught so much as a hint of it he would at once have been sent away. Leonie loved Hilary and no worker would have been allowed to trouble her peace for a moment. So he quietly hung on.

"Are you willing to search for your family's matrix?" Hilary pressed on. "Whatever we may discover, or not, Leonie is right; it would be good practice."

Ronal demurred. "I do not think my father will want to give it up." But he already knew that he would do whatever Hilary wanted.

"I am sure Leonie will be able to persuade him," Hilary said. "When shall we start?"

"Tonight, then?" they agreed, and separated, arranging when to meet again.

Later that night, Hilary and Ronal met in the deserted tower room—they had decided they need not disturb the others, although they were accompanied by Callista, who had agreed to monitor for them. She was about thirteen, no more, a tall slender child without as yet the slightest sign of oncoming womanhood.

"Shall I search for it?" asked Ronal. "I know exactly where it has been kept all these years."

"If you wish," Hilary agreed, "and Callista shall monitor for you, then."

"See you later," he said, and was off into the overworld. Ten minutes later he was back, a matrix clenched in his hands. "Found it lying about on a high shelf in the library," he said. "Nobody but my father even knew what it was. I heard of another one, too; one is lying on an altar of the forge-folk. Father spent some time in a

Tower; that is how he knew what it was. He visited the forge-folk to have them make a sword, and saw it there. It is supposed to be a talisman of their fire-goddess; but it is at least ninth-level. I do not know if I can get it—''

''No, that is work for a Keeper,'' Hilary said. ''Leonie would want to do it herself, I suppose; although I am perfectly capable of it. Except that I should know where to look; there is, after all, more than one village of forge-folk. Meanwhile, let us see what you have here,'' she said, taking the matrix from him. It was coated with dust, dull blue. She brushed away the dust. ''I can well believe that it has been lying about in a library all these years, forgotten. It must have been overlooked when we called in all the matrixes, a couple of generations ago. One like this would be easy to overlook. Let me see if it was ever a monitored matrix.''

She laid it carefully in a cradle and activated a small screen. For a long time she was silent, light from the screen coming and going, and reflecting on her narrow face. The other two leaned close. At last, Hilary switched off the screen, the lights fading, and said, ''I still do not know all its history, and it is not important enough to do timesearch to find it out; but it is very old. It may have been made before the Towers—oh, yes,'' she said in reply to Ronal's startled glance. ''It is an artificial one, perhaps one of the first ones made. I wish I knew who made it. Oh, well—'' She wrapped it carefully in insulating silks and said, ''Your father did not mind giving it up?''

''No,'' said Ronal, ''I don't suppose he knew he was; when I appeared to him, he thought he was dreaming of me. When he finds out that I have really been home, even in spirit, he will be so busy saying I should have first shown myself to my mother that he will not get around to scolding me for the loss of the matrix for years—if ever. It means nothing to him, and so it belongs here; Leonie may discover a use for it—or if not, destroy it.''

''Which will be safer for all concerned,'' Hilary agreed. ''Do you want to go after the one the forge-folk hold tonight?''

''No,'' said Ronal, a little reluctantly; Hilary looked

tired and ill, and he knew if she overstrained herself Leonie would be angry. Much as he enjoyed working together like this, elementary caution could not be neglected. And another thing: "Leonie might wish to seek for this one herself. It is a large and an important one, perhaps not to be left to a couple of apprentices."

When Leonie heard of the ninth-level matrix, she was eager to seek it for herself. Therefore they gathered in one of the Tower rooms the next night.

"Which village of forge-folk holds it? I think I have heard of it—this great lost matrix. It will not be altogether welcome to them—that such a matrix should go behind Tower walls and be lost to them, but I think I can persuade them."

Ronal did not doubt it; it would take a braver man than he knew to stand against the wishes of Leonie Hastur.

He supposed she had once been remarkably beautiful, this Keeper; certainly she had been behind Tower walls all of his life, and during most—if not all—of the lives of his parents—and for all he knew, of his grandparents. He found himself wondering how old she was; with some women, especially of Hastur blood, after they reached a certain age, it was impossible to tell their age because although they were not actually withered, or emaciated, there was something about them; they might have been any age or none. It was still possible to see that Leonie had been beautiful, just possible; it was perhaps the only remnant of her humanity. She looked almost unreal in the stiff, formal Keeper's veils of deep crimson.

"I will go," she said. "Keep watch for me."

Thus saying, she slipped out of her body. To the young people watching, there was no apparent difference, except for an almost imperceptible slumping and a somewhat vacant look in the eyes that were still as blue as copper filings in flame, but they all knew she was not there. She had gone heaven knows where into that strange unknown realm of the overworld, where time and space were not tangible, and only thought existed. Things were not what they seemed in the overworld, but could under certain conditions be manipulated—by thought alone.

The night wore away; after a long time, Leonie—who had, to all appearances, remained motionless in her chair—began to stir and struggle. Callista, instantly alert, murmured, "She's not breathing," but before she could intervene, Leonie pitched out of her chair, falling forward, in a flutter of crimson, breathing heavily in normal unconsciousness.

Ronal cried out, bending over to lift the Keeper. She half-roused at the touch, murmured, "Too strong for me—" and slipped back again into unconsciousness. Ronal lifted the apparently lifeless body and carried her into her shielded room. He waited there until Leonie's attendants had applied various restoratives and determined that she was suffering only from shock and exhaustion.

When he returned to the others, Hilary had already slipped into Leonie's vacated chair.

"No, Hilary," Ronal demurred. "If it was too strong for Leonie, what do you think you can do alone?"

"Do you know how much Leonie has been overworking lately?" Hilary shot back. "That is what led to her collapse; any task she might have undertaken could have done the same. And I will finish what she started. There is no question now that there is something to find, and it must be found before they have time to transfer it to a better hiding place." As Ronal still hesitated, she added persuasively, "I might as well; I will be good for nothing tomorrow, and probably not for another tenday."

"Perhaps if you rest now—" Ronal began.

"No." Hilary shook her head definitely. "It doesn't work that way. Right now I'm riding on the wave of energy I always get a day in advance. We might as well take advantage of it."

Ronal shrugged helplessly; stronger men than he had failed to deter a Keeper when her mind was set on something.

"Besides, if I go now, at once, I can follow her traces," Hilary said.

And Ronal could say only, "You know best."

Hilary took her place in the chair, wrapping herself in

a long woolly robe over her regular working robe, shrugged a bit to make herself comfortable, and slipped out of her body.

Hilary found herself at first on what appeared to be a gray featureless plain, without visible landmarks except, behind her, the rising Tower of Arilinn—not the real Tower as it appeared in the outer world, but what she knew to be the idealized form of that structure. It had been a landmark in the overworld for many generations, and before it, Hilary saw shining footprints, tracks with a faint silver luster. *Leonie's? Did she leave these marks for me?*

Since her main thought had been to follow in Leonie's footprints, she set out quickly along the trail, knowing that it would fade to invisibility all too soon. She moved without conscious thought, unaware of the motions of walking; her only aim to follow that almost imperceptible trail before her where Leonie had gone. She was so intent on following in Leonie's footsteps that it seemed to her to be no time at all—though to the watchers in the outer world it was a considerable time—before she found herself at the entrance to a great dark cave, one of—she was not sure how she knew this, perhaps some intangible trace of Leonie's thought—a great labyrinth of caves which made networks all through the foothills of the mountains. This was the home, she knew, of the strange people known as the forge-folk.

She had no personal knowledge of them, but she had been told by Leonie that they were the first group on Darkover to discover mastery over metals. Darkover was a metal-poor world; from the very earliest days, metal had assumed an almost sacred significance. The small amounts of metal necessary to shoe a horse, to edge a weapon, and other uses, dictated by necessity—in the beginning it had been necessary to make certain that the allocation of metals was made by real need, and not by greed. Still, human nature was always at work, and economic forces had also dictated some accommodation to human status desires which had nothing to do with actual need. Therefore, various political expediencies had made it desirable for powerful persons—and above all the Hasturs and the Comyn—to keep in favor with the forge-folk. Therefore they had been given certain privileges, especially relating to the use of matrixes, traditional from the days before the Ages of Chaos. *But even with these privileges,* Hilary thought, *they should not be keeping a ninth-level matrix, even if it has become a sacred object to them.* She should reclaim it for the Comyn, and for the Towers, where it could not be abused by anyone who might have a fancy to do so. Such a matrix represented a very real danger to the Comyn and to the people of the Domains. And if Hilary could recapture it, the danger was lessened.

The movement, at the speed of thought, had brought her past several glowing forges, and she began, dimly through the darkness of the caves, to sense, if not quite to see, the glowing nexus of a great matrix. Above it, shadowed—not perhaps a physical figure at all, Hilary could see, sketched dimly on the darkness, the figure of a woman, kneeling, golden chains enshrouding her, all faintly glowing flame-color. Sharra; the goddess of the forge-people, here imaged, not on their altar, exactly, but so near as made no matter

Now she could see it. In the Ages of Chaos, when this thing had first been shaped, it had been traditional to house these things in the shape of weapons; and this one was fashioned to be set in the hilt of a great two-handed sword. Hilary moved swiftly to take up the sword in both hands. It was surprisingly heavy. In the overworld she was accustomed to moving without weight, but an object like this—a matrix, she knew, had form and body through all the various levels of consciousness—had weight and substance even in the overworld. *Now,* she thought, *I have it in my hands, and I shall return to Arilinn as swiftly as I can.* She turned to retrace her steps, but as the matrix moved away from the altar, she heard a great cry.

Sharra! Protect us, golden-chained one!

Heaven help us, she thought. The forge-folk, even the guardian of the altar, were aware that the matrix had been touched by an intruder! Now what to do? In her astral form she could not physically struggle for it; her only hope lay in getting back to Arilinn so swiftly that they could not overtake her.

But which way was Arilinn? In the labyrinth of caves, she had become confused. Somehow she must find her way out. The traces, faintly shining, of her own footsteps on the way in were still there. She began to move along them, fighting for breath—it was smoky and hard to breathe. Well, that did not matter; Callista, monitoring her bodily functions would see to it that she kept breathing. She told herself firmly that the heat and smoke were illusions, and struggled on.

As she went on, retracing her earlier steps, she became aware of a glow. Neither ahead or behind her; it seemed to be actually beneath her feet. Down below, on a level somewhere below these astral caves, there was fire. *They have set it here to frighten me,* she thought, and tried to quicken her step as much as she could without losing sight of the faint trace of her own footsteps she needed to find her way back—back to Arilinn.

Beneath her feet, the very ground was beginning to burn. She went on, stepping carefully through the spreading patches of fire, reminding herself that the fire was illusion, intended to frighten her; it was not real. *It cannot hurt me.*

Now the very soles of her slippers were beginning to smolder; she felt sharp pain in the soles of her feet. *It is only illusion*, she told herself, clinging tightly to the matrix, stepping gingerly over the floor of the cave and across the glowing flames. *It is all an illusion—*

Anguish seized her, and faintness; she stumbled, dropping the matrix. Before she could seize it again she was spiraling, choking, through layers of smoke, into a well-known room. She was in Arilinn, abruptly back in her body, conscious of burning pain through the soles of her feet, and Ronal and Callista were looking down at her in fright.

When she could speak she gasped, "Why did you pull me out? I had it—"

Callista murmured, "I'm sorry, but I had to. I dared not leave you longer. Your feet were burning!"

"But that is all illusion, isn't it?" Hilary asked.

"I don't know," said Callista, bending to pull off Hilary's slippers with deft hands. They all gasped at the scorched and blackened shoes, and looked in dismay at the mass of blisters on the reddened flesh.

"You won't be doing much walking for a few days," Ronal said harshly.

Hilary sighed, feeling the familiar preliminary stabs of pain through her abdomen.

"Oh, well," she said, "I wasn't planning on doing much walking for about a tenday anyhow. Callista, will you help me to my room? And I'd better have some golden-flower tea, too."

Later that day, Leonie came to visit her. At the tender solicitousness in the older Keeper's face, Hilary burst into tears. "I nearly had it, but Callista and Ronal pulled me back," she said, weeping.

"No, no, child; they did it to save your feet—if not your life. I heard you were badly hurt."

Hilary wriggled her bandaged toes. "Not as badly as all that," she said.

"All the same, I think they did right. We must let the big matrix go, at least for now. At least, if it is so well guarded by the forge-folk, no outsider can use it to do us harm," Leonie said, "and the forge-folk do not have the type of *laran* to use it as a weapon." But she looked somehow troubled, as if touched by a premonition of the future.

Friends

by Judith K. Kobylecky

Judith Kobylecky writes: "A couple of years ago, I brought home THENDARA HOUSE *and settled down for a good read. I . . . found myself feeling frustrated: the characters kept breezing by all the things I wanted a better look at. I have read other books that captured the feeling of a place, but few have made me want to stop the action and take another look, maybe do a little exploring around an interesting corner. I think the anthologies are proof that I am not alone in this."*

Here then, with a sure hand, are some of the interesting corners she has explored around; seldom has an absolute beginner told a tale so well. She says "I have always mentally 'redone' stories I've read but I had never actually written anything before." That she has done so to some purpose this story proves.

She says she is 36, and has a husband and two young children, respectively 5½ and 2½. She adds that she also has two dogs with "a little too much personality."

I hope this will encourage her enough that it's only the first of many stories . . . not necessarily all on Darkover.

Elorie opened her eyes slowly, the light from the single candle dazzled them painfully. There was another storm raging outside, the window by her bed creaked and rattled with the force of the wind. *Glass*, she thought, *it has been a long time since I have seen a window made of glass. Where am I?* The candlelight was broken up into glittering rainbows by the beveled and faceted glass. *It would be easy to lose myself in them.* Already the rainbows were forming new patterns; she heard the voice of the storm speaking to her. Frightened, she turned away toward the room. *I must be in the Great House. How long,* she wondered, *how long have I been here?*

As if in answer, the door to her room opened; two women and a man entered and sat beside her, the eldest leaned forward, enfolding Elorie's hands between her own. "There, child," she soothed, "you must not worry now. You have been ill for weeks now, but we are here to help you if you will only allow it."

There was something about her voice. Vainly, Elorie tried to remember. Looking at the other two faces, she saw a woman still young, watching her with open impatience and a dignified older man who met her eyes and smiled. It was the smile that warned her. There was no warmth; his eyes remained cold and untouched. She recalled that they wanted something from her and they wanted it very badly. But what?

They saw her resistance growing and looked away from her, turning their concentration instead to a blue stone, the glow from which touched their faces with blue light. Elorie remembered now. She was in threshold sickness and had somehow managed to barrier herself against their probings. But those barriers were beginning to fail. Her *laran* had come late to her and its onset had been sudden and terrible. There had been no time to master it before she was overwhelmed. *Master it,* she thought ruefully, *I cannot even comprehend it.*

When she was first plunged into chaos, she had reached out to the minds around her for help, but had instinctively recoiled from their touch, sure that to accept the aid they so eagerly offered would be a kind of suicide.

The three turned to face her. *Like* kyorebni, she thought, *the carrion birds of the mountains.* The older woman she now recognized as the highly trained telepath they had brought in at her first sign of threshold sickness. After her arrival, the pressure from their minds had become almost unbearable. Why were they so interested in someone who works in their stables, without family or friends? They were not the kind of family who would care about hirelings. What did they want of her?

Already battered and weary, she now needed all of her

dwindling strength to maintain her mental walls against their onslaughts. The energy needed to hold off the delirium of the sickness was gone. Once again the world shifted and splintered; it was the slide into a nightmare of new senses giving too much too soon. Apprehensively she watched the glow from the stone grow and spread slowly toward her. No longer could she hope to hold them off. Exhausted and desperate, she leaped to a new place.

The quiet was a relief. Elorie now stood alone in a blue stillness. Had she left her body behind? She was not at all sure. All her life she had heard stories of an overworld wrought of blue light, but she actually knew very little about it. The remembered stories could not have prepared her for what it was like actually to be there. An uncomfortable thought came then, no one had ever mentioned how to get back.

Dimly she felt their fury at her escape; they were unable to follow, apparently. She smiled, perhaps they were afraid to follow her into madness. Not knowing what else to do, she began to walk through the mist. *At least,* she thought, *I believe I am walking; it is hard to be certain of anything here.*

Stopping after a while, Elorie looked about her. There were no recognizable landmarks, not even familiar contours. The only constant in this place was the soft breeze that blew the mist past her without ever disturbing her clothing. Determinedly she began to walk toward some vague forms in the distance but after what seemed a long time she was no nearer; if anything they had retreated before her. Elorie walked faster and then ran wildly but came no closer. It was then that she was forced to recognize the fact that she was truly lost and in need of help. Any contact with the others had long since been broken. Besides, she still shivered at the thought of having to trust the telepath who looked at her with such hungry eyes.

Elorie began to shout. She had hoped the sound of her own voice would strengthen her in the silence and give her an anchor of reality to hold on to. But her voice was curiously flat and quiet. Badly frightened, she continued shouting until exhaustion faded her voice to a whisper. At last her terror was lessened by fatigue and her only thought was of rest. *Would it be so bad,* she thought, *just to lie down for a while and close my eyes? I wonder what it would be like to drift.* The thought was so pleasant; she closed her eyes as the caressing mist blew soft and cool on her cheek.

No, fight. Listen, Elorie, you must fight.

Who is that? Those voices cannot be real. It is almost as if I can see you. I am afraid, voices, that I will never find my way back.

Yes, we are real. Hold on, or you will be truly lost forever.

I am too tired. Too tired to care now.

We care. We can give you some of our strength. Please let us help you. You must join us, if only for a moment, or we will be too late to save you.

The thought of letting down her guard was terrifying; she had held on to it for so long, and yet she had to trust them. It was with tremendous relief that she at last let her barriers fall. Surprisingly it was easy to reach and blend, their strength renewing her own.

We must return you to your body; already it is almost too late. Do not worry, we will maintain contact with you until you are stabilized. Trust us.

I will.

As the blue mist slowly faded around her, the familiar room came into focus. Only this time the world ordered itself as her new senses shifted and blended, now harmonious with the old. She was still tired, but now wonderful things shimmered at the edges of sight.

Elorie was alone in the dark room where they had left her for dead, but she no longer needed the candle to see the beauty around her.

Yes, it is beautiful, Elorie, but please, no exploring now. You really do need to rest.

How could anyone rest with the pressure from those other minds? I can feel their astonishment that I survived; their determination to control me remains as strong as ever.

We are not yet sure what they are after, but we have

suspicions that concern us. There is no need to worry for a time. Your instinctive barriers are extraordinary and we will show you how to further strengthen them.

Thank you. I owe you my life. You are not of this Domain, are you?

Laughter. *No, we are a circle of telepaths far from here.*

But who are you and where?

We are friends. From across the mountains. You see, you wandered farther than you would imagine, your laran *is very powerful. All we can tell you now is that we work in secret to establish a sanctuary. From the stories that have reached us we fear that it will be needed sooner than we thought.*

Who has need of such a sanctuary?

We fear the knowledge would endanger you in your weakened state. They must not suspect that we have helped you. Please, we will tell you more when you are stronger.

The acceptance and warmth that filled her was all she needed to know for the present. She allowed her eyes to close and felt herself slipping into the first restful sleep she had had in weeks. *Thank you, my friends.*

Hours later, Elorie awoke to find herself still confined to a room in the house of the great family of the Domain. Her quarters were luxurious, but she remained a captive. When she was stronger, all that was required of her were regular sessions with the telepath they referred to by the new title of *leronis*. From her Elorie gained some skill with her starstone, but it was from her friends that she learned more. The barriers they taught her to erect stood firm against the combined efforts of her teacher and the lord and lady of the house to overcome them. The voices kept regular contact with her and were her secret resource against all efforts to control her and her emerging powers. The family found this resistance intolerable.

One morning *Domna* Darela was especially irate as she began her almost daily lecture on ingratitude. Knowing that she would be trapped for quite a while, Elorie assumed the vague, cheerful expression that she had found worked best in these circumstances. Darela was wearing the most magnificently embroidered gown Elorie had ever seen. As she paced by, the stiff folds of her dress blew Elorie their sweet scent of herbs. Failing to stifle a yawn, Elorie saw that the *domna* had not missed her slip. Almost enclosed by the high stiff collar the lady's doughy face worked over this latest insolence.

Darela has outdone herself this time. She can hardly move in those clothes.

"The ingratitude of you hill folk. The weather turns a little colder and everyone comes swarming onto our lands. If you people think that any of those so-called ancient rights apply here . . ."

A little colder, she said, Elorie mused. Those with the weather gifts had seen the change of climate coming for decades. Most of the hill folk were familiar with the old lore of weather patterns and had wanted to outlast their fluctuation; they were determined to hold on to their independence from the emerging Domains and their twisted ideas about the old gifts. Time passed and it became clear that the change would last generations. A small ice age, the elders had called it. The increasingly bitter weather meant that the land could support far fewer households. She thought sadly of all the communities dispersed, all the painful farewells. Telepathic networks that had taken generations to build were broken forever. She had herself hoped to work someday in the small village circle. While few were wonderfully gifted, most had some small talent and in a close-knit community they were able to combine their strengths. All who had even a small portion of what was now called *laran* were glad to share in one of those circles at one time or another. It was both the duty and the right of all Darkovans.

And then the famine came. Many weakened by hunger succumbed to disease. It was an old horror that still woke her at night to weep for her dead. Even though the population had been decimated, the survivors still faced the agonizing choice of who would have to leave so the others could survive.

Breaking away from her painful reverie, Elorie once more listened.

"While you, you overeducated donkey, must learn decent Domains behavior and forget all barbarian ways . . ."

Elorie had heard this many times, but it was still amusing. *Barbarians? We are the ones still civilized.*

"I heard that. You barrier yourself so well that only a little of your disgusting comments can be heard, but do not worry; every day we are closer to breaking through. You are lucky we have taken an interest in you."

A look came to *Domna* Darela's face of someone who was at last going to achieve a long-worked-for goal. She smoothed the furred trim of her dress and patted her intricately curled hair in anticipation.

She is very pleased with herself, Elorie thought, *she must be up to something. Perhaps they still think I will become their trained pet telepath. That would be quite a prize for an ambitious family.* As much as she wanted to discover their plans, however, she dared not lower her mental wall. Uneasy, she decided to pay attention.

"We took you in when we could have sent you on with the other hill folk we did not place on our lands. Time to forget that independence and serve the blessed descendants of Hastur and Cassilda . . ."

This was too much. Elorie, knowing an outburst from her would only lengthen the lecture, began to fidget. Looking at Darela's ridiculous hair, she reached with her mind and gently pulled a strand loose and left it swaying straight up in the air. She had only some small ability in this area, but she might as well enjoy it.

". . . the great lord Hastur who fell from the sky . . ."

We all fell from the sky, in a starship. In the mountains, we still remember. When she had first heard the story as a small child, she had imagined a starship to look like one of the sailed vessels on the river near her old home. She had pictured its sails full of starlight, passing across the moons. Elorie wanted to shout that to the smug Darela, but she did not want to die for shouting a Domain heresy, or a mountain truth.

She pulled another strand loose and looped it over the *domna's* ear.

Elorie had been one of those displaced by the changing climate and she had chosen to go to the newly organizing

Domains where at least one could be warm sometimes. The great families who controlled the lands would never admit it, but they benefitted from the abundant cheap labor. Hungry people were all too willing to work for food and shelter. What was disturbing, however, was the way some of the families had begun to pick through the refugees for those with certain *laran* abilities, although what exactly they were searching for was something they kept to themselves. What people did know was that a number of telepaths had formed circles unlike the old networks. Only whispered about were tales of unbelievable power as well as a suspicion that the great families were attempting to channel all the old gifts into their own hands. This would have been unthinkable not so many years earlier, but life on Darkover was changing.

Elorie was sure that they wanted her to join one of those new circles, something that she was determined never to do. What price would these new Domains pay to give so much power over to so few? With the old hill communities broken, what would Darkover have to pay?

". . . so you now have the opportunity to pay back this family."

When I escape from here, maybe I can arrange a payment.

A tuft of hair tied itself into an intricate knot at a right angle from Darela's temple.

". . . and immediately after your official adoption into this family you will be wed to *Dom* . . ."

Elorie was bewildered. *Wed? No, they wanted me for a* leronis.

"The *leronis* has determined that together your children would have some very useful traits."

Children. Now for the first time Elorie realized the full impact of what was happening. The whispered rumors had been right in a way. They wanted to fix *laran* into the families by controlled breeding. She had not been able to believe the warning the voices had given her. It had been too monstrous.

"No, never. You cannot make me. What ever gave you the idea that I would consent to such a grotesque idea? What kind of life would the children of such a marriage have? I have heard of that man. Many of his children have died in threshold sickness and all his wives in child-birth.''

"At last she speaks. You are strong and can bear many children. Enough of them will survive and bring power to this family and they will, in turn, do their duty as you yourself eventually will. You need not worry; we would never entrust their care to you. The honored *leronis* will undertake their training from infancy. You need only bear.''

"I refuse to do this. It will not happen.''

"It will,'' the *domna* had spoken very quietly. Even through her barriers Elorie had heard the triumphant shout, *At last.* For a second she saw herself through Darela's eyes, her own face sick with horror. The link between them broke instantly, a relief to them both.

"We have not been able to break you of your ways, but your *laran* we will not wait for. The arrangements were made in the most complete secrecy to prevent your attempting an escape before we were ready. Prepare yourself, you will indeed wed. In three days' time.''

Domna Darela gathered up her voluminous skirts and left the room triumphantly.

Three days. So closely watched was she that she seldom dared to contact her distant friends. Now it was a risk she had to take; she needed their counsel. What sane person could have believed the stories? Quickly she leaped to the overworld and extended her thoughts to them.

I made a mistake by not acting sooner, I should have chosen to flee over the mountains immediately. Perhaps I still can. I must. Can I seek that sanctuary of which you spoke? Does it now exist?

It will, her friends consoled her. *We will come for you.* There was a pause. *This is what we had feared would happen. You must know that it is necessary to inform our own lord and lady what is happening and we cannot be sure how they will react to our plans. We will need to enlist many others in our cause and it will inevitably become known to the other Domains. It will go hard on our land if our lord tolerates such a haven. But we promise you, we will not abandon you.*

But I only have three days.

We will come as quickly as we can.

The promise consoled her little; it was impossible to cross the mountains in three days. While she sat straining to hold contact a great commotion began in the hall. *Domna* Darela was shrieking in fury.

She must have caught sight of her hair in a mirror, Elorie thought to herself. Picturing Darela's face puffing out over that collar lifted her spirits and she began to plan. Her *laran* was of enormous power, she knew that now, as the family must always have known. Her distant allies promised that they could provide the necessary skill and focus for all that raw power. Theoretically, that would enable her to maintain her barriers and still use her own considerable gifts. At least that was what they thought.

Wasting no time, she removed the lovely overdress and tunic and donned her old breeches, the practical hill clothing, for travel. For weeks her old clothes had lain carefully hidden in her present quarters. It had taken her considerable powers of illusion and a gift for subterfuge to retrieve them from her old room above the stable. She was thankful for the impulse that had made her do it before it had seemed necessary. Now she was too carefully watched to be able to carry it off. It was going to be a long climb down from the room and she did not think it would be possible in the clothing they had provided her.

Looking at the fine clothes carefully laid on the bed Elorie could not help but give them a few fond pats before bundling them into a hiding place she had hollowed out in the wall. They were beautiful and warmly lined. Crossing inlaid floors she ran her hand a last time across the wall panels of carved wildflowers; she had to admit she would miss all the luxury. And the warmth, though even in this grand house the growing cold reached inside to cover outer walls with frost. Reluctantly, she threw the soft blue-dyed boots on top of the rest of her clothing. Boots like that would not last a day on the trails she

would be following. She buried bare toes in the bright
carpet and smiled.

*And I had thought that carpets like this were so waste-
ful. I think that I will miss them most of all.* Reluctantly,
she pulled on the heavy boots with the warm felt liners.

The voices laughed. They thought this was all very
amusing. *Just remember Darela's foolish face when you
are missing this all too much,* they taunted. *Will you miss
her, too?*

Wrinkling her nose at the thought, Elorie started to
haul herself out the small arched window and froze. It
had not seemed such a long way down when the plans
were made, but now that her leg hung out over nothing
she began to get queasy.

*How can someone raised in the mountains be afraid of
heights?* they asked.

*I lived in a house like anyone else, not at the edge of
a cliff. Besides, I am not afraid of heights. I am afraid
of falling, there is a difference.* Hard as it was to be
dignified while crawling out such a small window while
groping for handholds in crumbling mortar, she did her
best. The fact that the family knew of her fear and to
deter her escape had had her placed in one of the highest
towers only made her angry enough to go on. As she
began the long limb down, she was thankful that their
great vanity had made them add a huge relief of a falcon,
the new family emblem, to the wall. It took her a long
time to get that far and she spent as much time as she
dared clinging to its beak while trying to get her breath.
That bird was the last secure handhold she knew of, and
before she continued on she patted it with affection.

It was unknown hours later when she clung shaking
not very far from the base of the sheer wall.

*I never really thought I could get this far, and now I
cannot seem to move at all. My shoulders are cramping
and my hands are too numb to find a handhold.*

The domna *would never think you could make it either.
She had other plans for you and maybe she was right.*
Into her mind they projected a picture of Elorie as the
proper Domains *domna,* complete with hair done to look
remarkably like Darela's.

I had thought that no one could look as foolish as Darela, she thought wryly. *I was wrong. You people think that you are so amusing.* Aggravated she continued her descent, ignoring her pain and fear as best she could. *Well, if I am going to fall, I might as well aim for the manure heap. It is soft and maybe then the family would not want me back.* Several minutes later she found herself at the base of the tower, shaking so badly she was unable to stand.

I am down. I did it and you, my friends, mocked me on purpose.

Now she is learning. Besides the only other choice was the manure pile.

Wearily she climbed to her feet and tried to keep her bundle from banging into her legs as she crept toward the stable with its familiar comforting smells. She had worked there for almost a year before her emerging *laran* had made her so valuable to the family.

I would have almost been content to stay there for a while. Honest work was all I asked for, not to be used by them. The rumors of horrifying gifts appearing were probably true, then, too. The result of the breeding program. Shuddering, she fought down the nausea the idea always gave her.

At least that thought has renewed my courage, which is not much.

Elorie, it is enough, but hurry.

She chose a mountain-bred pony that she knew well and saddled it. Turning quickly at a soft sound behind her, she saw the large hound she had brought with her from her old village. It bounded over, almost toppling her with ecstatic tail wagging. "Good dog," Elorie thumped its great side with affection. "I am glad to see you; I was so worried that you would not be able to come when I summoned you. Now if we can all be quiet, we can slip away." After giving the animal a hug, she climbed up on the pony. The dog rested its great head on her foot and gave her its patented agonized look.

"Stop that," she hissed, "before you make me laugh and then we will never get out of here. Yes, you are coming, too. I could use a little company." *And protection,* she thought. *It was a long way over the mountains.*

Allowing one of her distant allies to help her focus her *laran,* she rode out undetected and found herself in one of the worst rainstorms she had ever seen. She tied her hood tightly under her chin but knew it was not really going to help.

"A good sign," she said miserably. "What fool would ever think of venturing out in this?"

On the day of her wedding the silent bride was led from her room surrounded by honor guards in the newly designed livery. *Domna* Darela could not help but admire the effect, her own design. The family was rising rapidly and this new alliance was just a measure of its success. She pulled aside the captain of the guard. "Remember Captain, the *dom* and I want you to watch her carefully. We want no more of her tricks so you are not to tolerate any scenes. Any measures are acceptable, just keep her quiet."

Smoothing the gown that befitted her new rank, she strolled over to her husband and smiled happily, relieved that her troublesome charge had succumbed to depression and was about to be unloaded on her new husband without any scenes.

"She is silent but seems resigned," she told the *dom.* "I do believe she has come to her senses and is going to do her duty at last."

"As she should, to repay us the trouble of taking her in."

Contented, the *domna* sighed. The groom the *leronis* had chosen was going to make that donkey wish herself back in the stables. Altogether, it was a satisfying day.

Surrounded by her guards, the bride paused and looked confused, but continued to where her future husband stood. He turned slowly and looked at her with contempt.

The pony's hooves crunched through the layer of ice that covered the mud. Elorie laughed and shook the snow off her head; with the weather changing so rapidly it was hard to tell just what season it was. It was good to be so close to freedom; in two days she would at last meet some of her friends. Three days of rough traveling in addition to the constant strain of using her *laran* over such a distance had exhausted her, even with the focus and strength given her by the growing circle over the mountains. She knew herself to be staggering with fatigue and her nerves were raw, but now the end was near. The only thing that kept her going was the knowledge that the promised sanctuary did in fact exist. The *dom* and *domna* of that far Domain had just agreed to offer a haven to any who fled the madness of the breeding program. It was a courageous act to oppose the powerful *leroni* and their allies in the other Domains. They would surely try to crush such a show of defiance. A dangerous time lay ahead of them all if the other Domains could not be made to see the insanity of the plan. Possibly the beginning of a long and bloody conflict. Elorie could take some comfort from reports that gifted individuals were already seeking out the same haven as she; surely they would be as willing as her to defend it.

While she feared for herself and the future of her new homeland, her overwhelming feeling was still one of great thankfulness. Now when the time came for her to have children, she would raise them in the old ways and tell them of the lost starship that fell to Darkover.

Are you ready, Elorie?

Yes, I am now at the limit of my powers, even with all your help. At the same time that her friends withdrew their support she released her hold on the illusion and the animal.

I almost wish I was back there at the hall so I could have seen their faces when the illusion broke. Imagine, the great Lord Durraman finding himself married di catenas to a donkey.

Singing and laughing she picked up the pace, tired as she was. Some of her new countrymen were making plans to free others from this madness and she wanted to be a part of that. But for now she was happy to be riding on to her sanctuary. To brave Aldaran.

Manchild

by L. D. Woeltjen

"Manchild" was actually submitted to Red Sun of Darkover, *the last anthology; however, the anthology was
full, so I asked Linda to resubmit it this year, and here
it is; I liked it.*

*She says: "As for biographical information, everything
is much the same as when you bought "Hero Worship"
earlier this year. My three children are a bit older and I
seem to find a bit more time for writing." (She must be
unique in this; I found much more time for writing when
the kids were small and portable—i.e., stayed where you
put them—and as long as they were fed and dry, made
no demands. When they're old enough to have their shoe-
laces tied and ask you to make a peanut butter sandwich,
demands are endless—until they're out of college, which
all three of mine are now.) She adds, "Currently I'm
branching out by working on a horror-suspense
novel. . . . I've had work published in* Modern Liturgy
*and a couple of gamer's magazines." I ought to add that
I heard Linda read at a convention from a sword-and-
sorcery novel in progress and am moved to say, "Keep it
up; you've made a good start." (MZB)*

"What kind of a man are you?" the boy asked, contempt
clear in his voice.

"A very content one," the scholar answered. He removed his eyeglasses and stared back at the boy. "Just
what do you think a man should be?"

"Strong, brave," Ewen answered, trying to think
quickly, "adventurous."

"I'm strong enough to do the farm chores," the man

said, pulling absentmindedly at his gray beard. "I'm brave enough to travel light-years across space to make my home on a strange, forbidding world called Darkover. And I'm greedy when it comes to adventure."

"*Terrannan,*" the boy muttered. The old man ignored him and continued his speech.

"I wasn't willing to settle for just one world, just one quest. I wanted them all." He thumped the ragged, loosely bound volume in his lap.

"Books!" he said as Ewen scowled. "Books, my boy. They're my mode of adventure."

"Ugh!" the boy spat. "All you do is take care of cattle and read. I need to be taught the things men do. Show me how to hunt or practice swords with me. Those are the lessons I want, not learning letters like a Nevarsin monk." Ewen wadded his writing paper into a ball and threw it on the floor. "I'm eleven years old. It's past time for me to be learning to defend myself and to provide food for my family."

"If you want to learn to hunt and fight, ask Tara. She knows both skills far better than I do."

"Women don't teach men," Ewen argued.

"Mothers teach boys."

"But Tara is Pier's mother, not mine." His answer was smug and cold.

"Then wait till Shani comes back," Mikhail's steady tone made Ewen wince. How could he have let the old man back him into this corner? "If you gave her a chance, she'd be happy to teach you all the things you want to know."

"She doesn't care about me." Ewen tried to make his words sound final. He edged toward the door.

"Doesn't she?" Why did the old man persist?

"She left me here, in a home even the Free Amazons scorn. I know they call this the 'Renegade Guild House.' "

"If you remember, your mother was reluctant to leave you here until Tara convinced her that we weren't trying to undermine the Guild."

"Well, if she's so convinced, why doesn't she stay here, like Pier's mother?"

"Shani's business is trading. She has to travel. Once the two of you get acquainted, and she trains you, I imagine she'll take you with her on her journeys."

"No, she won't," Ewen insisted.

"Not if you keep sulking every time she shows up," Mikhail said. "How do you think she feels when you act like you can't stand the sight of her?"

"I hate her." Ewen clenched his fists. He was angry, and not just at Mikhail for goading him like this.

"Do you?"

"Yes," he hissed.

"Why?"

"Because she's an Amazon whore!"

Mikhail raised his hand to slap the boy, but stopped. Lowering his arm, he returned Ewen's defiant glare.

"Do you even know what that word means?" he asked softly.

Ewen did not answer.

"To me," the old man lectured, "you sound like a parrot—a bird that mindlessly repeats whatever it hears. Don't use those words again unless you're sure you mean them, because you will pay the consequences."

Ewen stalked out of the room. When he was beyond Mikhail's view, he ran out the front door and headed to the barn. He wanted privacy, but little Pier was there, building a play farm in the dirt with twigs and bits of straw. Ewen refused an invitation to join in the fun. He looked toward the forest that lay beyond the farmland. There he would find refuge.

It's finally time to go, he thought as he ran. Since the day his mother brought him here, he'd been planning to run away. Ewen had been waiting until he had a satisfactory plan for escaping from the farm. The hard part was thinking of a place to go. He could not go home. He no longer had a home.

Why did my father have to die? he wondered angrily. No one else had perished in the forest fire. They told Ewen's stepmother it was ill fate. Eduin had stayed behind to put out one smoldering spot and the wind had changed, trapping him.

Tears blurred Ewen's eyes as he remembered that day.

He stopped running, feeling alone and unloved, just as he had then. No one comforted him. Instead, the death of his father caused an immediate change of status. Ewen was no longer part of the family. A *nedestro* child, his presence in the household was tolerated only long enough for his mother to come and claim him.

Ewen cringed from the memory of his older cousins sniggering as he rode out of the courtyard behind the woman. Her dark hair, the color of his own, was trimmed short, curling obscenely about her neck and ears. Though she wore trousers and boots, her femaleness was all too obvious.

His hatred for her was born then, the red flame of the humiliated boy's cheeks burning its way down to his heart to smolder. Shani's aloofness fed the embers, and when she abandoned him here among strangers, the fire flared up, engulfing him as the forest fire had consumed his father.

Some part of Ewen knew that Shani had the power to quench the anger that flared in his soul. But another part, perhaps the fire itself, did not want the fury to subside.

She'll be back soon, Ewen thought. He sat on a rock and began to plan in earnest. *I wonder if she'll even care when she learns I've run away. But where will I go?*

Ardais and Nevarsin were closest. *No,* he quickly eliminated the latter, *I've had enough of living among* cristoforos. Mikhail and his freemate, Mhari, had not forced their religion on him, but Ewen had been exposed to their piety, nonetheless. Besides, he thought, winter is coming and Nevarsin is supposed to be colder than Zandru's fifth hell.

Ardais would have to do. He stopped, finally determining that he would need to go east. Just as he rose to set out, he heard a sharp "thwack!" There was movement close by. Ewen crept toward the sound.

Tara! She was kneeling beside a dead rabbit-horn. Ewen watched the expertise with which the young woman bound the creature and added it to the string of small game she had already brought down. *Mikhail was right, she could teach me to hunt. Running away will wait,* he decided. Knowing how to catch his own food would keep his stomach full on the way to Ardais.

"You've had a fine day hunting," Ewen called as he left his hiding place.

"Ewen?" Tara looked up, surprise and puzzlement mixed in her voice. "Are you finished with your lessons?"

"Mikhail said I should come to you to learn how to hunt."

"I see." She hefted the string of game over her shoulder. "I've about enough, but Mhari won't mind extra meat to smoke for the winter."

Ewen tagged after Tara as she headed off through the trees. Soon she was showing him how to tell what animals had passed by their tracks on the ground.

Everything that Tara was willing to teach, Ewen quickly absorbed. In the following days, he became her hunting companion. Once her time had been spent solely in supplying the farm with meat. Now, with Ewen's help, Tara was often able to return to the house by midday.

The boy convinced her that it was time for Pier to learn to use a sword. Ewen gave Pier the little wooden sword he'd brought with him. His father had made it for him when he was six, but now he had outgrown it. After he whittled a practice blade for himself, he demonstrated what he knew for Tara. She complimented him on his skill and enlisted his help in training Pier.

"You know," she confided, "we Renunciates don't often use swords. We are forbidden to wear them. What skill I have comes from using a long knife, but some of the principles are the same."

Unaware, Ewen grew fond of Tara. He forgot his plans to run away until the day Shani came back. Tara and Ewen were returning from hunting when Pier brought them the news.

"Your mother's here!" he called out as he ran to meet them. "Now you won't have to share mine."

Ewen's belly seemed to twist in knots. He followed Tara to the house without saying a word. Pier skipped along, babbling about the circlets Shani had brought them from the city. "Hurry up. If it gets too near meal time, Mhari won't let us have them now."

"Hello, *chiyu*," Shani said as she met him at the front door.

Ewen stiffened at the words, but did not acknowledge them. He walked past the woman as if she were nothing more than a shadow of the door frame. He heard a sudden bump behind him and smiled secretly. She had either punched or kicked the door in frustration.

Later that afternoon, Ewen overheard Shani talking with Mhari as they cleaned the game.

"I thank you for inviting me to stay, but I don't think any of us looks forward to spending the winter locked up with a sullen child. From what you've told me, Ewen is becoming used to his life here. I don't want to spoil it for him."

"The very fact that Ewen overcame his prejudice regarding Tara proves that he can change," Mhari said. "Given a chance to know you, he may lose his resentment. He's almost a man. You don't have many more years to win him over."

"Do you really believe I can?" Ewen swallowed hard when he heard the sincerity in her voice. There seemed to be a lump of something caught in his throat.

"Isn't it worth trying?" he heard Mhari ask. "You have to hole up somewhere when the snows come. Why not here?"

Shani did not answer.

"In truth," the old woman almost whispered, "we need you here. This is the first winter we've had such an empty house. Rumors of banshees coming down last year gave us quite a scare. I think we'd all be safer having an experienced fighter here."

Shani stayed. At first Ewen showed his contempt for his mother by avoiding her. He did not join them at the dinner table or around the fire in the evening when they gathered to hear Mikhail's tales. But no one seemed to care that he did not eat. No one came to coax him to the table. Even Pier would not smuggle him food in the evening.

"Your mama's nice," the younger boy said. "Not as pretty as mine, but kind. Remember how she brought us candies?"

It's no use trying to explain to Pier, Ewen thought. *The lad has a full belly and still his tongue longs for sweets.* His own empty stomach grumbled and Ewen relented by the third day.

Once he became accustomed to his mother's presence, Ewen found she did not seem too different from Tara. Now other suspicions nagged at him as he watched the two women working together or sitting before the fireplace. What had they called the Amazons? Lovers of women?

Ewen had only a vague, uncomfortable idea of what that meant. He studied every word and gesture of the women. At night, shamefully, when Pier was asleep, he put his ear to the wall that separated the boys' room from the one their mothers shared. He was not sure what he expected to hear, but there was never more than idle gossip.

They called each other "sister," but even Mhari used the term. Nor did Mikhail seem overly familiar with either of the younger women. Yes, Ewen did know what was meant by the names his mother had been called. The more he thought of it, the less evidence there was to support those accusations. His mother dressed and lived differently than the women who had raised him, yet she seemed no worse, no less human, than they had been.

"How can you live like this?" he heard Shani ask Tara one evening as he listened at the wall. "Do you know what they say about you people in the Guild Houses?"

"Do you know what they say about Renunciates?" Tara laughed. "Gossip is gossip. Believe it if you will. The truth is still the truth. I'm happy here, and I haven't violated the Oath. I can see my son grow and know that he's not being influenced by the foul-mouthed men that his father calls friends."

Shani's voice was sad when she answered.

"I don't think I'll ever be able to make Ewen forget the things they've told him about me. He hates me."

"By what you've told me, he doesn't know you. Mhari

has seen this over and over, since the first of our sisters sought refuge from a storm here. She birthed a son and lamented that she would have to be separated from him. Mhari offered to keep him and to shelter the mother whenever she visited. The Renunciate stayed, and others after her. Some, like me, bring their sons straight from the Guild House, but many are like you, Shani. Mhari was right to ask you to stay. I see signs of his softening already.

It was true, Ewen realized as he eavesdropped. He was aware of the effort Shani put into reaching him. She cared and he was beginning to care in return.

No! came the searing emotion from deep in his soul. *She leaves me too often. She goes off, just as Father went off. Someday, she won't return.*

Ewen shivered. At times ice burns just as painfully as fire. This was not anger that he felt now, but something cold and horrible; fear. Ewen struggled to make sense of his feelings.

She risks her life, he told himself, *just like Father did, every time she ventures out on the mountain trails. I will not love her. I will not lose another parent. If she truly cares about me, she will stay here, as a mother should.*

For now, it would be as Ewen wished. Shani could not leave until the snows melted and the passes cleared. But some travelers were not deterred by snow and ice. Late one night, Ewen was awakened by eerie wails. It was the first of many such hideous calls. Soon, the household was gathering to discuss the approach of the banshees. Even the boys were included in planning the defense of the farm should one of the monstrous birds come too near.

"Perhaps we should just accept the loss of a few cattle," Mhari suggested. "It's what they prefer."

"And if they finish off the animals and still hunger? If they decide to move their nests to these woods?" Shani asked.

"Surely they'd never migrate this far for more than a tenday or two," Mikhail argued. "There's no record of them ever nesting this low."

"There's never been such a good market for marl fur," said Shani. "The *Terranan* hunger for Darkovan trinkets has made the trapping industry double. That's at least one of the reasons the beasts are ranging farther for food.''

"Then it's likely we'll have to defend ourselves?'' asked Mikhail.

Shani shrugged. "Who can say, but the time to build a shelter is not when the blizzard blows.''

"Preparation is our best defense?'' Mikhail paraphrased.

Shani nodded. "And, if we're ready to fight the banshees, why let the cattle be lost? We'll protect them, too.''

"How?'' Tara wondered aloud. "They're taller than men. I've heard that one can gut a horse with a single blow.'' Sitting on her lap, Pier wriggled closer to her, seeming to sense her fear. "What good is a knife against claws like that?''

"Perhaps I could requisition some blasters from headquarters,'' Mikhail suggested. All three women seemed shocked by the idea. "Well, do banshees honor the Compact?'' He tried to say it lightheartedly, but no one was cheered.

"You've fallen from the Coordinator's good graces, at any rate,'' Mhari added. "But, with all your books, you must have some weapon that would be lawful, as well as effective against the creatures.''

"Hmm . . .'' Mikhail pulled his beard, then turned to Tara and Shani. "Come with me, you two. Mhari, have the boys help you take stock of the supplies we've stored in. Might have to stretch them . . .'' He was already in his library, Renunciates close at his heels.

In addition to Tara's hunting bow, the farm family armed itself with lances modeled after pictures in one of Mikhail's books. These were carved from long, heavy tree limbs. Ewen helped whittle one end of each shaft, bringing it to a sharp point. Mikhail taught everyone but Pier how to brace the lance against the ground.

"If my theory is correct,'' Mikhail explained, "the charging creatures will impale themselves on the poles.''

"I don't think banshees travel in packs,'' Shani told him. "Even one will be trouble enough.''

"If any come, they'll be drawn toward the barn,"
Mikhail continued. "Tara will try shooting them . . ."
Seeing Shani's arched eyebrow, he amended his words,
"it, first. If she fails, the lances will be ready."

"Still seems to me," Mhari grumbled, "that it would
be wiser to sacrifice some of the animals. What's one or
two cattle, compared to human life?"

"Would you fend off a wolf by feeding it a chicken?"
Shani countered.

Mhari only sighed. It was decided. Each night, the
boys lay awake, listening to the horrible shrieks getting
closer. They prayed to the god of the *cristoforos* that the
banshees would not come.

Perhaps the god half-listened, or maybe Shani was right
about them not traveling in packs. When the banshee
came, it was a solitary visitor. Its wailing echoed in the
farmyard, drowning out the terrified calls of the cattle.

Ignoring the chill the sound sent up his spine, Ewen
joined the others as they stood by the front door.

"It's moving toward the barn," Shani whispered. She
was watching the yard through a crack in the door. Tara
came up beside her, bow and quiver in hand. After Tara
had removed one shaft, she gave the quiver to Shani.
Ewen stepped back as his mother pushed the door open.
At the same time, Tara was setting the arrow on her bow-
string. She moved into the doorway, took aim, and drew
back the arrow.

Cold winter wind made Ewen shake even more. Mhari
had bundled Pier in a shawl and was carrying him to the
corner by the fire.

Tara loosed the arrow. As soon as it left the bow, she
reached for another, which Shani supplied.

"Glanced off," Mikhail announced as Tara readied her
second shot.

"Hit!" Mikhail said moments later. "It doesn't seem
to notice."

Ewen dared to peek around Mikhail. The creature was
clawing at the barn door. Its head was higher than the
lintel. Tara's arrow dangled from the loose skin at the back
of its skull.

A third arrow entered the shoulder, where one of the

bird's useless wings hung limply. The banshee's head craned around, then its body followed. Ewen saw the beast lumbering toward the house as Shani slammed the door shut. From the corner next to the door, Mikhail was bringing out the lances. He distributed them to the Renunciates and Ewen.

"Take Pier to the pantry," Shani told Mhari. "There are no windows or doors there for the banshee to enter."

The creature was beating its body against the corner of the house, even as Mhari was carrying Pier out of that end of the room.

"Why?" Mikhail mouthed to Shani.

"It's attracted to the warmth of the fireplace." The wall rattled at the impact of the bird beast's body. "Do we wait till it tears a hole in the house?" Shani asked.

"Maybe Mhari was right," Ewen found himself saying. "We'd be safer if we'd let it eat the cattle." These were the first words he'd ever spoken directly to his mother.

"Too late for that now, lad," said Mikhail.

"If that's what you want to do," Shani rasped, eyes grazing Ewen with anger before turning to the old man, "there's a way. I'll distract it while you fetch a dainty morsel from the barn." Her voice was fierce and frightening, but she seemed to realize it. Shani took a deep breath before completing her instructions. "Take it slowly, though. They are drawn by movement."

Ignoring Mikhail's protest, Shani went out into the yard, lance held tight. She crept along till she was behind the bird. It was too preoccupied with bashing itself against the wall to notice her cautious steps. When she was even with it, Shani began running toward the woods. The banshee stopped hitting the wall. It raised its grotesque head as if sensing something. Shani was still running as it turned its sharp beak toward her. The body shifted on huge claws.

Now Mikhail began his measured journey to the barn. The bird, turn completed, was following Shani. Its speed made Ewen gasp. He slipped past Tara and into the snowy yard. Shani spun around to face the beast. She pushed the blunt end of the lance into the frozen ground and braced herself. Ewen glimpsed the huge beak plunging toward her.

"Mother!" he screamed.

The pointed shaft ripped out of the bird's back. Shani disappeared beneath the falling creature's massive body.

"Mother!" Ewen called again, racing forward. The bird still writhed and he feared it would crush the woman below. Frantically, he jabbed his lance at the bird. Its flesh seemed impenetrable, but as his panic ebbed, he realized he needed to find a vulnerable place. A huge, dumb eye turned toward him. Ewen thrust the lance into the blank stare, pushing it hard, till it would go no deeper.

Tara came up beside him as the beast stopped moving. She drove her own lance crosswise through the banshee, wing to wing. Together, they used her lance as a lever to topple the corpse off Shani.

As soon as the weight was lifted away, Shani inhaled sharply. Ewen dropped to his knees in the snow.

"Mother?"

"Ewen . . ." she breathed before sucking in another lungful of air.

Tara crouched next to him. Her hands gently probed the fallen woman's blood-drenched torso.

"May have broken a rib or two. No serious wounds that I can see. What do you think, Shani?"

Ewen watched his mother nod reassuringly. She did not take her eyes from his.

"Mikhail," Tara called, "help me carry her to the house."

The man came and bent to lift Shani's shoulders. Tara grasped her feet. As they raised her, Shani grimaced. She turned her head so she could smile at Ewen.

"Let's get her in by the fire," Mikhail urged. It sounded good to Ewen, who walked beside them, shivering.

Startled, Ewen recalled the fire that had once raged inside him—the anger at losing his father. He remembered the icy fear that kept him from reaching out to his mother. Now both were gone. Tonight, the two had been forced to confront each other: the fire melting the ice, the melting ice quenching the fire.

Feeling whole, Ewen followed the others inside.

"Now I know where the boy got his hotheadedness . . ." Mikhail was saying.

Just A Touch . . .

by Lynne Armstrong-Jones

I'll start by saying that she's no relation to Lord Snowdon; as far as I know, she can't even take pictures. She currently works as a psychometrist; which is not, as in this country, laying your hands on an artifact and psychically telling where it comes from—or claiming to—but in Canada, where she lives, of giving kids tests to measure their intelligence and abilities (I did that for a while; here they call them guidance counselors; and what they mostly do, instead of measuring intelligence—that's thought to be undemocratic—is to find out for kids what college will take them or for what job they might be qualified.)

She says, "I've been writing all my life, but most of my ideas have remained inside my head as—well, fantasies, what else? This changed when I discovered how easily stuff could be edited on a word processor."

She is 37 years old and resides in London, Ontario with two cats, one computer and a "challenging three-year-old son." She's also a prime example of "if at first you don't succeed, try, try again." For a while I found a story from Lynne on my desk every couple of weeks, until by sheer persistence, and practice, one got good enough to print. Her first published story, "The Lady, the Wizard, and the Thing," appeared in the second issue of Marion Zimmer Bradley's Fantasy Magazine. *Her first seven or eight stories, I think, were submitted for the first issue; in fact, one of them was the first story I read for the magazine. Even though I rejected it, I remembered her name, and was pleased when she finally sent me something I could print. (MZB)*

Donalla ran. She ran blindly, not caring where she was going. It would not have mattered at any rate, the tears were blurring her vision so.

Such had become a pattern for her of late; whenever the frustration had turned to anger, she had sought the opportunity of running in the woods as an outlet.

There seemed to have been a great deal of frustration of late. *Laran!* Would they never speak of anything else?

Oh, yes, my good brother, thought Donalla. *You have the great talent and they have wondrous plans for you! You are now wed to an equally gifted woman, and will soon produce children with powers which the* leroni *have only dreamed of!*

Donalla had slowed her pace and given in to the tears which sought to escape her eyes. She sat down upon a log and wept, wondering why she had been the great disappointment. *Laran* had not descended suddenly upon her brother and sister when they had reached adolescence, but rather had seemed to somehow grow with them.

Here am I, thought the young woman, *nearly fifteen and still no trace of* laran *at all!*

She sighed, thinking of her parents, and their confusion: in spite of her bloodline, what Gifted Family would wish her as bride to their son when she had shown none of the gift herself?

I shall probably end up as wife to a ragpicker, she thought with a sigh.

Oh, there had been times when she had been quite certain that *laran* was coming to her—for what else could explain the strange emotions which seemed at times to surge through her for no reason?

Yet—"no," they had said, for the household *leronis* had shaken her head, her starstone still in hand. If the *leronis* had indicated thus, then it must be so.

The cry of a kyorebni somewhere above startled the young woman back to reality. Donalla rose, her eyes scanning the sky for some sign of the great bird.

Seeing none, she had just begun to relax once more, when—

Her breath came in a gasp. Suddenly, she could feel her heart begin to beat more rapidly . . .

She was running, running—*No,* she thought, *I am standing still . . . why does my mind feel as though my body is running?*

She felt the pain—but it was not physical. She felt the terror and saw death before her eyes—yet she did not.

Somehow, she knew where it was coming from. Her gray eyes looked toward the trees to the west, and she moved in that direction . . . hurry, hurry!

She could hear him, now. Quickly, she pushed the bushy growth aside.

There—a child. She hurried to his side. Blood dripped steadily from a gash upon his forehead, and seeped into both eyes so that he could not see clearly. Murmuring comforting noises, Donalla ripped a strip from the bottom of her gown and began to clean the boy's face. She secured another around his head in an effort to stop the bleeding. She smiled with relief when she saw that it had begun to flow more slowly.

He was a small child—no more than four, perhaps—and looked as though he might have come from the village. He sobbed something about being with his older sister and becoming lost—and falling down a hill and striking his head.

The rest of his babble sounded to Donalla like the fancies of a frightened child. She smiled.

"Come with me, then," she said gently, "for I know where there is a hill like the one you have described. Let us look for your sister together, little one."

He was quite happy to take her hand.

They had not ventured far before they could hear a female voice calling the boy's name. It was a very relieved sister who embraced the child.

Donalla's walk in the forest seemed to be a much more pleasant one now.

She had told her mother, *Domna* Jamilla, of her experience, but she had learned to omit any mention of *how* she had found the child. They would only be certain to mention, after all, that it was not *laran.*

Yet, that night, when the rest of the household slept, Donalla was sitting at her window and gazing at the sky.

"Idriel," she murmured to the mauve moon, "what is wrong with me?"

Though she said nothing of the recurrence of her "problem," Donalla found herself thinking more and more of it—and trying to make some sense of whatever was happening.

"What is it, *chiya?*" *Dom* Mintus was asking. "Are you ill, child?"

"No, my father," she whispered. "I am sorry—I was preoccupied."

Her father said nothing, but stroked Donalla's reddish locks, and wondered how hair as red as his own could grow on a head which was completely devoid of *laran*.

Suddenly he felt the young woman tense, as though struck.

"What is it, child?" Mintus knelt beside his daughter, wondering if she was, indeed, ill.

Donalla tried to reply, but the fear which took her was overwhelming: terror, a desire to flee—yet an inability to do so. *Death!* Death's face seemed before her.

Suddenly, she was standing: half herself, yet also half someone else.

Someone else who was terrorized.

And she knew where he was!

"Father," she managed to gasp, "quickly—get some help. We must go to him!"

Before Mintus could question her, she had fled out of the door. Her father followed quickly, shouting at a servant to bring one of the chervines and hurry after them.

His hand upon his sword, Mintus ran into the wooded area after his daughter. She had headed toward one of the roadways, but then turned away and in the direction of one of the cliffs.

For a moment, he was fearful that she was not in her right mind and might fling herself over the edge—but then she was slowing and stopping to peer downward.

"He is there," she gasped between breaths.

Dom Mintus did not need to use his own *laran* to pinpoint the man's location. He was on a ledge, obviously injured—attempting to fend off one of the more zealous birds of prey.

The servant secured the rope to a nearby tree and clambered down to the injured man, the bird deciding that there must be an easier meal elsewhere. Mintus and the servant managed to fashion splints for the broken arm and leg, and somehow, the man was brought above.

It was a quiet journey back.

The man was bedded and tended to. He thanked *Dom* Mintus profusely for saving his life. Donalla was in the corridor and heard him ask, "But how did you know where I was?"

Mintus gave an evasive answer and looked into his daughter's eyes as he stepped out of the room.

"Perhaps," he said gently, his hand against the young woman's cheek, "perhaps—just a *touch* of *laran*. It would seem very narrow in its scope, yet also very sensitive. You must learn to use it wisely, my daughter—but I do not know how . . ."

"Do not fear, Father," Donalla whispered, "it is clear to me what I shall do."

The winter had finally come to an end—and an end, as well, to the dangers brought by the wind and the cold.

Donalla smiled when she thought of the many travelers whom she had assisted to find their ways. Their feelings of fear and panic had been like beacons to the young woman.

She knew now that she would not marry: her *laran* was still too weak to render her desirable among the Great Families.

"Are you quite certain, my daughter?" *Domna* Jamilla asked yet again.

"Yes, Mother," smiled Donalla. "Although spring has come in our lands, there are many more where winters last longer. It is there that my 'touch' can be used most effectively. Think of the lives I may save!"

" 'Tis a noble thought, daughter."

As Donalla mounted the horse and headed away, she looked over her shoulder at what had been her home.

My parents, she thought, *my poor parents! How it concerned them when their daughter did not fit their desires!*

The saddest part of all is that they truly do not see that a "touch" used for the good of all can be more worthwhile than the most powerful laran *there is.*

With a sigh, then a chuckle, Donalla urged the beast forward.

Mind-eater

by Joan Marie Verba

*Elsewhere in these introductions I mentioned a contro-
versy as to whether the Darkover stories were science
fiction or fantasy. The one thing they've never been accused of is being horror fiction except in the most limited
sense; but I think even Ms. Verba would agree that
"Mind-eater" is one of the rare horror stories written
about Darkover . . . in the rather special old sense of
stories which give a* frisson *of horror or dread, an at-
mosphere of terror, instead of the all-too-frequent modern sense of "If you can't scare 'em, gross 'em out."*

*Joan Marie Verba was born in Massachusetts, but says
she has lived in Minnesota since she was four years old.
She attended the University of Minnesota and the University of Chicago, and holds a degree in physics; she
worked for one year as an assistant instructor at the
Graduate School of Astronomy at Indiana University, and
for ten years has worked as a computer programmer. I
think after all that I'd write horror stories, too. She began
reading Darkover books in 1978, and has previously had
stories published in* FREE AMAZONS OF DARKOVER
and in FOUR MOONS OF DARKOVER. *(MZB)*

Domenic MacAran tried to shake off the sense of fore-
boding that increased with each dogged step up the ancient stone stairs. A *nedestro* son of the Altons, he had
the Alton Gift, but his mother had been a *nedestro*
daughter of the Aldarans, so that Domenic had also had
occasional flashes of insight about the future. It was this
sense that nagged him now. But he could not go back:
the tower where he had been under-Keeper was now in

ruins, destroyed in the lowland wars that raged in the Domains. No, the only cure for his war-weariness was to get away, go as far into the Hellers as he could, find a village so isolated that the Domains were only a rumor, and *laran*-weapons a fairy tale. He'd been raised by a family of modest means; he could earn a living as a herdsman or a carpenter or stonemason. He'd served in the Guards; he might earn a living as a bodyguard, if one of the mountain lords in this area could support one. Wherever he settled, he must do it quickly—winter was fast approaching, and he could not wander the Hellers, alone, in the inevitable storms and blizzards that would come.

In the meantime, there were the stairs. They had appeared at the end of an overgrown dirt track, the rock splintered by years of frost, but not worn smooth by use. Weeds sprouted from the cracks. He had thought it a natural rock incline until he saw a spot where two stone slabs had been fitted together. He took his matrix, the starstone around his neck, and examined it more closely. The foundation showed no mortar or mark of any tool. The stairs had been laid by matrix workers, long, long ago. To be sure that there was no existing Tower, he had briefly gone into the overworld, where any Tower would leave its mark. There was none, but his sense of impending danger had begun at that moment.

He reached the top of the stairs. Looking up, he saw night fall, the ragged edges of a dark starry blanket coming toward him, over him, then behind him to the far horizon. Idriel and Liriel had risen, lighting the way.

A stone road appeared in front of him. He came to a village. There was a fountain in the village square. He stopped to drink, and wash, and fill his water bottle. He looked around for a likely place to knock on the door and ask for shelter for the night. Light shone through the shuttered windows of the small stone houses, but his attention was drawn to the dark face of an edifice beyond the village.

No! Leave me alone!

Domenic put his hand on his sword hilt, stood, and turned. No one was there. He had heard no sound. Hand

on his matrix, he peered into the overworld. He saw a
youth, with the physique of a runner-messenger, sprint-
ing across the gray plain. A youngster with newly-
developed *laran* having a nightmare, Domenic guessed.
In that case, if he could find the house, he could offer his
assistance as a *laranzu* to the family. *Laran*-gifted children in remote areas suffered unless they could teach
themselves control or had the milder forms of threshold
sickness. But as he turned to the houses, the overworld
image was gone. Before putting his matrix away, something about the houses caught his attention. They, too,
were matrix-constructed, just as the castle in Thendara
had been. Who would waste Tower energy on village
houses? And in an area where the nearest Tower was a
tenday's ride away?

Clouds obscured the moons. It began to snow. He
knocked at the door of a house. Before he could say anything, the woman who answered spotted his starstone,
said *"Laranzu!"* in a startled whisper, and slammed the
door in his face. At every other house in the village, it
was the same. Domenic sat in the snow powder and
wiped his forehead on his sleeve, though he was not
sweating. In the lowlands, he had been treated with respect, even awe, but he had never been shunned. In the
Domains, even the most ragged beggar might find shelter
for the night in the rudest of huts. Why did these villagers
refuse him?

Domenic turned back to the edifice. It was larger than
the castle in Thendara; had he not seen it earlier by
moonlight, he might have mistaken it for a mountain. No
light came from any window or door. He might have tried
to spend the night in an animal shelter instead, but the
smell of straw and hay would stop up his nose. He walked
to the castle.

He halted before the wooden double doors. These were
in good condition, on their hinges, latched, but not
locked. He unfastened the catch and pushed. The door
swung open easily, silently. He called inside. Nothing
answered. With his matrix, he kindled a cold blue light
in his hand. Domenic stepped in, closing the door behind
him.

He stood in an entry hall. In front of him and to his left was a stone staircase. Beside that was a hallway. To his right, there was another door, presumably leading to a chamber. To his far left, there was an open entryway to a vaulted hall. Holding the light in his hand in front of him, he walked in.

The bare wooden floor was clean. His sensitive nose detected no dust. In the middle of the long wall was a fireplace, taller than he was, with dry wood stacked next to it. He walked up to it, put down his pack and sword, laid fuel on the hearth, and kindled a fire with his matrix. Then, he extinguished the blue light. Hungry from the long day's climb and from the use of his *laran*, he ate a large meal from the store of food in his travel pack. Spreading his bedroll in front of the hearth, he prepared to sleep.

A hideous scream made him sit up and reach for his sword. Shrill curses echoed in his ears; the vilest language he had heard since leaving the Guards. It echoed in the hallways, reaching his ears in this large room. Then it stopped.

Domenic sat quietly, his heart racing. In his mind he recalled childhood tales of haunted castles and demon-possessed artifacts. But he was a Tower-trained telepath, and he knew such things were not so.

Are they not, little man?

Domenic stood, clutching his sword, and swung around before realizing he had not heard a voice but had, instead, received a telepathic message. "Show yourself!" he called. Although he was small in stature, he had become the best swordsman in the Guards, and when he received a wound serious enough to be sent to a Tower for healing, he became the most skilled telepath there, who would have succeeded the Keeper had he lived to lay down his office. No one mocked Domenic MacAran for his size and went unchallenged.

As if in answer, something ripped at his mind, as if banshee claws were scraping his brain. Domenic put a hand to his face, breathing heavily. After the shock of the attack had passed, he recognized the tearing rapport as a reflection of his own gift. Angrily, he thrust back, putting all his strength in resistance. A cry echoed in his thoughts. The pain stopped, and he fell to his knees.

His first instinct was to flee. A single telepath could not have a range he could not get away from. But there was a snowstorm outside. He would have to go beyond the limits of the village. by that time, he might be dead of the cold. No, whoever it was, whatever it was, he'd have to face it. Here. Now.

Putting his sword down, Domenic sat and took out his matrix to find his opponent. In the overworld, Domenic's image of himself was that of a large, muscular man. Let his opponent see that, if he would! But he saw no opponent. The runner-messenger was there; a woman, tall and silent; an *emmasca,* huddled and frightened; a clawed crustacean, like the ones from the ocean beyond the Aillard Domain. Dream images, none menacing. His opponent was hiding telepathically, but he—and Domenic sensed his opponent was male—had a physical presence, and *that* Domenic could find. He took his Keeper's kit of small matrixes and telepathic tools, and his sword, and walked from the hall, leaving his bedroll and the rest of his pack behind.

Domenic had invaded fortresses before. He knew how to search for hidden opponents, knew what precautions to take. Sword in one hand, blue matrix light in the other, he padded up the stairs to the topmost level. The floors were swept, the beds made, but no one was there. He wondered how such a large castle could be kept so clean. It should take a army of servants to maintain such a large building.

He went to the next lower level, and the next. Again there was a shriek, followed by cursing. He crept toward the noise, sword raised. At an intersection of hallways, he looked to the right, then to the left. The dim blue light revealed a bulge in the wall.

"I see you," called Domenic. "Show yourself."

The bulge did not move, but Domenic could hear stressed breathing. Cautiously, he moved forward. A form took shape. It was a large young man, his arms and legs twisted at odd angles. Shakily, the man's thick fingers reached for a matrix at his throat. Not wanting to be taken again by his own Gift, Domenic reached out and overwhelmed the figure's mind. The younger man cried out softly in response to the forced rapport. Domenic saw the image of the runner-messenger and withdrew immediately.

Domenic held the blue light to the figure's face. "I'm sorry," he said. "I thought you were someone else."

The figure turned toward him, tears of pain in his eyes. Again, the fingers reached for the matrix, which, unlike Domenic's, was unshielded.

My name is Ruyvil. I cannot speak clearly, the figure said into Domenic's mind. *I was born with my limbs twisted so.* Putting his hand down, Ruyvil moved away from the wall. He took a couple of steps, dragging one foot, and stopped in front of Domenic.

"I see," said Domenic. "I was looking for another, Is there another man here, a *laranzu,* perhaps, like myself?"

The round face puckered, the expression pinched, as if in pain. Ruyvil shook his head repeatedly, compulsively. Domenic tried to reach his thoughts, gently, but he was barricaded, and Domenic hadn't the heart to force himself into his mind again.

A shriek made Domenic turn, sword raised. He walked back into the middle of the hallway intersection. He heard a shuffling. Ruyvil walked toward him, one twisted arm extended, as if pleading. Domenic heard a string of curses. A woman came into view. She walked normally, but her head twitched.

A touch on his shoulder made him start. Ruyvil had his other hand on his matrix. *Her name is Mirella. Truly, she is harmless.*

Mirella stopped in front of them. A thick cord ringed her neck. Her matrix, threaded by a strand of spider silk, was tied to that cord. She thrust a trembling hand under the cord to steady it, and touched the matrix with a finger. In his mind, Domenic saw the quiet, still woman he had spotted in the overworld, a contrast to her real self.

A tall figure came from the shadows. Domenic did not hear him coming, did not see him until he came into the view of Domenic's blue hand-light. The *emmasca?*

"Yes," he said aloud. "I am Gareth. We . . ."

Mirella, Ruyvil, and Gareth shrieked and crouched, hands to their ears as if shutting out a painful noise. Domenic slammed his mind shut against the effect, but not before he caught the thought of his opponent:

Fool! Do you think you can escape me? All here are under my control!

This was intolerable. Even using his full Alton Gift to shield himself, Domenic could feel something thrumming against his barriers, like a battering ram against a gate. He strode ahead to the nearest door. Any Great House occupied by telepaths had to have a room with a damper. He'd find one if he had to go through every room.

Fortunately, he found one on that floor, probably a small presence-chamber used by the forgotten lord of this castle. He went back to the intersection and hauled Mirella and Gareth, one on each arm, to the room. Then he went back for Ruyvil. He half-dragged, half-carried the young man, but got him there at last. He took one of his matrixes, keyed to his own brain pattern, and locked the door with it. Then he turned on the damper.

The other three telepaths collapsed, moaning. Gareth sat up first. "Thank you," he said.

"Speak quickly," said Domenic. "Our adversary could come up at any moment, break the door, and turn off the damper."

"No," said Gareth, "he cannot do that."

"Of course he can," said Domenic. "The matrix will keep the door locked, but won't keep him from breaking the hinges."

"Gareth is right," said Mirella. She shrieked. "Castimir has no legs. He cannot go anywhere—" She let out a string of loud curses. "—faster than a crawl."

"I read of some of his life in his mind," said Gareth. "He was born of a mother raped in a lowland campaign. She fled to the house of a minor lord and became a servant there. Castimir made a name for himself as a mercenary soldier. He showed nothing but contempt for those who had any physical defect. Somehow he got involved in a blood feud. Knowing his mind, those he fought against drugged him so he could not use his *laran,* then cut off his legs instead of killing him. When he recovered his strength and his *laran,* he used his gift to kill those who had disabled him. Then he overwhelmed the mind of a strong man and compelled the man to carry him on his back, away from the lowlands. He forced the man to feed him, clothe him, find him shelter. By the time the strong man climbed the steps to the village here, Castimir had worn his caretaker out. The man died, and Castimir compelled the people of the village to house him here, feed him, clean for him, wait on all his needs, as if he were an overlord here.''

"Has anyone tried to kill him?" asked Domenic.

"Those who have . . ." Mirella whooped. ". . . have died.'' She let out a string of curses.

"He can compel people to jump off a cliff, fall into a well. . . .'' Gareth shrugged.

"Does he have a matrix? A starstone?" asked Domenic.

"Yes," said Gareth. "He took one from one of the lowlanders he killed and keyed it to himself.''

"Damn! If we were only near a Tower," said Domenic.

"We are," said Gareth, "in a way.''

Domenic turned to him.

"We are a small village," Gareth said, "but a proud one. Once we were the center of *laran*-skill in Darkover. We were kin to the *chieri,* as you can still see in some people, like me. The first telepath circle was in this castle, only underground. Towers were built later, as our knowledge spread to the lowlands and took root there. We are not what we were, but the babes here learn at their parents' knee what a matrix is, what *laran* is, what to do when it comes upon a body, and how to live with it after. Our skills and knowledge are not now what they are in the lowlands, but it all started here.''

"How many telepaths are in the village?"

"We are the strongest," said Gareth, "which is why Castimir keeps us here because he can control us more easily.''

"That is not . . ." Mirella let out a string of curses. ". . . all."

Gareth hung his head, embarrassed.

Mirella explained, pausing when her head twitched, or when she whooped or cursed. "We are not only here because of our . . . *laran*. We are here because when Castimir came . . . and began to control the *laran*-gifted . . . the villagers bargained with him. . . . If he would . . . take us for himself . . . they could send their *laran*-gifted . . . kin out of his reach."

Domenic nodded. Now he knew why he had been turned away from the houses. The villagers thought he was another Castimir. "But you said he forces the villagers to care for him, too."

"Yes," said Gareth, "that was also part of the bargain. In exchange for leaving their kin alone, they must provide for him. He forces them if they forget."

Domenic sat. After some thought, he said, "You said there was once a telepath circle here?"

"Yes," said Gareth, "but underground, on the lower levels of the castle."

"Have any of you ever been there?"

They looked from one to the other. Gareth said, "No. There's no reason to go there."

Domenic stood. "Show me."

They looked to the door, terrified. Mirella shrieked. Gareth said, "But outside this room, he'll control us again."

"We can't stay here," said Domenic. "For one thing, there's no food. And we must defeat him."

"How?" said Gareth.

"If there was once a Tower circle here, there has to be at least a second-, third-, or fourth-level matrix around. All of us working together, with that sort of screen, should overwhelm him."

"But we know nothing . . ." Mirella cursed. ". . . of such sorcery."

"I know," said Domenic. "There is a risk, since there is no monitor for us, and none of you have worked in a Tower circle before. But none of you are new to the use of your *laran*. I can draw you in and keep you steady.

Provided it does not take all night, we should be safe. What do you say?"

They looked from one to the other. Gareth said, "We are agreed, but how to get down to the matrix-chamber without Castimir ripping our minds apart? For he surely shall if he senses what we wish to do."

"Let me try this," said Domenic. "The damper will have thrown him off our scent, so to speak, and when I turn it off, he might not realize immediately where you are. With my Gift, I can overwhelm your minds, and thus protect you with my own resistance. Then I can lead you to the lower levels by the hand. Can you trust me to do this? I can only do it if you are willing."

The others consented. Domenic turned off the damper. One by one, Domenic put their *laran* under his control. As he worked, he thought that this also would help them work smoothly within the matrix circle, for by the time they reached the lower chambers, at Ruyvil's pace, they should be deeply in rapport and attuned to each other.

Once their minds were protected by his, and his own thoughts barricaded, he linked arms with Mirella on his right, Ruyvil on his left. Gareth took Ruyvil's other arm to steady him. Slowly, slowly, they walked down the hall and descended the stairs. Even barricaded, Domenic could sense Castimir's thoughts searching him out on the surface of his awareness:

Fool! Do you think you can thwart me so?

Domenic ignored his adversary. It was taking a great mental effort to protect them all from Castimir: Domenic could understand how he could keep three telepaths and one village under his sway. But the matrix—and he hoped there was a matrix—would amplify their thoughts at least fourfold.

At last, the four reached the lower regions of the castle. There was a door there, with an ancient matrix lock, still activated. Domenic uncovered his matrix, gathered the other three in his rapport, matched resonances with the lock, and released it. The door swung open.

Domenic led the other three into the room. There was a damper there. He released the three others and turned it on. Then he closed the door. The matrix lock reactivated, making the room secure.

"What now?" asked Mirella. She cursed.

When he had turned the telepathic damper on, a dim glow issued from the ceiling. "We find the matrix," answered Domenic. He strode through the chambers of the underground levels. There was a familiarity about them. He could well believe that there had been telepath circles here, perhaps even the first telepath circles on Darkover.

He found a room with a third-level matrix. He walked around it, examined it, and found it workable. Turning toward the entrance, he saw Mirella, Gareth, and Ruyvil looking on curiously.

"This is where we will work," said Domenic. "Mirella, you sit here; Gareth, here; Ruyvil, here. I will turn the damper off from here. When I sit, we will begin."

"What will . . ." Mirella cursed. ". . . happen?"

"We will fight him in the overworld," said Domenic.

"The gray plain?" said Gareth. "But that is illusion."

"It can be," said Domenic. "But the effects can be quite real. Tower battles have been fought in the overworld before. Injuries and deaths to the participants have been recorded."

"Could we die?" said Gareth.

"We could," said Domenic. "But working together, with the help of the matrix, we should have the advantage. If you don't want to do this, I will try it alone with a lower level matrix or with only one or two of you. If you have the slightest doubt about this, I want you to quit *now*. There is no disgrace in standing aside in this matter, for anything less than full cooperation from any of you could kill us all, once we begin."

"I will help you." Mirella let out a whoop.

Ruyvil motioned that he wished to join the circle.

"Death would be better than being his tool for the rest of his life," said Gareth.

"Just think *with* me," said Domenic. "The rapport will be very much like it was when I brought you down here." He sat and turned off the damper. Again, there was a respite—the damper apparently threw Castimir off-balance, temporarily unable to reach his victims. Dom-

enic fell into a tentative rapport with the large matrix,
then drew the others in, one by one. Mirella, despite her
body twitch, was rock-solid as a telepath. Ruyvil, in contrast to his handicap, was strong and supple. Gareth was
energetic and steady. Just as Castimir made contact, Domenic thrust them all into the overworld. Here, Domenic
was a tall, muscled warrior fending off Castimir's attack,
which was represented in the gray dream-stuff as spears
against Domenic's unyielding shield.

That's Castimir, said Ruyvil, whose thoughts were
speech in the overworld. *The shelled creature.*

Peering over his psychic shield, fending off Castimir's
barbs, Domenic spotted the shelled crustacean he'd noticed before. *So that was how Castimir pictured himself,*
thought Domenic. *Impregnable and unreachable.* But
Domenic had been by the sea, and eaten such creatures
for dinner. He knew how to break their shells. Keeping
up his shield, he altered his dream-shape to that of Zandru at his forge. His companions quickly picked up on
the image, and as Domenic grew, towering over Castimir, arms bulging, Ruyvil became a hammer in Domenic's hand, Gareth formed a wall to protect them from
Castimir's barbs as Domenic took shape, and Mirella became an anvil that slipped under Castimir's form. Startled by the change in strategy, Castimir had time only to
raise his claws in a vain attempt to fend off the hammer
as it came down on his shell.

With a gasp, the four telepaths returned to their bodies
in the matrix chamber. Domenic quickly checked the overworld with his personal matrix. The Castimir image
was gone. There was a mental silence. Domenic reached
out for contact with Castimir's mind. Their adversary was
either barricaded or dead.

''Is he gone?'' asked Gareth.

Ruyvil touched his matrix. *I will not be satisfied until
I see his body.*

''Where does he usually stay?'' said Domenic. ''We
could check those rooms.''

Gareth led him to a suite in the middle of the castle,
on an upper floor. There, lying on a bed, was a legless
body. It looked as if he had been crushed.

Gareth leaned against a wall and slid to the floor, exhausted. "It's over."

Mirella came in soon after, leaning on Ruyvil's arm. They looked in on the body and sighed.

"It's over for Castimir," said Domenic, "but I am uneasy about there being a third-level matrix close at hand. If Castimir had known of it, and known how to use it, he would have been all but invincible. Or, worse, if a group of Tower-trained telepaths had descended on you with ill will, this whole castle, and the area here, could have been reduced to rubble."

What is to be done, then? said Ruyvil.

"Stay and guard it against misuse," said Domenic. "Then, too, we can put it to good use—a small circle with even a relatively low-level matrix could do a bit of mining close by, keep the roads in repair, and the summer fires under control. I could teach you, if you wish, or I could teach the *laran*-gifted in this village, who will probably return when news of Castimir's death reaches their kin here."

We will fare no better anywhere else, said Ruyvil.

"I bear no ill will toward my kin in the village," said Gareth. "They did what they thought best to save themselves."

"I will . . ." Mirella whooped. ". . . stay."

Domenic nodded. "Good. We can probably earn our keep through mining alone. I think, after this, the villagers will leave this castle to us. One day, when the Domains stop fighting, we can send to a Tower to have the matrixes here recorded and monitored. Until then, we have our life's work ahead of us."

No one can play the tyrant with us again, said Ruyvil.

"No," agreed Domenic. "Here we can have peace, if we work to keep it." His foresight assured him that it would be so.

Mists

by Meg Mac Donald

This story was originally called "In the Mists of Hali," and I held it to the bitter end for one of the previous anthologies, RED SUN OF DARKOVER, but finally found I couldn't use it. The characters in this story made an appearance in the story "My Father's Son" in FOUR MOONS OF DARKOVER, and I, at least, was glad to know more about them. That sale, she says, "inspired me to do a major rewrite, which not only shortened the manuscript by over 1500 words and tossed out extra characters, but tightened the plot."

That's the way to do it; the major fault I find with beginners is that thy are too much in love with their own "flawless" prose. Even when you're as experienced as I am, second thoughts are often better than first, and short stories are better than long ones—unless very good.

Meg Mac Donald lives in Michigan—and although I don't know too much about Michigan, I know that every time I go there, I am again struck with how much the climate resembles that of Darkover. For some reason I always get stuck to go to Michigan—or Minnesota—in February, and Phoenix in August; anybody with brains would reverse the times. (MZB)

Tell them! Seanon swatted a ball of dust across the floor, determined to elicit a response this time . . . *this time* . . .

His young cousin glanced up briefly, cocked his towhead as if in response, then yawned before turning pale eyes toward the red sky outside the unshuttered window. Listening, Seanon waited a full ten count, breath held, anticipating, anticipating . . . Dori sniffled loudly and began to rock to an unheard tune, his inner-song which played louder than the argument of Seanon's parents and their guest in the next room.

Exasperated, Seanon dropped to the hardwood floor, thumping doe-hide bootheels against the boxy window seat before he spun around on rumpled pleats. Hiked almost to his knees, undyed moggins stretched out from under his belted plaid to rest against the unswept floor. He shoved the broom away roughly. Already crimson splashes of sunset transformed the small room from egg-shell to rose; soon the long shadows of early eventide would stretch across the walls and it would be time for dinner. Below the back of the house, chilled autumn waves rushed against the shore as the tide rose with violet Liriel. They would have to leave soon.

Fingering the pendant at his throat, Seanon traced the lacelike thistle carving. The blue stone head winked invitation. A suffocating beauty awaited him, mist and mystery beyond comprehension.

Behind drawn curtains, Jaes Mac Domhnall's voice interrupted Seanon's thoughts. The sound of splintering wood punctuated his father's quarrel with kinsman Damar Morough.

Seanon's nose wrinkled at the thought of the thane's bulging belly and gaudy trews. Shameful, it was, for the plump old oyster to sweep a seemingly witless child out of his fine estate and into their cottage just to avoid having equally gaudy northern-bred guests thinking it was his own son, and not the half-witted brat of some milking maid. Worse to steal him out of the only family he'd ever known! This debt of kinship, for the sake of Seanon's aunt Doria, was being redeemed in excess.

For five summers Morough had been content to leave Dori in the Mac Domhnall household undisturbed; now he showed a renewed interest in the child. His visits wreaked havoc. He professed readiness to raise his wife's son . . . if Dori could be ferreted out of hiding on that fateful day. Dori's foot at the back of his neck made Seanon start.

"Ye've nae blood o' tha' mean pisser," Seanon said,

tugging an untied brog playfully. Dori pulled his feet out
of reach, legs tucked up under Seanon's castoffs—an
oversized plaid and drooping blue and white tartan leggings. Pale eyes glinted red in the setting sun.

"Ye must show 'em, Dori," Seanon told him. Dori
didn't even bat an eyelash. "They 'ave to know for sure
'e's not yer papa, before it's too late . . . ah, here,"
Seanon wiped his foster brother's nose then sank down
to the floor again. His jeweled starstone pendant
scratched against his neck like a live thing seeking its
master's favor.

Matrix, he corrected himself. Torm called it a matrix,
and the northern wizard, a *laranzu,* had taught him
enough about the mysterious gem when Seanon was eight
and seeing things from some otherwhen to know it was
not simply a stone. Seanon had already heard the stories
about the gentle forest folk and starstones. Why, the folk-
songs had been taught to him even as he wove his first
net; he knew them all by heart.

Torm called it a science, though. It was a science to
direct power through the matrix—a dangerous science.
Seanon respected that, uncertain as he was what science
meant. Alaric Hastur-Elhalyn had insisted he trust Torm.
He had trusted Alaric, too, as captivated by the young
man who walked at the bottom of Hali as Doria had been.
Hali, the lake that wasn't a lake though Seanon didn't
know what else it could be.

Alaric had been the first stranger among them, appearing on the snow-dusted Ridge one morning without a stag
pony, without a cloak, with nothing but a bewildered
look on his face as he stared with fascination and horror
at the winter whitecaps.

Itching fingers played with the pendant again. Last time
he looked into the stone, he had been lost following Dori
in blue swirling confusion, waking to find his worried
parents sitting over him. But Alaric had urged Seanon to
explore his talents, had often praised his sharp instincts;
it was Alaric's voice that beckoned in the mist.

"Dori," Seanon said, leaning against the window seat,
watching fading colors lick at the opposite wall. He

closed his eyes. *Dori, what are ye waitin' for?* The child ignored him.

At least talk to me . . . Seanon kneaded his temples, wishing Alaric was still alive and could help him solve the puzzle of the mist . . . and of Dori.

As the voices beyond the drapes rose and fell like waves, Seanon Mac Domhnall's imagination wandered to the tales Alaric had told him, of people bound together using their matrixes in unison. A melding, blending, perfect joining of minds limited only by the weakest member. Seanon imagined the music of joined minds was like the wistful strength of pipes at eventide. And if many circles joined? It must be as glorious as when the Clans gathered in the summer for ceilidhs, the sounds of pipes and drums and voices groaning and straining into a melody as sweet and piercing as a tragic tale.

The blue stone glimmered at Seanon's throat. Without another thought he slipped the pendant over his head. Cradling it in his hands, he worked his way deeply into the glow until he was swimming freely, reaching with untrained ability for Dori to follow as he immersed himself in the wavering cerulean light.

The misty, flat landscape appeared again, translucent flowers bending under a noiseless wind. The image filled the space around him as he pushed deeper, reaching through the haze for his foster-brother's hand. Someone called, and he turned. A voice, Alaric's voice, called softly. He walked with effort through the fog, feeling the rolling, tumbling current moist and heavy around him, almost like the sea, washing him, sucking him farther and farther into a reality he had only passed over cautiously before. He called, listened, called again. Only a limitless silence wove around him, filling the mist with the luscious, comfortable dreaminess of slumber. Seanon swayed, bare feet shuffling through pink sands and tangling weeds. A glimmering, fluttering mass swarmed around him; a school of birds like undulating fish slithering by in the air. He sank slowly into the blue softness, hearing a voice beckoning in the mist, urgently calling him, but having no source. Then only sharp, cold blackness.

Seanon's eyes blinked open as his stomach heaved. Struggling against the urge to vomit, he focused on Dori's blue-edged form hovering over him, a tiny finger drawing away from the starstone pendant clutched awkwardly in Seanon's hand. Seanon squeezed his eyes to clear them, fighting back a moan as he struggled to lift his heavy head. Tremors bubbled down his spine, spasming his hand until the matrix slipped free to rest on the wooden floor. He stared, a cry caught in his throat, as Dori retrieved the thistle pendant, carefully slipping it over Seanon's head. The pain subsided swiftly as Dori tugged at his arm, urgently pointing with his other hand toward the window.

How'd ye do tha'? Seanon wondered, his sight clearing of the mist. Another pang of nausea struck him as he struggled to his knees, leaning on the windowbox to look where his foster-brother pointed.

At the edge of the blushed forest two men spoke with Morough and Seanon's father. His mother stood back, arms folded tightly. Red-haired strangers, they were dressed richly, one with a fine sword at his waist. Tall, well-bred stag ponies stood idly behind them.

Seanon . . .

Why didn't you answer before?

Take me to the mist, Seanon—now!

Laddie, not now, we can't go back in, I . . .

Seanon! Dori's fingers brushed against his cheek, touching the moisture still there from their last foray. *Seanon, please . . .* a voice whispered, not Dori's but coming through Dori's mind. The flood of rapport made Seanon sway, dropping back to the floor, Dori in his arms.

A lake beside a half-built Tower, red with sunset and calm with summer. Alaric's robust form, capped with golden locks, wading into the misty waters. Then a sharp-featured man with red hair, angry, jealous, following. An agonizing, deafening roar caused the flowing mist to billow. The stranger appeared again, clutching a starstone and howling with mad, perverse joy as he dropped the flaring blue gem on the pink sand at the shore of the ghost lake. Morough, laughing wildly at the sight, was hurrying down the shore to where the blue glow shone in the sand; smashing it with a rage that shook the scene until it splintered in Seanon's mind.

Seanon gasped. Alaric had been his friend; Seanon had cried for days when he heard Alaric had gone into the lake, never to return—his matrix crushed on the shore. It *was* Alaric's gentle voice calling from beyond a watery grave whenever Seanon looked into the swirling mist of his starstone. *Morough* had crushed Alaric's matrix, and he had the help of one of the strangers standing a stone's throw from their house!

Lifting Dori, Seanon stood, staggering toward the back of the house before his parents and their unexpected guests reached the front door. The bleakness, the coldness, the fear and loathing of thane Morough hung in his mind. The memory of something Dori should not remember—he had not yet been born! Alaric's bride, Doria, had come back to the Ridge shattered, taken in by the thane who professed such love for her. The murderer of her husband!

The salt-crusted door leading to the cellar groaned on its hinges. Seanon stumbled down the slippery steps, nearly dropped his cousin. His head pulsed. Had Doria Muir known what old Morough had done? She had borne him a child all the Ridge called witless, dumped on Seanon's family when Doria died. A child Morough had refused even to name. Of course! How could he? Dori was not of the old man's blood; he was Alaric's child, born of mist to haunt the old man.

Seanon kicked the cellar door closed behind them, catching his breath for a moment in the damp, fish-scented air. He shouldered his father's traveling packs and slipped a *skean dhu* into his belt. Outside the cellar the vast ocean stretched before them, cold with nearing winter and shimmering with sunset. Dori buried his head against Seanon's shoulder.

"Shhh, *alenya,* I know ye don't like the water." He set the trembling child in the larger of the two boats, tying Dori's loose brogs, hiking up the drooping moggins on the boy's calves. He paused, staring into the little boy's frightened face. "This sure ain't the best time, ye know . . ." he swallowed deeply, then ruffled Dori's hair.

In another moment the little craft was free of the dock and Seanon clambered in, straining with the oars to battle the rising tide as he rowed them out of the cove and into the expansive sea.

The night air was chilly; dutifully, Seanon wrapped his foster-brother in a blanket. His mother would have his skin if Dori were to take a cold. Pale eyes sparkled under the glow of the moons and Dori smiled as they drifted with a favorable current. The wind was low, and Seanon had yet to set the small sail. For now, early-night stars guided them.

"I never liked 'im, Dori. But I never knew he did that to yer papa . . ."

Sitting beside the child, Seanon stared out across the dark ocean, watched silver-edged waves rise and fall gently. He scanned the horizon, looking for clouds, a tickling fear in his stomach warning him that a storm would mean danger he wasn't prepared to face. All his plans for a safe journey had gone into the sea when Dori insisted they leave at once. He wondered what his parents had thought when dinner was served and he and Dori were nowhere to be found. Somehow they would know, they'd have to.

"Whene'er I looked in the matrix, I was seein' Hali," he said softly, turning his thoughts to other things, "and I always heard Alaric."

Ridiculous, he thought. No one could live at the bottom of a lake—magical or otherwise. His hands played with the chain around his neck, swinging the pendant back and forth. Mist beckoned and he dropped the winking stone against his off-white shirt. Alaric's voice, far away, whispered softly.

"Ah, no," he said to himself, "not now, not now." He looked down at Dori sitting between his knees. "Well, lad, we've done it now, 'aven't we? There's no goin' back," Seanon told him. "It'll take some doin' to find the Elhalyn folks, but they'll help us just as soon as they git a peek at ye. Don't worry, *alenya*—I'll let nae harm come to ye. We'll keep our secret." Dori sighed at that, leaning his white head against Seanon's chest.

Secrets . . . aye, Seanon, secrets . . .

Seanon smiled at the word softly intoned in his mind. "Our secret. Kept in here," he said, tapping the thistle pendant Torm had given him when he came to Marcone with Alaric when Seanon was eight. "Even thane Morough don't have one. He'll never know where we are. He won't be able to get ye. I promise."

Seanon rolled over when he heard his name called. He blinked in the star-studded darkness, listening to the breeze slap the patched yellow canvas. He had set the sail earlier in the night, and the stiff wind blew them swiftly along. Beside him, curled under two blankets, lay Dori. Seanon himself had drifted to sleep twice and struggled now to stay awake. It was dangerous, so near the coast, to fall asleep. If the small boat went off course, they could run aground.

He scratched at a sudden hot spot at his neck, sitting up. His shirt must have rubbed the tender skin there raw. Already woolen moggins, damp from splashed water, made his legs itch. He scratched again, his fingers brushing against the chain. Stopping, he listened. Had a voice just called his name? He looked at Dori's sleeping form. Torm had spoken of one mind reaching to another in dream. *Dori?*

Again a sensation of burning. A pulse at his throat. His matrix! Someone *was* trying to reach him. Resisting the urge to open himself wide to the call, Seanon thought quickly. No one had the skill. . . . he shivered. The two strangers with Morough were northerners—red-haired northerners!

Answering their call meant risking everything. Clamping down on his barriers the way Torm had taught him, he put the intrusive thoughts aside, busying himself with the boat, readjusting the billowing little sail to take in the most of the moderate tailwind.

The pulse was stronger the next time. More than an irritating pinch, it made Seanon swallow hard, flinching. *No,* he thought, *I won't answer ye. If I ignore ye long*

enough ye'll think I canna hear, that I'm too far away
. . . but what was too far? Alaric had allowed that distance influenced the simple working of a matrix. One
person could only do so much—but what about Alaric
himself? The man who disappeared for days in the mysterious misty waters at Hali? Alaric, who had come to
Marcone as no one had ever done before—from nowhere!

Seanon's temple throbbed with the next pulse and he
gasped. Dori stirred at the sound, sitting up under the
pale light of the moons, gray eyes staring at his foster-
brother.

"Someone's tryin' to find us, Dori. 'e wants . . . 'e
wants . . . ye, 'e wants ye back." Seanon closed his
eyes, pressing fingertips to his temples, battling the more
powerful, infinitely more schooled mind invading his.
The image of a hawk-nosed northerner bathed in blue
light burned in his mind. The boat rocked as Dori
squirmed out from under his blankets, reaching for the
starstone pendant at Seanon's throat.

"No," Seanon's eyes blinked open. "Dori, don't, ye
could kill me . . ." But it didn't kill him, and the searing
pulse stopped, the vision of the strange *laranzu* shatter-
ing in his mind. Seanon stared at the pale-eyed boy
kneeling before him, both of them trembling in the cool
breeze. His breath plumed in the night air, their breathing the only sound besides the slap of waves on the boat's
wooden hull and the flutter of the sail. "Torm told me
that only a few people can do that," Seanon whispered.
"I didn't believe ye did it the first time, and here ye do
it again."

A slight smile parted Dori's lips, and Seanon almost
expected an answer when he felt another jab in his mind,
more insistent than any of the others. Pain shook his
body, pitching him sideways. His head struck the tiller
and the little boat rocked as the rising wind played with
the flapping sail.

"Stop! Please, ye're hurtin' me!" Seanon pleaded,
tears squeezing out of the corners of his eyes. "Dori,"
he whispered, "Dori . . ."

Small hands reached for the flickering pendant. The
boat stopped dead in the water, the wind dying. Dori fell

forward, hands grasping for the thin rail. Their combined weight against the tiller spun the boat into a cross wave. A moment later the cold darkness of the water engulfed them.

Pain forgotten, Seanon floundered in the salty spray toward the capsized boat. Soaked woolen moggins dragged at his kicking legs.

"Dori?" he sputtered, "Dori, where are ye?" A tug, not in his mind this time, but at his feet. Dori! Catching his breath, Seanon ducked below the surface, shedding heavy leggings and boots as he propelled himself with his legs. Eyes closed against stinging salt, he searched blindly, the heaviness of the swirling cold water reminding him of his matrix-vision. Cerulean blue beauty, rolling, waving peace. Fingers closing on the tattered edge of his cousin's kilt, Seanon pulled Dori close, wondering if they would be better off sinking slowly, safely into the salty depths, away from the persistent touch of an acid mind. He butted the overtures away as he would have the snout of a sharp-toothed fish.

What do I do now? he wondered, feeling his and Dori's desperation merge into one powerful, fearful cry of terror in his mind as they struggled upward. Fear swirled in him like an inky stain on milk, darker and darker until it exploded in every direction. *Torm, hear me, please, what do I do?*

Inquisitions. Questions scattered into the landscape of his mind, silver etching across the ink-black surface. Battling fatigue, Seanon pushed himself upward through the water, hauling Dori after him, pushing up, up, through bubbles from his escaping breath, through the sudden questions spinning around him, stitching shining cords of sanity into his confusion.

Torm, who is that? a voice asked. A mind wondered.

Blessed Hastur, what power! Torm, what sort of matrix could that be? What have they found now?

With that they could . . .

Peace, friends. Seanon knew Torm's voice, knew the gentle, reassuring touch of his mind, far away, far, far away. *We must be as one. We are a circle, we are as one mind, we are as one soul, we are in unison, one power.*

Flowing acquiescence surged around Seanon as he swam, warming him for a short time, though the surface eluded him. Was he going the wrong way? To the murky bottom and not the air above? To one side he felt the insidious mind's return, slicing toward him, to the other, Alaric's voice surged through the depths, rising from a whisper to boom through the darkness. Confused, Seanon stopped swimming. The two forces collided, crushing the air from his lungs.

Seanon? Torm called him now. *Seanon Mac Domhnall? Where are you?*

Torm? Alaric? Help me, Seanon cried in the darkness, legs beating the water furiously, lungs cramping as he squeezed from between the opposing forces, *they've come for Dori! Torm, I can't find the boat! We'll drown!*

Slower, slower, chiyu—*I hear you, we all hear you. What matrix are you using, child?*

The one ye gave me.

Denial. Seanon smashed against something in the dark. Relieved to find the boat, he ignored the splintering headache and reached up. The cool smoothness of ice pressed against his hand. His fingertips burned. Still dragging Dori with him, he kicked back and forth, staring up through the clear crystal barrier at the star-filled sky.

Torm? Torm! Something's wrong—I can't get out o' the water! He pounded against the barrier; the resounding hum echoed in the water, waves turning him in somersaults. He struck another barrier, bounced off, hit another. Trapped, he sank down to the cold smooth floor of his impossible prison.

Dori, I'm sorry, he thought, looking down at his cousin's lifeless form slumped against the icy, matrix-inspired floor. *I'm so sorry . . .*

Through a rising blue haze Dori's body began to shimmer, passing into the crystallike barrier sealing a watery grave.

"No!" Seanon's hands passed through Dori's body. *NO!* Above, he detected Alaric's face peering down at him, crystalline tears anointing his cheeks, running along the hard edges of Seanon's prison, leaving hissing streaks in the ice. His moving lips made no sound, his slim six-fingered hand could not touch them. Brandishing his *skean dhu,* Seanon chipped furiously at the floor. The knife disappeared.

Alaric! He glanced up, met Alaric's flickering gray eyes, *Alaric, help me! I'm losin' 'im. Alaric, do something!* He reached up, straining to match his fingers to Alaric's on the other side of the barrier. Closing his eyes, he pushed himself through blue haze, screamed at the searing cold until his hand met Alaric's. His rapport with Torm shattered, ice fragments exploding into darkness.

Seanon swayed, falling into the softness of the mist. His hands clutched the fine, soft sand; gentle, wet specks of snow kissed his tear-stained cheeks.

Raising his head from Hali's mist-cloaked shoreline, Seanon peered through the heavy fog oozing across the blurry mantle of the lake. A hand touched his shoulder, lifted him to unsteady feet. He squinted up to see Dori riding against his father's broad chest.

"Alaric!" Torm's voice pierced the silence. The *laranzu* met them on the beach. "Alaric, how did . . . we never expected to see you rise from those waters again."

"The child . . ." Torm touched the little head as Alaric settled wearily in the sand. Seanon sat beside him, his soaking plaid half unraveled. "I was forbidden to see him."

"Of course," Alaric said softly, stroking the boy's wet hair. "Of course you were, my friend."

"Your matrix was destroyed . . ." another northerner said, draping a blanket around Seanon and another around Alaric and Dori.

"I found another."

"That's impossible! You keyed yourself into another matrix?"

"Not so hard when the matrix is the seed of your own child. I didn't know that it couldn't be done . . ."

"You didn't die," Seanon said weakly, shivering under the dry blanket. His teeth chattered.

The young man—young, for age had not crept upon him in Hali—smiled. He looked down at Seanon, a gentle fingertip pushing dripping locks from the boy's eyes. "No, lad. But I suppose I must find another matrix now."

"Can ye?" Seanon asked. "Can ye have a new star- . . . *matrix?*"

"Impossibilities never stopped Alaric, *chiyu*," Torm told him. "Or you, it seems. Someone pass me some food before this child goes into shock. Alaric said you were gifted, but he never said anything about this."

"But I didn't do a'thing. Alaric . . ."

"No, Seanon," Alaric shook his head. "You pulled yourself out of my dear cousin's trap; and you pulled me with you. You've tried for years—yes, I know, I felt it," he smiled. "You finally learned just how to use a very powerful matrix, lad."

"But I didn't know!" Seanon whispered, his eyes wandering to Dori's waterlogged frame in Alaric's arms. "I knew I had to get away from . . ." he glanced around, listening for the other *laranzu*.

"He's gone," Alaric assured him softly. "When I felt your mind touching mine, and his touching yours, I flung him out before he knew for certain I was there. I seem to have more influence in these matters than I realized."

"Where did you . . . fling 'im?" Seanon hazarded, accepting bread from Torm. He inhaled the sweet aroma deeply, mouth watering.

"Oh, the overworld maybe. Or Hali. I've always been poor with directions. That's how I got to Marcone. Missed the castle at Elhalyn . . ."

"Seanon," Torm touched his shoulder, "we'll send word to your parents that you're safe—you'll need a lot of rest before going home."

"Please, can't I stay?" he asked, shifting painfully. He hadn't realized until then just how sore he was. He looked around at strange, compassionate faces. "Is this the circle? Can't I stay? I want to learn, Torm. I want to learn how I did this."

"Don't count on it," someone snorted, handing him a second piece of nutcake. "You'll never know how you did that. It can't be done."

"You've already learned more than some people learn in a lifetime," Torm told him. "These are dangerous times, Seanon, very dangerous. Are you sure you want to be a part of it?''

"I know that if I go back to the Ridge I'll never learn more about me matrix. All they use is precognition anyway." He heard intakes of breath and chuckles around him but pressed on. "I'm not keen on carpentry; maybe I could be a better—? I don't know. What does one *do* with *laran*?''

The adults laughed at his question, shaking their heads. Dori slipped out of his father's arms and went to kneel in front of Seanon. His little fingers touched the thistle pendant at Seanon's neck gently and he looked deeply into the older boy's eyes.

"Ye are the impossible one," Seanon told him. "But I'm glad for it, *alenya*." He hugged the younger boy to him. "I couldn't go back without ye, Dori. And ye wouldn't 'ave me, would ye?'' Dori smiled.

"How did ye ever stay down there, Alaric? Is there something in Hali?'' Seanon looked out over the misty water that was not water; it made his eyes moist.

Alaric smiled. "Something like that," he replied.

Dori smiled, the secret still hidden behind the veil of his sleepy, misty-gray eyes, and Seanon sighed. He would find the answers someday. He had time to learn, and he knew there were many things to be learned before he could share with others. But not now, Seanon thought, yawning. Now, he was tired, and Hali's rolling mists lured him to sleep.

Our Little Rabbit

by Mary K. Frey

Mary Frey says that this story concerns itself with a new form of laran *known as the Cassilda Gift and is laid somewhere in the darkness of the Ages of Chaos, between* DARKOVER LANDFALL *and* STORMQUEEN.

She says of herself that years ago, she told herself that by the time she was forty she wanted to write something good enough to sell professionally and that she "made it with exactly two months to spare."

Her story in the first Darkover short story contest (ten years ago, when I was editing a fanzine and running contests, instead of editing professional anthologies and a magazine) was called "Journey to Newskye" and tied for first place. She says that I was "extremely kind to seek me out personally at a convention to explain why it was not suitable for THE KEEPER'S PRICE—*the first of these anthologies. She adds "It* does *pay to try to write to the editor's guidelines."*

She is a high school French teacher and has "made two Darkovan outfits for costume competitions, and won a prize for each one." I remember one of them very well: a Free Amazon costume, down to elaborately styled underwear; she came on the stage in properly constructed cloak and boots, took them off, and kept on removing garments; the overtunic, undertunic, down to embroidered petticoat and drawers—without the least impropriety. Free Amazons don't usually strip in public, but if they did, this is what they'd look like.

Reminds me of the one time I ever had any input on a cover; people are always asking me, "Why do you let them put those covers on your books?"—as if I had had anything to say about them. About most covers I am quite

*happy to leave all that to the Art Department; but when
I wrote* THE SHATTERED CHAIN, *whose original title
was simply* FREE AMAZONS OF DARKOVER, *I had
just seen a costume contest where a so-called Amazon,
nearly naked as a Frazetta cover, won the day. So I remarked to Don Wollheim, ''Don, if you put a naked or
near-naked Amazon on the cover, I'll never speak to you
again.''*

He didn't. (MZB)

It was nearly dusk when Kelan Darriell turned his chervine off the trail toward the gray stone travelers' shelter.
After three nights of sleeping on the ground, he was
looking forward to a real bed. More important, he was
now only two days from Nevarsin. He would sleep much
better, bed or no bed, once the papers he carried were
safely inside the monastery walls where no woman had
ever set foot.

There had been no actual threat made, but for the past
few months he had been unable to shake the tiny voice
persistently reminding him that *Domna* Ysabet certainly
must consider his knowledge a danger to her safety. To
what lengths would she be prepared to go to preserve her
secret? He did not think she would send Aillard's women
warriors, as appropriate as she might find their use to the
task, for news of their presence in the mountains would
spread too quickly. There were men, however, who would
be glad to take her money and not question too closely
the whys of what they were told to do.

The shelter was small and simple, much like the other
seldom-used buildings he'd come to know well in the
course of this roundabout journey. It was far too risky to
travel the main north road where other travelers would
have questions about who he was, where he was going,
and why. Someone might recognize him in spite of the
shaggy, slow-moving animal he now rode, the drab farm-
er's clothing he wore, and the strong tea with which he
had rinsed his hair to cover its reddish highlights.

Kelan led the chervine into the half of the shelter which
was meant to serve as a stable and relieved her of the

saddle. When she had been fed and watered, he carried his packs into the main room of the shelter and lit a small fire, hoping to dispell the chill. Then he took the little hand ax and checked through the closest part of the woods for deadfall to be chopped for this evening's fire. So long as the weather was dry, it would be wrong to deplete the stores of firewood with which the mountain guards had stocked the shelter. If it had not been so close to dark, he would have liked to set a snare. A small bird or bush animal would be a welcome change from his usual evening porridge of meal, dried fruit, and nuts.

He wished it was possible to go directly to *Domna* Ysabet and tell her he meant her no harm. At midsummer council last year, long before he had begun to comprehend the full story, he had gone to the Aillard suite in an attempt to gain an audience—how foolish that had been, to let her know who he was! And although he had revealed none of his true suspicions to the young woman she'd sent to put him off, she must have realized how close he was to the truth. After that was when he had first begun to fear for his life.

How many precautions could a man take? He'd lied to his own family about his reasons for this trip to Nevarsin, hoping that ignorance would keep his brother and his brother's sons safe from harm. He'd avoided his friends, reluctant to let them see how far he'd gone beyond the original challenge that night in the tavern.

His arms filled with freshly chopped wood, Kelan pushed the door of the shelter open with his shoulder and backed inside. For a moment, whatever was wrong did not quite register, and then he realized someone had lit candles in addition to the fire he'd started earlier on the hearth. He could smell rabbit stew.

Had another traveler or travelers arrived while he was in the woods? He had not thought to look into the stable as he passed by to see if other animals had been put there. He turned around and saw a woman, her back to him, stirring the pot which hung over the fire.

"I think you will find this a tastier meal than the one you had planned, milord," she said without looking at him.

"I am at your service, *domna*," he replied politely, "but your husband must still be in the stable seeing to your animals." Her voice was not that of a farm woman, and what he could see of her gown looked to be of expensive stuff, embroidered heavily as only a woman who had many servants to see to daily tasks had the leisure to stitch. He was thinking that the shelter was so tiny, with no drapery to pull across the center, and wondering how he would give this highborn couple sufficient privacy short of joining the animals in the stable.

She turned around and he felt the hairs rise on the back of his neck and along his arms as he recognized the ginger-colored hair and face of the young woman *Domna* Ysabet had sent to speak with him in the Aillard suite in Thendara. "I have neither husband nor animals, *Dom* Kelan," she said. "Not even a guard or servant this time. There is no one here except the two of us." Kelan just stared at her. "Why not set down the wood and come here by the warmth of the fire so we can talk?"

He pushed the door shut with his foot, crossed the room to lay the wood down in the box, and waited to see what she would do next.

"I am not going to *do* anything," she smiled. "You needn't be afraid to speak. Or are you remembering the mud-rabbit who will not drown in the rainstorm so long as he has the wits to keep his mouth shut?"

He cleared his throat. "I am curious. How did you come to be here?" If *Domna* Ysabet thought to catch him off his guard, why had she sent Liane Delleray, the one person he would recognize?

"Perhaps that is not the best proverb to cite just now," Liane went on, glancing at the bubbling kettle hung over the fire, "since there is already one little rabbit here who has found himself in the stew whether he kept his mouth shut or no."

Kelan knew the beads of sweat had broken out on his brow. Merciful Avarra, protect me from. . . . He almost laughed out loud as he realized how he had unconsciously begun the prayer. "Did she send you because you are younger and stronger?" She was not dressed like one of the women warriors; she did not appear to be wearing even a meat knife; he was taller than she by at least two handbreadths.

"I promise you are in no danger of physical harm." He struggled to raise his mental barriers. Or would that even matter? "Won't you come and sit down? A glass of wine, perhaps, before our supper, to help calm your stomach." She stooped down to pull a bottle and two goblets from the leather pack at her feet. "You may pour if you wish, so that you know I have not slipped some drug or poison into your drink."

He took the dark glass bottle from her. His hands shook so badly he could hardly manage to pull the cork from its neck. She seemed to take no notice of his agitation but simply held out the goblets to be filled.

"We should make a toast first," Liane decided when he had set the bottle down and they each held a goblet. "But whom shall we honor? What about Truth? She can be a harsh mistress, and there are few who have the courage to remain faithful to her."

"To Truth," he agreed and took a sip of his wine. He recognized it as the famous apple wine from the orchards south of the Valeron.

"The stew will be a while yet," she remarked. "There is some bread and soft cheese if you are hungry right now—although I hope you are willing to save some room for the main course of the evening."

Kelan studied the pattern of leaves and flowers etched into the bowl of his goblet. He must remain alert to every trick she might try. "And that, I imagine, has very little to do with the stew. You haven't been sent here merely to share a meal and a fireside with a lonely traveler."

She looked at him over the rim of her goblet. "Considering what the rabbit is giving up for our sakes, it would be unkind of us not to oblige him."

Did she think he would be less wary when his stomach was filled with a hot meal and a few measures of wine? "I know who you are and *what* you are, *domna*. Let us get right to the point of why you are here. I know more than Lady Aillard thinks I should, and she is afraid of what I will do with my knowledge."

"We are not afraid, *Dom* Kelan. Even if you tell the

Hastur-king everything you believe to be true, and if he sends his armies to destroy the leaders of Aillard, and if they somehow succeed, there will always be women to follow the way of the Goddess.''

''Certainly there would be some danger to your lives, if not to your beliefs, from Hali.''

''Cassilda has many daughters, milord. We are a sisterhood, if you will, that extends far beyond a single family. No amount of noise and posturing by the Hastur-kings will change that.'' She set her goblet down on the little wooden table that sat to one side of the fire. ''Would you not be more comfortable if we sit down to continue this discussion?''

''As you wish, *domna*.'' He nodded and pretended to give his full attention to adjusting the stretch of his breeches over his knees as he settled himself on the bench before the fire. If the Lady of Aillard was not afraid, then why was Liane Delleray here? He could not rid himself of the feeling that she was going to do something to him, but if it was not done out of fear. . . . Just as when he had spoken with this woman in Thendara, he felt disconcerted that a woman had more control over the situation than he did.

Liane turned one of the simple wooden chairs that went with the table outward to face the fire, but rather than sitting down immediately, she stepped to the hearth to give the contents of the pot another stir. ''I don't believe you fully understand how little we are concerned with the doings of Lorenz-Rafael Hastur and others like him.''

''So long as he allows the families south of the Valeron to do things their own way . . .''

She sighed as she sat down at last and took another sip of her wine. ''As a man, there is no good reason for you to comprehend our ways, but I thought that in light of your searching and the information you claim to possess, you might have begun to perceive just a little bit. You are not a stupid man, or you would not have come as far as you have on nothing more than fragmented pieces of old stories.''

Kelan smiled. ''At least you no longer speak of amaz-

ing tales and bizarre stories that a madman created, as
you did in Thendara.''

"We made a toast to Truth a few minutes ago, *Dom*
Kelan. Would you not agree that it is time to dispense
with the verbal parrying and speak the plain truth to each
other?''

"I have never claimed to speak, or to seek, anything
else,'' he nodded.

"When you were in Thendara, you told me certain
things you believe to be true, but you said nothing about
the conclusions you have reached.''

"Conclusions?'' he asked.

"Conclusions,'' she repeated as she reached down and
drew the leather sack toward her, rummaging through it
until she found the bread and the soft cheese she'd mentioned earlier. "You must have given some thought to
what the existence of the heirs of Cassilda and the Cassilda Gift means.''

He watched as she twisted around to use the table top
as a board on which to cut the bread. "I have,'' he agreed
when she had spread the first slice with a bit of the pale
cheese and held it out to him. "Thank you. I would like
to think I am sensible enough to believe that the Cassilda
Gift has some other purpose than the one commonly attributed to it by so many young men.''

It was that "legendary'' Gift which had started him on
the road leading to this place three years ago. Everyone
knew the story of Hastur and how the god had become a
human man for love of Cassilda. When a boy went to one
of the Towers to learn control of his *laran,* sooner or later
a slightly older youth would confide the secret to him—
that somewhere there was still a woman, descended from
Cassilda, who had the Gift which could turn an *emmasca*
into a man or, the older boy would whisper conspiratorially, drive a normal man wild with desire.

It was a pretty silly story, but that night in the tavern,
after a few too many drinks, some of them had started to
debate whether it had any foundation in truth at all. There
had been more moments than the current one when Kelan
wished he had never boasted that he would find the truth

of it, for what he had found was so much more than some young men's fantasy.

Liane's mouth twitched. "You don't think I could do *that* for you if I were so minded?"

"I'm certain you could," he agreed, staring into his wine so that he would not even accidentally meet her eyes with his own. Would it be such a bad thing if he found himself in bed with this intelligent and attractive woman? The idea suddenly seemed much more appealing than it had when . . . No, he must keep his thoughts on the conclusions for which she had asked. "The Hastur-king claims the right to rule this world because of his descent from the Lord of Light when His Son walked the shores beside Lake Hali and got a son on Cassilda."

"And those same sons of Hastur, in their zeal to control others, have chosen to suppress the knowledge of Cassilda's daughter," Liane reminded him. "What fool thinks that a woman needs to take a *husband* in order to bear a child?"

"And yet the women of Aillard, who secretly call themselves the heirs of Cassilda, have done nothing to prevent the Hasturs from spreading their version of events. In fact, the secrecy is more your doing than the Hasturs'," he countered. He swallowed the last of his wine in a single, long draught. "Why, if your Gift is no less powerful than the one the royal family claims? A man with the Hastur Gift may be the channel for Aldones, but a woman with the Cassilda Gift is the channel for the Goddess, isn't she?"

He'd said it aloud at last. Not just thought it, or tried to argue his way to every other possible conclusion, only to find that this was the only one that fit the facts he had gathered. He had said it.

She did not reply, but leaned forward to study the progress of the stew. "I believe our supper is ready, *Dom* Kelan. There are bowls and spoons in the cupboard above the woodbox. If you would be so good as to fetch them down?"

"I asked a question and you have not answered it," he said as he stood up to step toward the cupboard.

"Yes, I think our little rabbit has cooked long

enough," Liane commented, lifting the long-handled spoon to sniff at the contents of the cooking pot. "I, for one, find I am looking forward to this meal."

If he had been wrong, Kelan decided, she would have said so. "Given that the power is there to directly oppose the reign of the Hasturs," he said while she dished up their supper and placed the bowls on the table, "I have to wonder why the Lady of Aillard does not use it. Why the secrecy about what she can do, when it is not secret at all that in the midsummer councils Aillard rarely agrees with the will of Hastur? Or can it be that you would have to admit that the God is more powerful than the Goddess, and that it is truly man's place to rule and woman's to obey?"

"There speaks a son of Hastur indeed," Liane sighed. She re-turned her chair and sat down facing him across the table. "You think the only possible contest is the one of physical strength, of the ability to control the lives of others? There is a contest, of course, but not in the way a man imagines."

"Are you going to explain, or am I expected to spend more years of searching to find the rest of the answers for myself?"

"Eat your supper, son of Hastur."

He picked up the wooden spoon and looked at the stew. It was the same sort he'd eaten all his life, but at the moment he felt uneasy about eating what had once been a living creature. Just a few hours ago, the animal had been going about its usual routine, blissfully unaware of what the future held in store. He put the spoon carefully into the bowl, scooping up only a few pieces of vegetable and some broth.

"We do not fight against the power of the Hastur-king because that is not our intent," Liane explained. "What we must do for this world can be achieved without fighting and killing other human beings. The sons of Hastur are the ones who believe that they must limit *laran* to a select few, to those who can somehow claim kinship with the sons of Hastur's son. They would kill anyone who tried to teach otherwise and wage wars in the name of extending what they think is the only correct way, *their* way."

"What is your way?" Kelan asked.

She watched him continue to avoid capturing any piece of the stew's meat with his spoon. "Your scruples will not save our little rabbit; he has already met his fate. You might as well eat it, meat and all."

He looked up at her. In the light of the candle which sat between them on the table, her face had taken on a golden glow. He noticed a scattering of freckles across the bridge of her nose and a tiny white line that followed the curve of her left eyebrow and might have been a scar. There was a danger, he knew, in allowing the evidence of her physical imperfections to lull him into a sense of security about her real nature. "What is your way?" he asked again.

"Our way is to persevere," she replied. "It is not for us to oppose the choices the sons of Hastur make, but to continue to offer another choice for those who cannot or will not submit to their tyranny. To you it is no tyranny, of course; you were born to the privileges of the system."

"My kinsmen are not wealthy. Life in the mountains is harsher than it is where you live. Many summers I have worked alongside the farmers and villagers to ensue the harvest, and my mother and sisters do not wear the elegant silks or the expensive perfumes of the court at Hali."

Liane dismissed those facts with a wave of her hand. "You and the other men in your family have sworn your allegiance to the Hastur-king, and he has granted you the benefits of his Towers. Where do you think you would have been able to learn to control your *laran* if Hali did not count you among the Hastur-kin? What Tower would have accepted you if you didn't carry the blood of Hastur in your veins?"

"I don't know," he admitted. Her hand had come to rest on the tabletop, only inches from his own, and he found himself struggling to resist the urge to reach out and touch it.

"The daughters of Cassilda would have found you and

seen to it you learned the necessary control so that you would not be a danger to yourself or to others.''

"Even though I am a man?''

"The Goddess care for *all* Her children, *Dom* Kelan, whether they choose to follow Her way or not. Can you say as much about the Lord of Light?''

"Your efforts cannot be as widespread as you make them sound, or they would not be such a secret,'' Kelan objected.

"There are very few who know as much as you do right now,'' she agreed. "The secrecy which strikes you as so ominous is nothing more than a way to ensure our system can continue. If we were to come into direct conflict with the aims of the Hasturs . . .''

"So you do admit that the king is stronger than you are, and that if there were a war, he would win?''

"Have to you listened to nothing I have told you, milord? We do not *want* to confront the sons of Hastur. That is not why we exist. We must remain as the other choice. Eventually, when the way of Hastur becomes too confining and begins to fall in upon itself, the daughters of Cassilda will still be here for those who seek what the Goddess offers.''

Kelan finally took up a morsel of the stewed rabbit on his spoon and chewed it slowly while he considered the implications of the existence of an entire network like the Towers but separate from them. Who bore the responsibility for it if not the Lady of Aillard?''

"Aillard has a seat on the king's Council. Is that so you can keep an eye on what he is doing?'' he asked.

"Aillard has had a place among the Hastur-kin from the beginning. We see no reason to change that, since it enables us to have a role in the Towers where we can encourage the development of those skills that are not yet widely accepted. We use every possible means available to us to see that every person, male or female, Hastur-kin or not, is given the chance to develop to full potential.''

"I have heard discussions in the council itself as to whether the ends ever justify the use of any means to hand. Don't you think it might be immoral for the Lady of Aillard to keep the true nature of her Gift a secret?''

''The Hastur-king and the others like him see only what they wish to see and know only what they wish to know. It suits the sons of Hastur to believe that the Cassilda Gift is of significance only to help an *emmasca* achieve the masculinity they prize so highly. If they refuse to admit the value of the feminine beyond childbearing and certain forms of sexual satisfaction, it is not *my* place to enlighten them.''

''Nor do I see it as mine,'' he assured her. ''You say you have no desire to confront the Hastur-king, but only wish to be left alone to pursue the way you have chosen. I also seek nothing more than to be left alone as I try to keep the truth from being lost. I am no threat to Lady Aillard.''

''Does the thought of what you believe she has the power to do to you if she wished distress you?'' Liane asked, scraping the last bits of stew from her bowl.

Zandru's hells, of course it does, Kelan thought. He remembered a time he had come across an isolated mountain farmhouse where a woman had been in childbirth with no one to help her but a young girl and how the woman had cried out in her pain, begging for Avarra's mercy. At the time he had wondered why the woman had seemed incapable of summoning her own inner resources to cope with the ordeal. Now he understood the sense of helplessness that came from being in the grip of a more powerful force.

He put down his spoon and pushed the bowl aside. ''I have finished my supper as well.''

''Finished, or only satisfied your appetite?'' She smiled and stood up to clear the dishes from the table. ''The little rabbit has played out his part to the best of his ability. Shall we leave him be and move along to the after-dinner sweet?''

''What will that be?''

''Oh, I'm certain there's something here that will strike your fancy,'' Liane replied, giving him such a bold look that if she had been anything other than an Aillard woman, he would have sworn it was a very specific invitation.

Liane busied herself with pulling the cooking pot away from the fire with the tip of a poker, beating down the partially burned logs, and adding new ones from the pile he'd laid in the woodbox. Kelan made no offer to help her, but only sat back in his chair and watched her. If she had been a mountain woman, he would have used the time to enjoy the outline of her figure revealed by her gown as she worked, to plan what combination of pretty words would make her most likely to agree to his notions of how to spend the rest of their evening, and to whet his own appetite by imagining the scent and taste and feel of her bare skin.

But she is Aillard, he reminded himself. She had been sent here to prevent his doing anything with the truth he knew about the Gift. He tried to review all she had said, looking for some clue as to what would come next and how he could best protect both his information and himself. On the one hand she had claimed to be opposed to killing, but she had also asked if he was frightened by what *Domna* Ysabet could do to him if she wished. He concluded the best course of action was not to show her he was afraid of the power of the Cassilda Gift and he might come out of this yet.

"You could make yourself useful," she commented when it was clear he was going to make no move to assist her. "There should be a small cake and a pot of fruit syrup in the leather sack by your feet."

He bent down, pushed the flap back, and felt around inside. His fingers touched something that felt like papers bound with a leather strap. He pulled the bundle up just enough to be certain. Yes, she had already ramsacked his packs and taken the results of his search. The sneaking, thieving, little . . . But there might be some advantage if she did not suspect that he knew she already had them. He shoved the packet back down and pulled out the wax-sealed syrup pot and the cake loaf wrapped in a damp cloth.

"I should have known that Maura would remember the groundberry syrup. She has been spoiling me since I was little and she and the other servants took pity on me because my mother was dead.''

Kelan tried to imagine this woman, who behaved with more confidence in herself than any woman in his own family, as a motherless child, relying on the kindness of a nursemaid or servant for affection. Had she ever cried herself to sleep, or wished that she was like all the other little girls who still had a mother, or dreamed of a man who would love. . . . *Stop it!* he scolded himself. *You are letting her lead where this goes. You must take charge of what happens. Do not permit her to direct the conversation or decide what we do next.*

"If it is your favorite, then by all means, you must have some. For myself, however, I think another drink of wine will suffice," he said.

"Let me refill your goblet," she offered, taking it from him and turning away to find the wine bottle. "No doubt your muscles are stiff after a day on the trail, and this will help you relax."

Relax was the one thing he knew he did not dare do. "Thank you," he replied curtly as she handed back the goblet. The surface of the wine trembled. Were her hands shaking? Could she possibly be nervous, or did she only want him to think that she was? "Don't you want the rest for yourself?" he asked when she started to put the bottle down on the table next to his arm. He had never known a woman who could hold wine well. Perhaps he could make her reveal more than she intended of what was going to happen to him. There was more wine among his own things if this bottle did not suffice to do the job.

Liane sat back down and refilled her own goblet. Or was this what she wanted him to try to do? How was he to tell which thoughts were his own and which she might have put into his mind?

"You know," she remarked when she had taken a sip of the wine. "I must admit to being rather surprised to learn how much time you've spent at Nevarsin. You don't look like a *cristoforo*."

"And how is a *cristoforo* supposed to look?"

"Pinched and weary, as if he hadn't had a decent meal, a soft bed, a woman, or a warm day in thirty or forty years. You don't look like a Tower worker either, although I have checked and found you were telling the truth when you said you'd spent five years in the third circle at Neskaya.''

She has been checking on me? ''What have you found out about me that you could not have learned just by asking me what you wanted to know?''

''Nothing, really, that I did not expect to find. You don't care for the politics of the Council—you take your seat, but you never express an opinion, and then you go away to whatever you were doing before midsummer. You served your time in the mountain guard. I suppose that's where those shoulders come from. Tell me, when you were a soldier, did you ever kill a man in cold blood?''

He nodded. ''Though before you brand me as a murderer, I must admit that he was a bandit who'd dispatched more than his share of innocent women and children, and I acted in self-defense.''

Liane shuddered. ''I don't think I could ever . . . to inflict a wound and then have to watch the dying . . . I don't even fly a hawk as many of the Aillard women do.''

She isn't going to kill me! Kelan almost shouted as relief washed through him. *Even if that is what she was sent to do, she isn't going to be able to do it!* And then came a more troublesome thought. *Certainly her distaste of such things was known to* Domna *Ysabet; why send someone who didn't have the stomach for the task?*

''Why are you here, then?'' he asked. ''If *Domna* Ysabet wants to keep me from telling anyone the truth about her Gift . . .''

''Lady Aillard does not have the Cassilda Gift,'' Liane cut him off short. ''She is only the head of the family to whom a Hastur-king once gave the right to seats on his Council. If the Gift had been awakened in *Domna* Ysabet, don't you think something in Lorenz-Rafael would sense it?''

''But the daughters of Cassilda . . .''

''Every woman with *laran* is one of Cassilda's daughters, *Dom* Kelan, even your own kinswomen who kneel before their husbands and fathers and claim to have no will of their own.'' The distaste in her voice was obvious, and the thought crossed his mind that a man could find marriage to one of these Aillard women a singularly trying experience. "Surely in all you have learned so far, it must have occurred to you that the 'daughters of Cassilda' are not precisely the same thing as the 'heirs of Cassilda.' "

"A daughter is only a child," he reasoned. "Even a man can have daughters, although they cannot be his heirs. His heir might be a brother's son rather than his own. That a man has an heir implies there is something to be inherited. . . . The Cassilda Gift is the inheritance, and only some Aillard women qualify . . . in an unbroken line of descent, through women, back to Robardin's daughter herself."

"Back to Robardin's wife's daughter," Liane corrected him.

"If *Domna* Ysabet is not the one who has the Gift," Kelan tried to turn the conversation back to what *he* wanted to know, "then who?"

"You've sat in the full Council sessions. You must have noticed *Domna* Yllane sitting at the Lady's righthand side."

Kelan tried to picture the council chamber. "To Domna Ysabet's left is her eldest daughter who will someday be the Lady of Aillard."

"Katarina," Liane nodded. "My mother's sister."

"And to her right . . . a very old woman. I assumed she was given that honor in deference to her advanced age. She—*Domna* Yllane?—must be close to ninety, a grandmother's sister or something."

"Or something," she agreed with a smile. "You are right; she *is* very old. Ninety-four in the rose month."

Kelan sat up. "Then *Domna* Yllane was the one, seventy odd years ago when Geremy, the *emmasca* son of King Ardran, needed to be a man in the eyes of the council? I knew that *Domna* Serena was the Lady of Aillard then, but also that she was with child that summer, and I was never able to understand how she had been able to accomplish both tasks at the same time." That one seeming impossibility was the only item that had not fit with the other things he had learned about the Gift. What else was there to do now but put all the information in a safe place?

"We are not finished yet, milord," Liane reminded him as he started to get up from the table. "You may have had your questions answered, but what about the rest of it? There is more to the meal than just the little rabbit who provided a flavorful stew."

"I am not trying to learn *all* the secrets of the daughters of Cassilda, *Domna* Liane. I have found what I was looking for. That is enough."

"No, it isn't. There is more for you to know, whether you will or not, and that is why I am here." There was an edge to her voice that sent a chill down his back. "You will know it before I leave. That is what She wishes."

"I would be happy to oblige *Domna* Yllane, if she really thinks . . ."

Liane shook her head. "Not the wish of *Domna* Yllane, *Dom* Kelan. The wish of the Goddess. You were impetuous enough to come searching where you had no business, and She intends for you to have exactly what you seek."

Despite his upbringing, he found it hard to countenance that the gods could have wishes in regard to human behavior. The gods were just *there,* somewhat benevolent, but essentially unconcerned with the little comings and goings of this world. "How do you know what the Goddess wants or does not want?"

"And I took you for an intelligent man," she snorted.

"Unless *Domna* Yllane told you before you were sent here, or unless . . ." Kelan shivered in spite of the warmth of the fire and he did not have to look down at his arms to know they were covered with goosebumps. He considered for a moment leaping up to run out into the chill night air, and then as quickly abandoned the notion. There was no place in this world to hide from Avarra. His earlier resolution not to show fear seemed utterly pointless. "You're the next one, aren't you?"

She did not look at him as she poured the last drops of wine into her goblet. "You need not feign surprise. Dishonesty does not become you."

"It's not dishonesty; it's . . . but you can hardly be old

enough. What are you, nineteen or twenty? And you don't look like a . . . a . . .''

"Like a goddess?" she suggested. "At least I have some basis for what I say when I tell you that you don't look like a *cristoforo* or a Tower worker. Just what do you think Avarra looks like?"

He could think only of the tapestry he had seen once in the Great Hall at Hali with the Dark Goddess hovering over the world like a giant bird of prey, with her eyes black as a moonless, cloudy night and a great, spiked headdress of glittering feathers. Vengeful, pitiless, more fearsome than even Zandru at the forges of his hells, for She treated the peasant and the lord, the kindhearted and the wicked, exactly the same. The woman sitting across from him was young, attractive; she looked almost vulnerable when compared with the image on that tapestry.

Kelan took a deep breath. "Is She here now, with you, as a part of you?"

"There is a part of Her in every person. If you mean, am I currently acting as a channel for the Goddess, so that you are really addressing Her rather than Liane Delleray, the answer would have to be . . ." Liane emptied her goblet, and Kelan realized that he was holding his breath and even his heart seemed to have paused for a moment. ". . . not yet. Perhaps if I fail to carry out Her instructions, or if you find some way to outwit me, then She will be here."

He started breathing again. "Outwit you?" he repeated. "How could I ever possibly hope to . . . I mean, if She is helping you, there is no way I could ever . . . She might as well just do what must be done and have it over with quickly."

"Are you so eager to meet Her face-to-face? Do you really think there is bravery enough in you for that moment?"

"Yes," he lied. "Or if not bravery, at least the belief that it is better to confront the enemy straight on."

Liane laughed. "She is not your enemy, *Dom* Kelan, and neither am I. An enemy is the last thing I want to be."

"What *do* you want?" It was very quiet. He could hear

a noise on the roof of the shelter that sounded like freezing rain or sleet. How would he have fared out under the trees tonight? He had some difficulty persuading himself that the current situation was an improvement over being cold and wet. The fire hissed and spat a little shower of sparks out onto the hearth.

"You." She spoke so softly that at first he wasn't even certain whether she had said it aloud. *Of course she's a telepath,* he reminded himself, *or she wouldn't have the Gift.* "You find that amusing?"

"No," Kelan shook his head. "I was . . . thinking of something else."

Liane sighed. "How very lowering, to have a man tell you he is thinking of something else when you've just announced you want him."

"You wouldn't have come here if you didn't want something from . . ."

"Not from, or of, or for, just want."

He glanced away from the fire and saw she was watching him. Her dark gray eyes had lost their calculating look, and he knew perfectly well what their current soft intensity could mean. For a moment, he almost let himself believe that she was sincere. "Is this what the Goddess told you to do, seduce me?"

She shook her head. "Not everything I say or do or think comes from Her, you know. I *do* have a mind and desires of my own. You don't think I spend my entire life being overshadowed by. . . ? If it were like that, I think I would have killed myself long before now."

Kelan told himself that she was trying to put him off his guard by arousing his sympathies. This woman, of all women, did not need to appeal to anyone's masculine instincts in order to find a man to protect her from the vagaries of existence. Although he liked to consider that he was a better-than-average swordsman, his abilities to take care of himself paled to almost nothing beside what she could do if she chose to. Did that mean that when she said she wanted him, it was just plain, honest physical desire?

"Why me?" he asked.

"Because you arouse my curiosity. You are intelligent

and much more clever than I think I would have been in your place. I *know* just from how you have reacted to what you've learned tonight that you are far braver than I could ever be. And I don't suppose I am the first to tell you that you are an exceptionally handsome man. Certainly you've made love to women many times with far less justification than that.''

Kelan smiled. ''It would not be very gallant on my part to respond to that particular charge.'' He shifted his weight on the chair. Damn, was he reacting to what she had said about him, or to . . . ''You need not use your Gift on me, *Domna*.''

''I'm not.'' She stood up and held out a hand toward him. ''Are we going to discuss the whys and wherefores all night, or are we going to move along to the next step?''

''As you wish,'' he replied, taking hold of the offered hand and standing up. He tried to force himself to look away from her and found he could not.

She raised his hand to her lips, but continued to look at him steadily. ''I have been told that north of the Valeron, the man is usually the one to take the initiative. I wonder, Kelan, whether in spite of all the times you claim to be too gallant to detail, you have ever had a woman make love to *you*. Do you think you might find that appealing?'' She gently turned his hand over, eased his fingers open, and brushed her lips across his palm.

He swallowed hard and struggled to breathe evenly. When the tip of her tongue touched his skin, he was only able to half strangle the moan.

''Is that a yes?'' she smiled. ''I hope so, because I really want to do this for you. And I hope you're man enough to enjoy it.''

''I . . . I'm sure I'll,'' he cleared his throat, ''manage.''

''Yes,'' she agreed, looking him up and down, ''I think you will.'' She let go and stepped closer, reaching up to take his head between her hands. She kissed him.

He closed his arms around her and pulled her tight against him. On a purely physical level, the kiss was definitely exciting. Emotionally, he wondered at the void.

Liane pulled back as much as she could in the embrace and looked up at him. "Can you not lower your barriers just a little, so that we can share at least some of our feelings?"

Kelan hesitated. Could it really be that this entire evening he'd been successful in keeping her from reading his thoughts and manipulating them? Was he more in control and was there less danger than he had believed? Lord of Light, he wanted this woman, all of her, wanted to touch her mind as well as her body, just so long as he could be certain it was *her* mind alone that joined with his.

"Avarra," he said at last. "Is there some way to make certain that She doesn't . . . isn't . . . ? I don't want to open my eyes after another kiss like that last one and find myself looking into Her eyes instead of yours."

She hesitated, too, as if she were searching for something in his face. She must have found it because she nodded slowly. "If it is so important to you, yes, there is a way. Her concern is the papers you are carrying to Nevarsin. If She knows that the truth about the Gift is safe from the prying eyes of the Hastur-king, She will have no reason to come here through me. If you were to put them into the fire . . ."

"No," Kelan said automatically. He had spent too much time on those papers to give them up so easily. To burn three years of exhausting effort just to make love to this woman, no matter how much he wanted her right now, was unthinkable. Every single line he'd written was fixed more firmly in his mind than any kiss or embrace would ever . . .

Fixed more firmly in his mind! Even if the papers were destroyed, he could write it all out again once he reached Nevarsin. He could have Liane now, and still keep the truth from being lost!

Liane ducked out of his encircling arms. He felt suddenly, terribly cold and alone. "Just burn the papers, and She will not bother us?" he repeated.

She knelt down to the leather sack and held the papers up to him. "It is your decision, Kelan."

He took the packet, undid the leather strap, and shuffled through them. Slowly, one by one, he crushed them in his left hand and tossed them into the fire.

When there was nothing left but blackness crumbling slowly to ashes, he pushed the mental wall back so that the only thing it shielded was his memory of what the papers had contained, turned from the fire, and took her back into his arms.

"Why are you smiling?" Liane asked.

"You'll soon find out," he whispered and bent his head to kiss her. She may have been able to outwit one little rabbit for the stew. . . .

What kind of wine did I drink last night? Kelan wondered as he tightened the saddle girth one last notch. The last things he remembered clearly were gathering wood for the fire and wondering if there was enough daylight left to set a snare for a mud-rabbit or some other small animal to add to his supper.

The remainder of the evening was a blur, confused with images from a strange dream he'd had in the night about a woman he'd met once in Thendara and the legendary Cassilda Gift. *How much longer,* he asked himself as he put one foot in the stirrup and swung the other leg over the chervine's back, *am I going to keep trying to prove my boast? There is not one shred of evidence anywhere between Nevarsin and the Plains of Valeron indicating there's any truth to the legend at all.*

As the chervine stepped toward the trail, something in the bushes caught his eye. Kelan dismounted and walked over to look. It was a snare. Had he set one last night after all?

The lines had been sprung, as if the rabbit had managed to extricate himself from the fatal trap. He did not see any signs of a struggle: no clumps of fur, no drops of blood, not even a broken branch among the bushes. With a sigh, he gathered up the snare, tucked it inside the overlapping front of his tunic, and pulled himself back up into the saddle.

Yes, it was time to stop searching for what wasn't there.

He turned the chervine's head and started down the trail toward home.

The Gift From Ardais

by Barbara Denz

Barbara Denz starts off a letter by saying that although she is not (yet) a frequenter of conventions or book signings, she is already being asked where she gets her ideas. I tend to admire Stephen King's version; he says "Ithaca." It doesn't mean anything, but it sounds good and gets him off the hook. There's also the bad old joke told by waggish old pros to newcomers (some of whom even believe it) about a magazine called Ideas *to which you can subscribe when you become a fully qualified member of SFWA or the MWA; and my answer has been, "Oh, I keep a little old lady chained in the basement to think them up"—about as good a description of the subconscious mind as I can think of. More recently I have taken up saying that I just leave a saucer of milk on the back porch.*

But if people are really trying—as I believe—to get some insight into the creative process, I answer more truthfully, as Pogo the Possum used to say, "Out'n my own personal headbone."

I would find it more realistic to ask of these people "How do you keep *from having them?" A writer, by definition, is a person with ideas; nonwriters are not.*

Barbara Denz says that her mother saw her need to create and enrolled her in creative writing classes when she was six. Now I have taught classes in fiction, but the mind boggles, wondering what anyone could teach *a six year old . . . at least about creative writing. She has a B.A. in Shakespearean and Medieval Literature, spent ten years working in libraries in the U.S. and Sweden, and worked in public radio for eight years.*

Recently she has been working in grants administra-

176

tion, but when asked what she does, she tells people she writes. (And after this story, I'd say she's entitled.)

She lives in Baltimore (but still considers herself a Northwesterner) with her husband David, who is a composer and lutenist, as well as a computer programmer (has it ever occurred to anyone that in this anthology we are up to our ears in computer programmers? Misty Lackey, Lisa Waters, Dorothy Heydt's husband, to mention only a few . . .) and their "lovely, lively ferrets." Huh; the last ferret I met bit me; which only proves that one man's monster is another person's pet; I once knew a girl who kept a Komodo dragon in her bathtub. I wouldn't have minded too much; but the girl who owned the ferret assured me solemnly that "ferrets never bite" and after it bit me, she assured me just as solemnly that because ferrets were so clean, their bites never got infected. Well, maybe it was the carbolic acid I used. . . .

Anyway, better you than me . . . I'll stick to dogs; but some people like ferrets, Komodo dragons, goldfish, or even teddy bears—which never bite. At least mine don't; or anyhow, none of my nine has ever bitten me yet. (But I'm taking no chances.)

This is Barbara's second fiction sale, and I doubt, judging by precedent, that it will be her last.

The winter winds had begun wagging their vicious tongues through the streets of Thendara when Larisa left her father's shop with the bundle of finely woven wools and cottons from which she would make the festive clothes for the Midwinter Festival. This would be the first year she would be allowed to do fittings in the Castle. Craftswomen of Darkover were rarely allowed inside those walls, and usually it was her mother or sister who went. This year her mother considered her old enough and mature enough at sixteen to work closely with the *comynari* and to tolerate the rigorous schedule she must keep to get the work done.

Larisa was proud of her creations. Her talent with ornate new embroidery designs, her eye for the perfect design for each figure shape, her speed at executing even the most intricate work, and her dexterity with a needle, along with the fine fabrics her father and brothers created, put her much in demand. She had been invited to join the Guild of Craftswomen when she was twelve, two years younger than her mother had been when that honor had been bestowed. Now Larisa rarely had time to rest, since the festivals were so evenly spaced over the year. She actually looked forward to the middle of winter when no one went out. It was during this short period after the Midwinter Festival and before spring thaw that she could recover and begin to plan new embroidery designs.

She sighed at the thought of rest, and lost her balance on the ice. An arm reached out from nowhere and held her upright. She whirled around, only to slip from the strong male grasp and tumble into the knee-deep snow which continued to swirl around her, her package of fine fabrics cast into a drift.

"The *comynari* who pay you well would be much dismayed to see how you treat their fine fabric," snarled a voice which froze Larisa's soul.

"My lord," she managed, and began to scramble away to retrieve the valuable package. Her father would scold her soundly if these pieces got wet and their dyes ran together. The wind caused tears to freeze on her eyelids, and she had difficulty locating the dark paper wrapped around the fabrics. Just as she located the bundle, the rock hard muscles again grabbed her and the bundle and pulled both up.

"You are hurting me, my lord," she forced through clenched teeth. "Thank you for your strong hand as I fell, but I now must be going." She turned and with tears blinding her progress, she stumbled away as quickly as she could. She hoped that she had not really heard his words correctly as she departed. What should be said to no respectable woman rang in her ears.

"My strong hand is not all you will feel, *grezalis*, but I can wait."

As she stumbled home, Larisa remembered the night she had joined the Guild. She had been allowed wine and to stay out late, and she was more than a little drunk on the honor. The summer air had been warm against her bare arms, and she still could feel the heady wonder and excitement of the night. With that lovely memory, she mixed the same drunken, sadistic voice she had just left behind.

"You women who think so much of yourselves. You were meant to serve men like me who are strong enough to control you. You are just like your mother, flaunting your freedom by walking alone. I'll teach you the same lesson I taught her."

Those words haunted her still. She had broken free of his drunken hold, but had come away with deep bruises on both arms and wrists. She had run, crying, just as she was now, and had found her way home. When her mother saw the bruises, the story and the description of the man had come out.

"Lord Kyril Ardais," had come the hiss through her mother's clenched teeth. The ashen face and shaking fists had told Larisa that this man was, indeed, known to her mother. Only then was she to know that this man who had accosted her was her real father, and that the circumstances of her conception were nearly identical to the assault she had experienced. From that day to this, Lord Kyril Ardais was someone she avoided at all costs.

Larisa threw herself on her bed and swore as her still shaking and nearly frozen hands tried to untie the bundle to check the fabrics. She had rushed through the house to her room without stopping to greet her mother and younger siblings, who were putting the final touches on a simple but plentiful dinner. Her father and three brothers were not long behind her, and the evening meal would be served as soon as they arrived.

She heard a light tap on the door of the room she shared with her two younger sisters. Before she could respond, her mother came through the door.

"Is there trouble, *chiya?* It is not like you to rush through the house without greetings."

"I slipped in the snow and dropped the fabric. I wanted to be sure it had not gotten wet," she said simply, keeping her eyes averted. Since the fabric was now being spread over the bed, it was a logical explanation.

"Are you sure that's all that is troubling you, Lari?"

her mother persisted, her hand now resting lightly on Larisa's shoulder.

Larisa braced herself. She never lied to her mother, but she knew this explanation would not be taken well.

"Lord Kyril caught my arm as I fell. He appeared out of nowhere," she blurted. She looked into her mother's eyes and saw the deeply passionate anger and hatred she expected.

"He is early in Thendara this year. He does not usually come from the Hellers until spring and is rarely here for Midwinter Festival. His duties are in his domain." The rigid recitation of known facts about Kyril reinforced Larisa's fear of her mother's anger. The disgust in that usually loving voice was almost too much to bear.

"I wonder why he comes for Midwinter. No matter. Whatever his reason, we will have to take precautions sooner than I expected. You were bundled and he has not seen you in four years—did he know you?"

"I do not know. He called me *grezalis* and made an ugly suggestion, but he may not have known who I am."

"You said you had just left the mill when he saw you? He must have been waiting. You carried fabric, and he is not so stupid as to not be able to count years," said the icy voice that again chilled her to the bone. "You will not leave the house unescorted until he leaves Thendara. I will tell your father and brothers."

Larisa had not raised her eyes again since she had first looked in her mother's face, ostensibly so that she could scrutinize the fabric. She heard the unmistakable whisper of her mother's soft boots and tunic cross the floor and pause by the door.

"The Ardais brat may have found *me* alone and raped me, but he will not be allowed to do the same to his daughter," the frozen voice said. "I suggest you carry the longest shears you can find and keep them freshly sharpened. Keep them with you from the time you wake until you sleep, and be prepared to use them. If you do not feel that you can, your brothers will show you how. Hear me, Larisa. That man is dangerous."

The voice caught, and before it could say more, it fled the room and she heard her mother's sobs echo down the stairs. Larisa threw down the fabric, letting it lie ignored in a rumpled pile.

Larisa's three older brothers and one older sister had been aware that something was wrong through the pregnancy, but were not told why until after Larisa was born. Her brothers were eight, six and five years older than she, and her sister seven years older, so they were really too young to understand anything other than that this was their long-awaited little sister, whom they adored and spoiled.

After the first encounter with Kyril Ardais, Larisa had been told all this. In numb silence, she absorbed the fact that her mother had been ashamed of the rape and had tried to abort the child when she found herself pregnant. But the gentle, loving man Larisa had always thought her father had shared the horror of the rape soon after it had happened. Besides, he had reasoned, this child might as easily have been his as Lord Kyril's. Larisa chose to believe that, too, although her mother did not.

Larisa was five when her twin sisters were born. She remembered those five years as quiet and lonely. She was secure in her father's love and that of her brothers and sister, but her mother always seemed oddly distant. Larisa was given to a wet nurse, and it was not until the twins were born that love and softness returned to her mother's eyes. Her two youngest brothers had been born during the next three years, and suddenly they were all a family again. But because of the distance in years on either side of her, Larisa often felt left out of the family and her mother's love. Just four short years ago, she had finally learned why. Since then, she and her mother had been working on decreasing the chasm that years of neglect had left in their relationship. They were now fairly close—drawn together by an assault.

Right now, however, she felt incredibly alone, drawing no comfort from the fact that her experience was like her mother's. And she felt humiliated even though she had done nothing wrong.

When she finally came down to dinner, it was obvious that her mother had told the family what had happened. Her father and brothers ate in poorly disguised wrath.

She was grateful that Eliann lived elsewhere with her husband and child, so she did not have to see Larisa's shame. The two younger boys were too young to understand what they had been told, but the quiet which pervaded a normally noisy table had them unusually subdued. Her oldest brother, Loren, spoke first. He had always been her protector and was closer to her than any of the others. He was so angry now that his gray eyes seemed to flash fire and he was beyond controlling his tongue.

"Lari, we will walk with you in shifts as you do your errands away from the mill. Promise that you will not leave here or the mill alone, and that you will avoid any of the places that *grezu* might be."

Loren slammed his fist on the table, shaking all the plates and overturning two mugs. Their contents splattered the twins, who jumped away from the table and grabbed for two cloths to clean up the mess. Their mother stared in icy silence and their father pushed back from the table and began to rise to demand order. Loren held up his hand, waving back the reprimand, and stood up. Their father sat down slowly, a warning look in his eyes. He would not tolerate such language in his home, nor such visible anger. It was not his way and he was ashamed of his son for showing it.

"I am sorry, Father, Mother. I should not have sworn so in front of the children. But what Lord Kyril is allowed to do unpunished is wrong. Why he should walk free to terrorize Larisa—his own daughter—is beyond me. It makes me very angry that Comyn can do as they please and no one passes judgment when what they do is wrong—not when Larisa was conceived and not now." Loren's anger was spent, and with its passing returned the gentleness Larisa loved in her oldest brother. It took extreme circumstances to anger him, and then that tide of anger quickly ebbed.

"Lari, we will protect you however we can, but you cannot do any of the fittings at Comyn Castle this season. Mother or Eliann will. I know it is important to you, but it is not safe."

An embarrassed silence followed his words. The frozen stare on their mother's face warned all the children that their questions were not welcomed just now. Larisa hung her head in bitter silence that this man who was her natural father could spoil so much for her so quickly.

"Loren, you must not talk like that about Comyn. It could cost you your life if anyone heard," said her mother in a voice still little thawed. She saw her daughter's anguish and felt that same sick feeling she had felt over sixteen years before. She could not blame her daughter for the disgrace of her own rape. And she must protect her from that same shame at all costs.

"Lari, *chiya*," began her father—the only father she had ever known. "You know we all love you, and we only want to be sure you are safe."

"I know, Father." Larisa's eyes filled suddenly with unbidden tears that threatened to totally undermine whatever courage she had. "It's just that I feel so soiled when he's so close and he is ruining everything." With that, her resolve failed and she ran. Her father began to follow, but her mother waved him back to his meal and followed instead.

In her room, Larisa threw herself on the bed with sobs of anguish and fear, pushing the rumpled pile of rich fabrics away from her leaking eyes. Every year since she was twelve, these scenes had ruined her life whenever the Ardais Lord was in Thendara. Although he had not yet done anything to her, the threat of his presence tore her and her family apart. Although she had only seen him in the distance since that first encounter four years ago, with today's incident, she was not sure how many more such encounters she could endure. In the past year, she had fallen in love with Garth, who worked at the mill, and they were to begin their own household in the spring. What would happen if Kyril interfered again? She had everything to live for, and only the sadistic, drunken Lord Ardais between her and a much sought after life. At times like this she hated him with a hatred close to her mother's.

She heard her mother's soft boots on the stairs, brushed her eyes dry, and began folding fabric as her mother entered the room. Another pair of experienced hands began to help. They were both glad for something to occupy their hands and they finished in silence.

"Lari, you cannot let this man spoil your life. This is what he most wants to accomplish, and to give in to what he wants is to allow him success. No," she continued and raised a hand as Larisa began to protest her innocence, "I do not mean give in that way. If you show fear or run from him, it will satisfy him as much as any sexual pleasure, perhaps more. He thrives on making strong women yield to his tormenting. I was not the first, and you will not be the last. Avoid him at all costs, *chiya*. Loren is correct in his word for that man and in his admonitions to you. Let your father and brothers walk with you when you go out. Come home early, before final darkness, and let your sister or me do the final fittings. Better still, work here and let us go back and forth."

Larisa's sobs began afresh and she rushed to her mother's welcoming arms.

"But it was to be my first time in the Castle, and I wanted to see my dresses as they will be seen, not just as I make them. It isn't fair. He's ruining it all."

"I'm sorry, *chiya*. Better he ruin the fun than ruin your life. Think about it." Her long, nimble fingers pulled her daughter's face up and stroked away falling tears. A tenderness she rarely felt toward her middle child suffused her face. She kissed Larisa's forehead. "Now come back and eat something. You'll need your strength this season if we are to finish everything on time."

The next few weeks passed uneventfully. Larisa found that working at home was actually fairly easy. Usually the younger children went to her sister's house to care for her sister's small son. She accomplished more at home where her mind was not distracted by questions, Garth, or the chatter of others. Still, she felt very alone and very isolated. Her absence was explained as necessary to finish the work in time, with no other clarification.

Before Garth was allowed to come to visit, a family conference was held. All agreed that he should be told the real reason why Larisa was not at the mill. Larisa was in despair that he might reject her for the bastard she was, and could not be consoled. Loren, who was Garth's closest friend and who had introduced the two, was chosen to do the explaining, and did so the next day as they left the mill. As Loren had predicted, Garth took the news with the same concern the family had—for Larisa's safety, not her paternity. From then on, Garth ate often with the family and Larisa became visibly less tense, even though they enjoyed no privacy and Garth was often too exhausted to be good company.

Larisa watched with tears in her eyes as her mother and sister took turns with the busy and time-consuming task of fittings, often leaving early in the morning and returning late at night, but she remained stoic. One or another of Larisa's brothers or Eliann's husband escorted the needlewomen to and from the Castle. Occasionally, Garth was also sent as he could be released from duty at the mill. With his deepening relationship with Larisa was coming additional responsibilities for the mill, and Larisa was pleased to see that he was proving to be a good leader as well as a good worker.

With the beginning of the final month before Midwinter Festival, the mill began shutting down for the season. All the necessary fabric was made, and it remained now only to finish the cutting and sewing for the easier Festival clothes. Those requiring the most embroidery and beading were already in the final stages of fittings with Larisa adding final touches to the fine decorative work she had done. As the mill's processes were less needed, workers began their own preparations for the Midwinter festivities, and Garth spent more time with Larisa.

During all this time, Larisa had never been left without another adult nearby. Although Lord Kyril was a known bully, the family was fairly sure he would not attack Larisa unless she were alone or with only the children for company. Garth had become fiercely protective and was usually the one who could be spared for "guard duty." Since he was always around, Larisa taught him some of the fine stitching and showed him how to follow her patterns. It kept him from being bored and hastened her work considerably. His handiwork was not of her measured quality, but neither was it sloppy or clumsy. They laughed often, and enjoyed the conversation time such work allowed. He became quite proud of his efforts, despite the teasing from Larisa's brothers.

With days growing short, Eliann and her family moved into the larger house. Since Garth and Larisa were there, her younger siblings and Eliann's son stayed with them during day and evening hours rather than trudging through the dark streets between Eliann's house and the family home. The younger children adored Garth, and he and Larisa gave them little tasks to do which kept them busy. With Garth as a role model, even Larisa's baby brother and Eliann's toddler son began to sew. With this time together, the couple's love deepened as they shared their fears, dreams, and embarrassments.

"It was not your choice who should father you," he had said on more than one occasion. "Nor, unfortunately, was it your mother's. That the man you choose to call father is not your birthfather is of little consequence. It is he to whom you turn and it is he who loves you as his own. That is enough for me. It should be enough for you, too."

Whenever he said it, Larisa would hug him and touch his face with a love which filled the room. Then they would stare in each other's eyes in silence until one of the youngsters broke the spell.

The final week before Midwinter began with a frenzy Larisa had never known. She was proud that her reputation was such that the *comynari* would settle for no less than her best work. She was working hard doing what she loved, and it showed in the delicacy of the works she created.

With a kiss on her cheek, her mother and sister had left early for the Castle and taken the children to a cousin's to stay until all the creations were delivered to the Castle the next day. Larisa worked in peace, but found the quiet house strangely lonely. All the men were finishing the final closing procedures for the mill for the season, which they expected to take no more than an hour or so. Kyril had not shown his face in Thendara in nearly three weeks, and the family thought that perhaps he had

decided to return to the Hellers for his Domain's Midwinter Festival. Larisa's mother and sister had said that
they felt like spies in the Castle, but they continued to
listen carefully in order to find out more about him. They
said that his name was rarely mentioned, and then only
derogatorily among the women. It seemed that no one
much cared where he was so long as he was not nearby.

Larisa was nearly finished with the embroidery on
the last dress when she discovered that she was out of
the fine silver thread she needed to finish. She sat by the
hearth not doing anything for what seemed like hours,
but what was really only a few minutes. Should she risk
leaving before anyone came home? Kyril had not been
seen, so surely she was safe enough in broad daylight to
venture the short distance to the mill. Once she got the
thread she needed, she knew she would not have a long
wait before Garth could return home with her. What was
her alternative? She could wait for the men to finish and
have one of them walk back to the mill they had just
sealed for the season.

No, she thought. *That would be silly. I will be safe.*

She dressed in several layers, each covering more of
her features until she was fairly well disguised in layers
of cloth. She took the long shears and tucked them into
her belt, leaving a path to them through which her gloved
hands could pass quickly if needed. She inspected the
overall impression in the long fitting glass and giggled.
If Kyril could tell it was her, he deserved to try to get
through all these layers. She instantly sobered, knowing
that was no laughing matter. Again quiet and pensive,
and more than a little wary, she carefully latched the door
and, looking all around her, set out for the mill at a brisk
walk.

The day was stunningly beautiful. It was the clear,
crisp kind of day which made her feel most alive. It
would probably snow later, since dark clouds were forming, and the snow of the past few days came nearly to
her knees, but paths had been crushed through which
she could walk, and the sound of the snow under her
feet made her feel oddly warm and secure. The streets
were not yet full of people, since the hour was still early,

but enough people were around to make her feel secure. Larisa felt lighthearted and happy for the first time in over two months.

As she skipped around th corner, the mill less than a hundred yards away, a hooded man stepped into her path and grabbed her arm.

"I've waited a long time for you to finally come back here. I knew you couldn't stay away forever," he hissed. "And you thought these layers were enough to hide that proud walk from me? Who else but you would dare this distance without escort? And if it had not been you, it would not have mattered. Any woman who dares walk alone should be shown that it is not safe to do so."

Larisa's heart stopped and she froze in place, a thunder in her ears blocking all but that hated voice. She opened her mouth to scream and an iron fist closed over it and her nose, blocking off all possibility for air.

"Now, little one, we shall see how you compare to your mother," growled Kyril. A maniacal laugh began deep in his throat and built to near hysteria. It cut off as quickly as it had begun. She heard his swagger in his voice as he continued. "I rather like the idea of this comparison. She fought hard, but provided excellent reward for the effort. If you are as good, perhaps I could try this on our daughter as well."

With those words spoken, Larisa's fears and need for air drove her to desperation. She kicked as her mother had taught her to do and bit the hand that held her. Kyril yelped and let go, flinging Larisa into a snow bank. She screamed and reached to find the path to her shears now not so clearly defined. She thrust her hands through the layers until her gloves finally felt the rounded handles. Before she could extract her hand, Kyril was upon her.

"Shut up," he yelled and shoved her back into the snow as she struggled to get her feet under her. "I'll not have you causing me trouble."

Kneeling with one knee on her stomach and the other in the snow, he clamped one hand over her throat and with the other, fumbled with her tangled skirts. By now, all the layers she had put on were acting as an effective screen from his intentions. She still could not extract her arms with the precious weapon which could free her, and he could not disentangle the cloth from her squirming body.

"Stop resisting the gift I choose to give you, or I shall have to knock you out and deliver it to your unconscious body, and I do not want to do that. I want you fully aware of what I am doing. You must learn to enjoy such gifts, for I plan to give them often."

Larisa continued to fight, and in the distance she heard the shouts that told her that her father, oldest brother, and betrothed had heard her cries and were coming to her rescue.

Kyril heard them, too, and tried to cover the daughter he had intended should bear his next child.

"If you say anything, I will kill all of you," he hissed.

Before he could turn around, Garth was upon him. The hands which had held Larisa with love and which had been so careful with needle and thread pummeled at the face and body of her assailant. Kyril fell back from the assault, screaming his innocence, and fell on Larisa, who screamed and went limp.

Loren pulled Kyril away and held him with fists ready to kill.

"Not now," yelled his father. "Hold him for the Guard."

While father and son argued over the Lord of Ardais, the daughter was cradled in her beloved's hands. She was limp and turning cold, but they could not see why. She had been alive and able to scream seconds before and Kyril's sword was not bared.

"Help me," Garth yelled. "Something is wrong with Lari."

He reached under her to free one of the folds of her cape while her father tugged at layers and clasps. Just as the hands which had held this life for the first time closed over hers and felt the rounded ends of the dressmakers' shears at right angles to her body, Garth cried out at the crimson stain on the cape and the punctures through his gloves from two bare points.

As the Guards rounded the corner, responding to Larisa's screams, they were greeted by Kyril's maniacal laugh joining the wails of anguish and making a chorus which echoed through the streets of Thendara.

The Horse Race

by Diann Partridge

Diann Partridge introduces this story by saying, "We had gone up to Five Springs Campground for a picnic, so maybe it was the clear mountain air, but the story was just there. There haven't been many stories about horses in Darkover fiction. . . . I grew up in Kentucky. I rode anything that would stand still long enough for me to get on and some things that didn't. I could never understand why other people didn't share this overwhelming love for horses that possessed me . . . and horses still occupy a good deal of my imagination."

Well, if you ride them, I suppose it's different; but I grew up on a farm and have not only no love for horses, but a real dislike for them; however, I am one of the few women under sixty who could still hitch up and drive a team. During the war (1939–45) when gasoline was rationed, I drove the team often enough; my brother wouldn't let me drive the mowing machine, but I drove the hay rake often enough and the hay wagon.

I do understand that horses on Darkover are a primary mode of transportation; and as such, I welcome stories about them from those who have sympathy for them. Personally, I prefer hawks.

She asks a question; do the Armida blacks grow white with age as the Lippizaners do? It should be obvious that, although I've researched horses for various Darkover books, I don't really know enough about them to answer that. What do you think?

Diann Partridge has three kids, one husband (isn't that par for the course, or the legal limit, or something?), two cats and a dog. The hamster died since I last asked her for a bio. She suffered from the smoke of the fires in

Yellowstone Park last summer (just like Darkover), and says that at times it was so gloomy that street lights came on in the afternoon. (MZB)

Arliss Aillard let the mare walk the last mile back to the stables. She had run well today. There would be no competition in the race tomorrow except for the Ridenow horse. The Ridenow lordling, in her opinion, was the only other Domain heir besides herself that could ride *with* the horse and not just on it.

She had named the mare Ondulara, meaning "she of the waves." Ondulara was a big mare, a cross between the rangy dune horses of Aillard and a new heavier strain out of Alton. Her coloring was that of the golden sand, with the white froth of the waves for her mane and tail. There was no other horse on the Plains of Valeron, mare *or* stallion, that could touch her for speed and distance.

The head groom, Tomas, came to take her reins when Arliss rode into the stable. She waved him away, preferring to rub Ondulara down herself. Even at this distance from the Festival grounds she could still hear the din created by a gathering of all Seven Domains; lords and ladies, servants, children, merchants and hucksters, and the ever-present tinkling of the bells worn by the *oudhraki* of the inner desert nomads. Everyone who could walk or ride had come to the racing Festival held at the Aillard Domain this year.

The red sun of Darkover had set by the time she was finished with her mare. She quartered an apple and fed it to Ondulara, then left the shining horse to her hay. The stable was dark. Tomas had not yet come back to light the lanterns. She had been sleeping in the stables of late. The young lords who swaggered around the Festival grounds, drinking and oogling young women and boasting of their prowess were not to be trusted. Ondulara gave a ringing neigh and Arliss whirled. She was seized from behind, her arms pinned by strong hands. In the darkness other hands fumbled at her breasts and someone tried to kiss her. Arliss gagged from the stench of the strong desert *kiri* and unbrushed teeth and tried to scream.

The slobbery lips were replaced with a callused hand. The man holding her mumbled viciously, "Uppity bitch! Teach her to try an' race like a real man!" She couldn't scream, but she lashed out with booted feet and was rewarded with muffled grunts of pain and curses. Then one of her assailants grabbed her feet and she was carried, still struggling, into an empty box stall. The other horses in the stables were all shifting around nervously. Ondulara shrilled out her anger and pounded on the heavy wooden stall with hard hooves.

"Silence the horse," one of them whispered drunkenly. Arliss went wild at the thought of someone harming her mare and got one hand free. She swung her fist and hit something, then curved her fingers into claws and raked.

"Yeow!" screeched the one she hit. "The *grezalis* clawed me!"

Pain exploded along her jaw and she saw stars and then nothing.

Pain.

It flamed red along every nerve in her body when she tried to move. Hands were lifting her gently and she flailed out, fighting.

"No, Arliss! Don't struggle. It's me, Anya. Anya. Do you hear me, Arliss?"

Arliss opened her eyes and sat up. Pain screamed along her raw wrists and into her shoulders. She looked into the concerned face of her sister. Two other sisters knelt in the trampled straw beside her.

"Is Ondulara all right?" Her first thought was for the mare.

"Yes, she's fine. She's a little sluggish acting, but nothing else. What happened here, Arliss? Who did this to you?"

Arliss struggled to her feet. The heated flare of rawness between her thighs took her breath away. She moaned and her sisters caught her before she could fall. They held her up, opening their minds to share the pain and soothe it. Their own furious anger at what had been done to their sister was pushed aside for the moment. When Arliss had the pain under control, she stood on her own.

"Who did this to you, Arliss? Who?" demanded Anya in a savage whisper.

"I don't know. Last night after I brought Ondulara in and brushed her down, I was going to sleep out here. Tomas was gone. Three men, I think it was three, jumped me as I left Ondulara's stall. I was afraid they would hurt Ondulara and I—"

She pushed past her sisters and staggered to the mare's stall. The golden horse stood at the back, blinking sleepily. Arliss reached out with her *laran* and touched the horse, but there was no warm glow of recognition between the two. Someone, and she cursed her attackers to Zandru's coldest hell, had cast a quietening spell on the horse. Whatever the spell was, it was beyond her power to break.

She opened the stall door and walked slowly to the mare. Ondulara just stood there, not dropping her head as she always did to nudge Arliss to scratch behind her ears. Arliss leaned her head against the mare's neck for a moment, struggling to control her rage. She would *kill* them for this!

"Arliss, we must send for the Guard. Whoever did this will be punished."

Arliss turned away from the mare and walked out of the stall.

"No Guard, Anya. We will deal with this ourselves. Arly, I want you to go and find Alarice. Then one of you go and get me some clothes."

"What do you want the Keeper for?" asked Anya.

"To break whatever spell has been cast on Ondulara. I can't ride today with her like this."

"How do you expect to ride today with *you* like this?" Anya pointed down at her sister's bare and bloodied legs. "Alarice will take one look at you and order you to bed. Alida or Alena will have to ride today. You won't be able to."

Arliss turned and glared at Anya.

"You just get me some water and soap and clean rags. I will wash right here in the stable. I *will* ride today, Anya. Those damned Domains men won't keep me from riding or from besting them. By the Piper, I swear it!"

Anya's mouth dropped open as she remembered. "The Piper! By all the Gods, Arliss! You have more to worry about than winning. The Mother wants to see you. That's why we came out here this early to find you. She sent for you last night and then went off to sleep before we could tell you. She will be furious this morning."

So Anya carried in two buckets of water while Arly went for the Keeper. The third sister, Alison, ran to find Arliss some suitable clothes. Being called before the Domain Mother meant you wore the very best you had. Arriving late before this severe old woman with your face as bruised and battered as Arliss' was meant—well, Alison didn't even want to think about it.

Anya helped her sister wash the blood and dirt off. She tended the cuts and bruises with a healing lotion they used on the horses. Arliss stood gripping the inside of the stall door, her legs apart as Anya wrapped strips torn from her underskirt around the worst of the abrasions. She folded a length of the fabric to make a pad for Arliss to wear, tying the ends around her waist.

"Most of the bleeding has stopped, *chiya*. But if you ride today the damage will be much worse."

"I'll ride. Those *sharug* scum won't beat me. The way they ride they couldn't beat their own grandmothers on a three-legged chervine."

"This will mean a blood feud. When Alarice sees what has been done to you, she will tell the Mother. And you know what *she* will do."

"Then we won't tell her. At least not until after the race. I want to beat them, Anya. That will hurt them worse than they could ever hurt me. Do you understand that?" She reached out and took Anya's hand.

"A pact, then," answered Anya, squeezing gently. "You tell me who did this and I will keep silent."

Arliss looked into Anya's green eyes, so like her own. And nodded.

"It was dark, but from what I could tell it was Radolv

Ardais. And those drunken cronies of his, El Halayn and
his Hastur cousin. You know how none of them wanted
to hold the Festival at Aillard. He has been shouting his
mouth off for the last few tendays about how terrible it
is that Aillard is run by women.''

Remembering, Anya nodded. "You're certain?"

"I am certain it was Radolv. And since the other two
are never very far from him, I would bet Ondulara's first
foal that they were with him."

"And where's Tomas?" she wondered all of a sudden.
"Why wasn't he around last night?"

"They killed him. We found him inside the tack room
with a knife in his heart when we came in this morning."

Just then Alison came back with fresh clothes for Arliss. She used a curry comb to rake the bits of straw out
of her short red curls, then they helped her into clean
drawers and a lace-edged cammie. The heavy cotton underskirt came next and she held up her arms for her sisters to slip the silken rose-colored blouse over her head.
Tiny shells were sewn around the yoke and cuffs. Anya
bent down and tied the gilded sandals on Arliss' feet.
Then she stepped into the heavy thistle-silk skirt. It was
dyed dark gold with a stylized wave pattern along the
hem.

"Now you are ready. No, wait. Here, take these,"
Anya pulled her earrings off and quickly slipped them
into Arliss' ears. Alison just as quickly pulled off her
rings and handed them over.

"Now, go quickly."

Arliss carefully gathered up the skirt to run, then turned
back to her sisters.

"You'll stay here, won't you, until Alarice comes? And
stay with Ondulara until I get back? Please."

"Yes. Yes, now go. Or you may not come back."

Arliss ran.

She paused outside the tall double doors of the main hall
to catch her breath and smooth down the skirt. Two of
her cousins stood guard. They grinned at her frightened
face and one whispered as she opened the door, "She's

in a rare fine mood this morning.'' Arliss took a deep breath and marched in.

The Domain Mother was an incredibly old woman, rumored to be well over a hundred years old. Her face was a mass of fine wrinkles above a tiny frail body. The thick, luxurious silver hair braided high atop her head was the only beauty time had left her. Her eyes were still as green as the sea and the power in them fastened on Arliss and pulled her reluctantly forward.

The girl dropped to her knees in front of the old woman, clenching her teeth against the pain between her legs. The Mother leaned forward, balancing herself on the gnarled driftwood cane she used and narrowed her eyes. Then she sat back and motioned with the cane, shouting, ''The rest of you get out. I wish to speak with this child alone.''

Her personal guard stepped down and began to usher the rest of the audience out of the room. When the room was cleared and the doors secured the guard moved back against the wall out of hearing range.

The Mother motioned Arliss up and beckoned her forward. Wincing and suppressing a groan, Arliss got to her feet. Shifting around, the old woman pulled a pillow from behind her and dropped it to the floor at her feet. Arliss sank down gratefully.

The Mother reached out and took Arliss' bruised chin in a surprisingly gentle hand. She turned the battered face up and identical green eyes looked at each other. Arliss felt the question in the old woman's mind and she opened her *laran* to sea-deep compassion and complete understanding. Then the tears came. She buried her face in the Mother's lap and cried. All the pain, all the anger and fear of the night before poured out. The old hand gently stroked the bright red-gold curls. When the worst was over, she pulled a handkerchief from a hidden pocket and gave it to Arliss.

Arliss dried her eyes and blew her nose. As she looked into those ancient eyes, she saw a reflection in her own mind of another young girl with red curls dancing down the beach under the light of the four moons.

''*Chiya*, I called you here today for something totally

different than what I have to say now. The other doesn't matter. Once, a long time ago, I, too, had to do something very difficult for my own honor. For what was done to you, daughter, I could have them all killed." The green eyes bored into Arliss. "What do you want done to them."

Arliss didn't hesitate to answer. "Nothing. Let them worry about it. I will beat them today and that will be their punishment. They have bragged too loudly of how they will beat the Aillard women and ride away with the best of our horses. I will see them *walk* back to Ardais Castle."

The Mother grinned like a dune sprite.

"That is the Aillard spirit. I was right about you. Here, take this with you today when you ride. It will bring you luck." She reached down into the pearl-encrusted bodice of her dress and pulled out a little bone pipe. Arliss thought her heart would stop.

A silent gasp went up from the guards. No one moved. Indeed, time seemed to have frozen as the Mother tucked the pipe away beneath Arliss' blouse. Then the Mother rapped sharply on the stone dais with the copper-tipped cane.

"Don't just stand there gawping like a hooked fish! You are all witness to this. I've made my decision."

She looked down at Arliss. "Now, girl, go back to your horse. I will be there to see you win today." With a wrinkled hand on Arliss' head she said, "Evanda keep you, daughter, and Avarra be merciful to you."

Then she gripped Arliss' hand and helped her to her feet. Arliss leaned forward and kissed the withered cheek. As they touched, she felt the old woman fold her in her *laran* and the pain went away. Shocked, she drew back quickly. The Mother winked conspiratorially at her and grinned again, then shooed her away with the cane.

As Arliss stumbled out, the old woman was again shouting for everyone to come back so she could get all the business finished in time to see the race. People rushed past Arliss in their hurry to obey.

Alison was brushing Ondulara's coat when Arliss ran into the stable. The mare trotted forward to meet her, rubbing her head roughly against the delicate blouse. Arliss threw both arms around the mare's neck and hugged her tight. She touched the mare with her *laran,* checking thoroughly to make sure the horse was well. Tears stung the back of her eyelids but she banished them quickly. Tears were for private, not for fighting.

"She's fine," said Arliss joyfully as Anya came over carrying Arliss' riding clothes.

"The Keeper said it was a simple spell and should have no lasting effects. Ondulara was worked up, but Arly walked her around. I am glad she's all right."

"What did the Mother want?" questioned Alison in a whisper.

"I don't know," answered Arliss in an abstracted tone, taking the brush and finishing Ondulara's coat. "She started to tell me, then she said it didn't matter. All she asked was what I wanted done to those men who hurt me."

"You mean you told her what happened?"

"No, she went into rapport with me and saw it all. She even took the pain from me. I wouldn't want to face that woman in combat. She has more strength than all of us put together."

"So what else happened?"

"Nothing. She gave me this and told me to win the race." Arliss pulled the little bone pipe from the top of her blouse and showed it to her sisters.

They gasped as one and drew back, wide eyed. Anya put out her hand as if to touch it, then jerked it back.

"Arliss, do you know what this means?" She said in a low shocked voice. "The Mother never passes on this pipe unless she is ready to die and has picked a—"

"I don't have time to worry about what anything means right now Anya. I am going to ride today and *win!* Now, are you going to stand there like an idiot or are you going to help me get changed? Oh, by all the Gods! There's the first warning bell."

They helped her strip off the finery. Arly bundled them carefully in her arms and ran to put them away. The earrings and rings were pulled off, too. Anya removed the bandages from her legs, shaking her head in silent wonder. The cuts and scratches on Arliss' back and legs looked days healed now.

Stripped to the skin she pulled on the bright scarlet-colored shirt that symbolized the Aillard Domain. Over this went a silver vest that laced tightly over her breasts. On the back were embroidered six scarlet feathers. Fine, thin black leather pants and boots completed the outfit.

She saddled Ondulara, checking the buckle and girth of the light racing saddle carefully. Satisfied, they all walked quickly through the stableyard and out past the main gates, down to where the Festival booths were set up and on to the starting line of the race.

Horses and riders from the other Domains milled about. Six riders and six horses. Corvan Aldaran, in a dark brown shirt and a white vest, the double-headed eagle of Aldaran embroidered on the back, rode a tall, rangy black that was already in a sweat. Next to him was Jan Alton, in the green and black of Armida, a silver lightening bolt on the back of his vest. His horse was a heavy-shouldered black who was built for distance and not speed.

Lords El Halayn, Hastur, and Ardais arrived after Arliss did. Marc El Halayn wore a silver shirt with a blue vest, the silver fir tree and crown on the front instead of the back. Arliss noticed that one of the Di Asturien cousins was riding today for the Hasturs. His colors were the same as El Halayn's, the exception being that the fir tree was embroidered on the back of the vest without the crown. Radolv Ardais curbed his stallion cruelly, his bright red shirt and green vest flashing in the sunlight. His eyebrows went up slightly at the sight of her on Ondulara, then he raised a gloved fist, his device, toward her mockingly. She looked pointedly at the deep scratches on his face. Her mouth worked and she spat on the ground directly in front of the prancing bay stallion. Other horses pushed between them before he could respond.

The last rider was the young Ridenow man. He wore the green and gold of the Syrtis clan, with five black rings on the back of his vest. His mount was a tall, clean-

limbed chestnut stallion. The horse stood patiently, occasionally shaking his head.

Dalereuth Tower's Keeper moved among the riders. She
passed out a spelled amulet to each of them. Wearing
these, none could use *laran* to influence the race in any
way, nor could anyone from outside the race harm them
or the horses with *laran*. The riders tucked the amulets
down inside their vests. Arliss' fingers touched the little
bone pipe. She smiled.

The last bell sounded. Horses and riders moved to the
starting line. The babbling roar from the crowd hushed
as the Keeper moved to a stand beside the line. She raised
her arm. The hush was complete. Riders leaned over their
horses. Arliss spoke softly to Ondulara, who flicked back
a delicate ear to listen.

The Keeper's arm dropped. The horses exploded forward and the crowd roared to life, each cheering on their
favorite.

As always, Arliss felt the thrill of the strongly surging
muscles of the horse between her legs. She held Ondulara
back, whispering to her constantly, letting the other, more
highly-strung horses take the lead. She had ridden this
course all her life. And for the past three tendays she had
watched the other horses and listened to comments about
them. There was no doubt in her mind that Ondulara
could beat any of them, except maybe the Ridenow horse.
His rider held him back, a little to the right of Ondulara. The stallion was built along the same lines as she
was, used to running in sand.

El Halayn was to the left of her. His horse was lathered
already and as she watched, he brought the braided whip
down hard. The horse put on a burst of speed and jostled
the Aldaran horse, who stumbled and nearly fell on the
uneven ground. The amulets were protection only against
laran; there was nothing to prevent an accident from
purely physical means.

Across and through the desert scrub they ran. The track
led slightly upwards toward the pearl-pink Dalereuth
Tower, around it, and back down the hard-packed sand
of the beach of Dalereuth Sea. It was a grueling course
under the mid-afternoon sun. Arliss wiped the sweat from

her face with a forearm and continued to urge Ondulara on.

Out of the corner of her eye she saw the Hastur horse go down, throwing his rider directly under the hooves of the Alton horse. The Hastur horse had a broken foreleg and his psychic scream of pain jolted the other horses and riders alike. The Alton horse managed to jump over Rafe Di Asturien, but it cost him his position. He batted the horse furiously to catch up.

On they ran.

Ondulara came up on the outside and Ardais moved his horse close to her. Before she could dodge him, he swung his stick and struck Ondulara across the face. The mare threw back her head and broke stride. Arliss freed a boot from the stirrup and kicked out. It caught Radolv Ardais high in the thigh, knocking him sideways. She barely had time to find the stirrup again as she felt Ondulara take the bit in her teeth and race ahead. As she passed him she raised her arm and waggled her wrist limply in insult.

The Ridenow man grinned at her insult as she came up beside him. He was the only other rider besides herself who carried no whip or wore spurs. His horse ran as a part of him. Arliss nodded slightly and the two horses raced on together.

Once they rounded the point, there was just a little over a mile to go. With the rest of the horses behind them, she settled down to urge Ondulara on with hands and knees to beat the Ridenow horse. The mane whipping her face was wet with sweat. They ran on and on.

Ahead she could hear the roar of the crowd that had moved down to the beach for the finish. The Keeper's flaming red robes became visible off to the right as she waited for the winner.

Arliss' breathing became one with Ondulara's. The big mare put everything she had left into this last stretch. Beside her raced the Ridenow stallion, his rider's knee almost touching hers. She lifted the reins a fraction and the knee was behind hers. As they passed under the Keeper's arm, her knee was between the stallion's neck and nose. A roar of triumph and anguish went up from the crowd and washed over Arliss.

It was customary for the winner to pick the best of the horses that the other Domains had brought with them. A few from each Domain. To nearly everyone's amazement, Arliss Aillard chose only from the Ardais clan, taking every animal right down to the last scrawny pack beast. A furious, tight-lipped Galan Ardais demanded a reason, to which Arliss politely replied, "Ask you, son."

The Ridenow's given name was Kemal. Privately, Arliss asked him only two favors; that he turn his stallion in with the Aillard mares for a few days and the other was a more personal invitation.

He declined neither.

At dawn on the day after the race, the bell in the castle tower began to toll. The psychic breaking of a life bond ran through each and every Aillard woman. They knew, without being told, that the Domain Mother had died.

When it was discovered that the little bone pipe was missing, a council was called. Arliss produced the pipe and told her story. The discussion was short. Each of the Mother's personal guard told her story and Arliss was proclaimed Domain Mother, much to her chagrin. It meant more harassment to her than honor. A seat on the Thendara Council would mean too much time away from Aillard and her beloved horses. Well, she would worry about that when the time came.

As the tide ebbed that same evening, they carried the old woman down to the sea. She was wrapped in a long scaled cloak and her body placed in a small boat carved like a shell. In a secluded spot six generations of women in the old Mother's line pushed the bobbing craft out into the sea. A little way out, generations of her *chieren* kin appeared and the land daughters surrendered the boat to the sea daughters. Off the point, giant sea beasts breached and keened their song of sorrow.

The bloody red sun of Darkover dropped beyond the horizon.

The Plague

by Janet R. Rhodes

It seems a little strange that although I did a lot of research on epidemiology and pharmacology for the first Darkover story ever, THE PLANET SAVERS, which was first printed in a magazine, and I did quite a lot of research for another book which never materialized, in space medicine, from that day to this I have written almost nothing on medical research or epidemiology on Darkover. But as always, others have come along to remedy my lacunae. Janet Rhodes tells me—apropos of "The Plague"—that she has a degree in microbiology, and has done considerable research on—guess what—sourdough starters. (Well, I guess you have to start—no pun intended—somewhere.)

This story—which deals with what can be done medically on Darkover—raises some crucial questions; and reminds me a little of a hysterically funny story by Jacqueline Lichtenberg, about a modern-day sorceress whose specialty was enchanting bread to rise. I guess magical gifts come in all sizes and shapes.

Janet Rhodes works for the Department of Ecology, and says she writes "regularly," but it's mostly warning people of ecological dangers. She also makes baskets—and has kept up on most of the modern trends in the health field, and alternative health care. This story deals with a kind of health care that's just as alternative as you can get.

This is her first fiction sale; she stopped writing when a high school teacher provided some "overzealous criticism." That's a problem for everyone: how do you give creative criticism without discouraging as-yet-imperfect

*talents? Tightrope walking would be easy by comparison;
if anybody finds out how to do it, let me know. (MZB)*

Thomaste was getting worse and Kirsten, Lady of Rockraven, wife to *Dom* Lennart, feared the strange illness
would take her only child. Patiently, Kirsten concentrated on the starstone cradled within the small silken bag
at her throat. Reaching out with her psychic powers, focused and enhanced by the stone, Kirsten released the
fluids building up in the glands at Thomme's neck and
groin. She settled the building tension in his stomach and
eased the cramping of his bowels. Fervently, Kirsten
hoped her limited powers would not fail and she could
keep her son's body functioning until he could heal. For
this seemed no brief summer fever come to taunt and
torment, then to flee, borne in and out again on the
breezes from the north.

Adonelle hesitated before the great wooden door to the
sickroom. Having supervised Kirsten's servants for years,
she had no fear of entering her mistress' presence.
Rather, knowing Thomaste had been so terribly ill for
two days, and *Domna* Kirsten had left his side for little
sleep, Adonelle feared adding to her mistress' distress.
Yet others needed her presence.

"Avarra, help us," whispered Adonelle through
clenched teeth. "A fire in the resin trees isn't bad enough,
Zandru has brought a plague upon us, too—with every
able-bodied man and *leronis* on the fire-lines!"

With a sigh, she swallowed her fears and entered. Startled, Kirsten turned toward the doorway. "Ah, Adonelle." Kirsten swept stray strands of hair, sunlight on
bronze, from her face, shook her head from side to side.
"Oh, Adonelle. What am I to do? I ease his pain and it
comes right back. If only my *laran* were stronger, or the
others—have you any word from Lennart, from the fire-
lines?" Adonelle shook her head. "Ah, well, how about
the village? Has this accursed fever reached the villagers?"

Adonelle straightened. "*Domna,* Lennette's oldest has
come with news that Donal, too, has taken the fever."

She glanced at Thomaste. "Lennette begs of you to please attend him."

"Ah, Adonelle, she knows what little skills I offer!"

"Domna, she says you have the healing touch and Donal has only worsened from the midwife's remedies."

"The herbalist's remedies aren't helping? Then I must do what I can. Tell the child I'll come before long."

"Yes, *Domna."* She started to the door, then turned. "I hate to bother you, but could you stop by the kitchens and look at the ferment? It's gone bad again, just sits there and smells like a banshee. I'd high hopes we'd have leavened loaves again; it's been a long tenday without! I've tried everything I can think of. 'Twill be another ten day, or longer, before we have loaves unless you can resurrect it."

Kirsten sighed. "I'll stop on my way out. Have some soup ready, will you? Haven't broken my fast yet today, and it must be past noon."

Kirsten turned to Thomaste who was tossing and turning feverishly as if dodging a course of obstacles. He lay there so white, even his freckles had paled to mere shadows, his red hair a shining halo surrounding his face. Lovingly, she rearranged the coverlets he had thrust off as the fevers returned.

With a deep centering breath, Kirsten turned her attention again to the starstone. Gently, her mind entered the fragile energy being that was Thomaste. With an effort, she concentrated on the glands filled with fluid, saw the many cells collecting there. She released the fluids into the blood; then found the boy's temperature center, turned down the fire in his body, and opened the blood vessels to the skin to take away the excess heat and bring soothing coolness.

How fragile he seemed, not the running, jumping joy of her's and Lennart's lives.

When Thomaste grew quiet, Kirsten hugged him to her breast, then quickly left the room, an unnatural sheen to her eyes. She stopped a moment in the hallway to give the serving girl, Suzonna, directions for Thomaste's care. "Stay with him, keep him covered, and use the cool cloth if he starts warming." Suzonna curtsied and murmured words of promise, but Kirsten stayed with her with an imperative hand, "If he worsens, at all, let Adonelle or me know immediately." Alarmed, the girl stumbled over oaths and more promises, then sped into the sickroom.

"Stop scaring the girl, she's hardly older than Thomaste," muttered Kirsten to herself as she went to her rooms for a splash of water and a dress to replace the one she'd worn for two days. Longingly, she gazed at the bath, always filled with warm mineral water from deep in the rocks beneath the manor house.

An hour later, Kirsten entered the great kitchens, discovered the fermenting crock at the sideboard where Adonelle had placed it to start the morrow's loaves. *Well,* Kirsten thought, as she pulled on an overdress, *at least what little* laran *I do have is good for something.*

With the familiarity of long practice, Kirsten centered, touched the starstone with a finger of her mind and plunged her psychic senses into pale greenish fluid, then the pasty mess below. Even through the touch of *laran* the stench was nearly unbearable, a sure sign of the imbalance in the batter. Rapidly, Kirsten sorted through the sensations. There were few of the tiny rod-shaped sticks that lived on the sweets from the flour added to the crock each day. The round things clumped together like purplefruits were more abundant. They, too, lived off the flours and, when put to the barley and bitter-flower, made the brew enjoyed on hot days and before the fires during the snows.

In the years since her late-blooming womanhood—when her *laran,* uncontrolled, had either killed the tinylife in the ferment or stirred it up to violent froth—Kirsten had learned to control her gift. But she had always known it was only good for ferments—and for easing the discomfort of sick little boys—not the real healing of a *leronis.*

Now Kirsten used her skills and knowledge to enter one after another of the sticks and balls, to nudge their inner fires, to repair these tinylives. Soon the fermenters were able to do their work again.

Kirsten moved about and looked through the pasty mess for the strange life which often invaded the ferment and upset the delicate balance in the universe of the crock. Yes, there were strangers, shaped like crescent moons. For a moment Kirsten wondered at the odd familiarity of the invaders, then moved on to upset their inner fires. Searching through the batter, she disabled all the crescents she could find. Finally, she was certain the ferment would recover.

Lennette's poor home at the edge of the village mirrored her family's status in the community. With no husband and six children, their fathers unknown, and no other family to call on, Lennette and her children had lived at the edge of existence until Donal's and Thomaste's births some ten years before.

Kirsten had not been able to provide sufficient milk for her child. He grew daily weaker until Lennette came forth saying she could surely feed two little ones, her breasts were so full. Lennette came to the manor house for a year as wet nurse to Thomaste. She and Kirsten developed a fast friendship.

The room was dark as Kirsten entered. A single candle burned. "The light hurts his eyes," whispered Lennette, nodding toward the dark-haired boy tossing feverishly on blankets at the back of the room. The nearby fireplace served as kitchen and heat and light for the one room that was home to seven. "He won't eat and cannot keep food or water down when I force him to take it. The fever comes and goes. Nothing I do seems to help."

"I know," murmured Kirsten, removing her wrap in the warmth of the room. "It has been the same with Thomaste." She reached out to grasp the well-worn hands of her friend, looked into the face reddened with sun, wind, and cold. "I will do what I can, Lennie, even if it is not much." Kirsten gently caressed a strand of black hair from Lennette's face, smiled at her reassuringly. *Your children are all you have, they are your treasure,* she thought.

One of the daughters brought a clean blanket and placed it by Donal's bedding for Kirsten to kneel upon. She looked shyly from under frizzy blonde braids pulled around her head and remembered, belatedly, to "curtsey to the *domna*" as her mother had reminded her earlier.

Normally, Donal's complexion was as ruddy as Thomaste's was fair, his body as sturdy as Thomaste's was slender and frail. Today, Donal was a pale wisp of his usual self, and his white face matched Thomaste's.

Kirsten knelt on the blanket. "Donal, I am here to help you. Can you hear me?" Unsure whether the boy, in his feverish state, had heard her, Kirsten prepared to enter into his body.

Centering on the starstone, she reached out a tendril of her mind and found Donal's body nonresistant to her touch. Moving gently, Kirsten became aware of his burning skin, the fast beating of his heart, and his shallow, quick breaths. Moving deeper, Kirsten found his glands filled with the cleansing cells of the blood. They seemed all mixed up with some other odd-shaped cells. The cleansing system of the body appeared to be clogged with dead and dying cleansing cells and those others that reminded her somewhat of the invaders in the ferment. *How curious!* she thought.

Donal was much stronger than Thomaste, and Kirsten cleared out the glands at neck and groin easily, slowed and strengthened the beating of his heart, brought the blood to the skin to help cool his body. Donal's inner fires responded to her touch and, as Kirsten brought herself back to normal consciousness, she heard Lennette, "His fever has broken! *Domna* Kirsten, you have stopped the fever!"

"Would that it was so easy, Lennie. You must watch him. The fever might return. Call me if it does. And keep the other children away from him; who knows how this sickness spreads."

"Evanda be praised! Thank you, Kirsten. Thank you." Lennette hugged her.

"It was nothing, Lennette. But I am tired and must return home."

"Evanda and Avarra grant that Thomaste will recover as easily as Donal. If I can do anything . . ."

"Thank you. If you can help, I will let you know."

And Kirsten trudged into the bloody sunlight, back to the manor.

Returning, Kirsten thought again of the warm baths in her rooms and of the few hours' sleep she would allow before returning to Thomaste's sickroom. But Adonelle, wearing a frown and with knitted brows, met her at the front doors and stood there twisting her overdress in both hands. "Adonelle?" began Kirsten, then she knew. "Thomaste?" she asked and started up the curving staircase to the sleeping rooms before Adonelle could answer.

Suzonna rose hurriedly and backed out of the way as Kirsten burst into the room. Thomaste, eyes glazed, jerked and writhed on the bed.

"*Domna,*" ventured Suzonna, "it just started. I sent for Adonelle; she was going for you. I didn't know what to do."

Kirsten paid no attention to Suzonna, so intent was she on Thomaste, and on his unbearable thirst and the spasms that wracked his gut. His pain and fear reached out and enclosed her in darkness. She had to force herself back, away from the waves of pain, to where she could think and plan something to set it right again.

Adonelle pushed a cup into her hands. "Drink, it is redfruit juice and will give you strength." Kirsten drank without lifting her head from the cup. The sweetness coursed through her, strengthening body and mind. She returned the cup to Adonelle, grasped the silken bag at the base of her throat and returned to the bedside.

Suzonna held a bucket on her knees and Thomaste's head above it as his stomach twisted and squeezed and tried to force up food that was not there. His stomach heaved again and again.

"Dear heart," whispered Kirsten as she gently wiped his lips with the cool cloth and caressed his stringy hair. Then she centered on the starstone, sent her mind questing into the tortured muscles of Thomaste's stomach and bowels. At first the maelstrom that greeted Kirsten sent her into a dizzying spin, but she soon righted herself and set about soothing the ravaged tissues. It took time and the little strength of the redfruit juice was failing fast.

But Kirsten knew she had to go carefully and slowly to repair the damage.

Kirsten strained to remember what little training she had received about healing; she pushed her skills to the utmost, then reached some more. Deep into the tissues she went, deep into the tiny cells—all pushed together so they looked like eggs thrown together in a bowl before she beat them.

Kirsten did what she could to release the buildup of poisons that caused the muscles to spasm. She moved from cell to cell, muscle to muscle, clearing out poisons and repairing damage. Kirsten was deep in rapport now, using her *laran* more fully than ever she had in her life, or ever thought she could.

The jerking and spasms steadily slowed and she was able to pull back and look over her work. The muscles seemed to be healing, and Kirsten was surprised and puzzled at the newfound skills that had allowed her to assist with that healing.

Glorying in the heightened sense of her *laran,* Kirsten moved through Thomaste's body. And suddenly stopped, jolted into seeing something for the first time—Thomaste was filled with tiny crescents. To all appearances, they were the same crescents that had invaded the ferment crock. So many of the creatures filled his body they seemed as blades of grass in the fields.

The shock, her complete exhaustion, her fear for Thomaste, all piled one upon the other. Kirsten's inner vision clouded, she lost control and slipped out of contact with Thomaste. Briefly, she seemed to wander through a gray, featureless plain, then an overwhelming lethargy engulfed her and Kirsten slid into unconsciousness. Her final thought was that, at least, she had stopped the vomiting and diarrhea. There was hope.

When Kirsten roused from deep, exhausted sleep, pale green moonlight cascaded from the skylight in her rooms. Suzonna slept on a cot at the foot of the bed. *Thomaste!* thought Kirsten, suddenly chilled, remembering the invaders in her son's body. She tried to push back the coverlet, to swing her legs over the side of the bed; found that arms and legs refused to obey. The fog of utter exhaustion rapidly recaptured her, the result of lack of food and rest and *laran* work far beyond her experience.

When Kirsten finally awoke fully, the sun was high in the sky and Adonelle was bringing in a tray piled with fruit, sticky rolls, honey, and porridge. "*Domna,* you must eat before you go anywhere. Please, it is well known that *laran* uses up the energies. You may permanently injure yourself if you don't." Adonelle looked up and realized that Kirsten was fully awake, sitting up in her bed and gazing at her in consternation. "*Domna,* are you truly awake now? Earlier, you frightened Suzonna half out of her mind, talking about invaders and falling out of bed. We had to put you back. You are all right now? I mean, truly awake?"

Speechless, Kirsten simply nodded and reached for the food. As if she were carrying a child, Kirsten knew, she ate for more than one. Somehow, she must decipher the mystery of this invasion of the body. As mistress of Rockraven she was responsible not only for her health and that of her son, but for the welfare of the entire village. Never had the weight of responsibility seemed greater, her body more depleted, her soul more barren and bereft of comfort.

The food nourished her body, if not her soul.

Hours later, after again easing Thomaste's discomfort, Kirsten had retreated to her baths for privacy and to ease her battered body. She had sent the two eldest of the remaining village boys to carry word of the plague to her husband. Left behind because they were too young even to carry pails of water for those fighting the fires, the boys were probably too young to send on a day's journey. However, they were all she had. The village, and Rockraven, needed the services of a true *leronis*—desperately. For Adonelle had brought word that most of the women and children in the village were ill with the fever. Some, such as Donal, experienced no more than a temporary disabling fever and vomiting. Others were deathly ill. Several had died during the night.

Kirsten grieved with the villagers this day. And in a

hidden part of her, Kirsten felt guilty at her inaction. *Domna* Helene, her mother, had instilled in her over and over, ''You will be the wife of a nobleman. You yourself are noble-born. Be proud of your heritage, but also be aware of your responsibilities. You are not simply the mistress of your house, children, husband, and servants. You are the servant of your people. They are as children to you. They look to you to love and guide them, to protect them from all harm from without.''

Kirsten had lost more children these past two days than she cared to count.

The polite throat-clearing warned Kirsten that Adonelle was near, but she made no effort to stop the tears sliding down her cheeks and into the pool. ''Do not hide there, Adonelle. Come forward and tell me the news. I fear it must be bad indeed, if the shadows are your friend. Come,'' she encouraged. ''I wish for no more to trouble me, but doubt not that the world will hear my pleas and go as it will.'' Adonelle came quietly into the room. Her eyes were puffy and red, her face streaked with tears she did not bother to wipe away. In her hands, a tray of dried fruits, sweetmeats, nuts. Something to nourish her lady.

Adonelle knelt on the rug, ''I did not wish to disturb you, but . . .'' She sighed, swallowed and continued. ''The sickness still spreads. And . . . Lennette has taken the fever.'' Kirsten made a small cry much like the rabbit-horn's when caught in a trap. ''Ahhh! Avarra, Dark Mother, Goddess of Birth and Death, must you take her?'' she cried, weeping anew.

Dried and robed, Kirsten made her way to Lennette's cottage. Heartsick, she hurried through the dust of the track from manor house to village, never lifting her eyes from the tips of her slippers to see the pall of sickness laying over the cottages, the few children and mothers sitting listlessly in doorways and on porches. Two bodies, a child and an elder, lay stiffening in the road, their families too ill to carry them inside or to the burial ground.

The stench of vomit and diarrhea mixed with un-washed, sweaty bodies hit her first. In the murky darkness of the cottage she saw the children huddled together in the corner by the fireplace. Donal, apparently the healthiest, peered up from where he bathed his mother's face with a damp, grimy cloth. *"Domna,* you've come! Please help us. Mama is so sick and the younger ones, too. Please!'' Donal's eyes brimmed over with tears ''I . . .'' The rest was lost in a whispered garble of sobbing.

Kirsten swallowed her own tears, spoke with a strangled voice, ''If there is anything I can do for your Mama and sisters and brothers, I will do it.'' Within herself, Kirsten damned her limited *laran,* and with a helpless gesture pulled on the overdress she carried. Kirsten went from one to the other, lightly touching the place where the pulse was easy to find, brushing her fingertips over fiery foreheads, whispering an encouraging word. Donal trailed after her on legs gone wobbly.

For the most part, Donal's sisters and brothers responded well to her ministrations. They were of strong stock. It didn't take long for her to reach into their bodies with her mind, reduce the swollen glands, slow and strengthen the beating of their hearts, help the little bodies to cool.

However, her work with the starstone took its toll. When Kirsten turned to Lennette, she was weak and consumed with trembling and she started at every little sound—her senses were so alert.

"Domna, would you like some water? There is nothing else to give you.'' He held out a glass filled with well water.

She took it gratefully and began to drink with long, full gulps. Suddenly, she flung the glass against the stone of the fireplace, causing Donal to shrink back in terror. Perhaps she had become sensitized by all the *laran* work the past several days. Perhaps her fear for Thomaste's life had broken a barrier to her full *laran.* Perhaps in her extremity of pain and exhaustion, Kirsten's awareness had expanded as the ferment grows in the bread bowls—from a small, cool lump of flours to the smooth, rounded dough topping the filled bowl.

Whatever had happened, Kirsten sensed, with every fiber of her being, the invaders permeating the water. They were the same crescent-shaped tinylives as those filling her dear Thomme and threatening to take him from her. The invaders that even now spread silently through her people in the water they drank.

Slowly, Kirsten realized that Donal and the others must think her quite mad. Carefully, she monitored her breathing and slowed it, tried to think rationally, to consider the possibilities. There had to be a way to kill the invaders in the water. All she had to draw on was her experience with the kitchen ferments. She knew she couldn't kill each invader. There had to be a—the tinylives in the ferment! They died when the loaves were baked! The heat destroyed them.

"Donal, stir up the fire and put some water on to boil. Donal, do you hear me? The water carries the sickness. We must boil it or the sickness will keep invading all of us." Donal, disbelieving, crept hesitantly toward the fireplace. "When the water's started, go round to the other cottages and tell— No, go to Adonelle and ask her to come here. Go on, Donal. I'll see to your mother."

Lennette was weaker than her children. There had been too many years of drudgery, of bearing and nursing children, too much isolation and tears. Kirsten did what she could, then sat back on her heels, cradling her forehead in both hands. Adonelle found her this way.

"Domna, Donal said something about the sickness being in the water. What nonsense is this?"

" 'Tis no nonsense, Adonelle. The water is filled with tinylife that causes the sickness. Tell everyone in the village to boil their water. That should kill it. Get servants from the house to help if the families are too ill to do it themselves. We must free our drinking water of this plague, else no one will get well. We'll keep drinking invaders over and over!" She smiled weakly.

"Will it help that much?"

"We can only hope. If only there were *leroni* to help . . ."

"There is you. I know you are overtired—none would have expected you to go on as you have—but there must be something you can do!"

"I know nothing more." Her voice was bitter. "Now, if people were like ferments. . . ."

While Adonelle went to her task, Kirsten brooded. In the daydream of utter exhaustion, Kirsten saw a handful of ferment crocks dancing in the light of dawn, little worlds where good and evil tinylife battled for existence. In some crocks, the invasion was quickly crushed. In others, the invaders swept over the sticks and balls and the ferment went bad—as Adonelle would say, "smelling like a banshee." *What is the difference?* wondered Kirsten. *What makes one ferment survive and another go bad? What is the difference?*

With a start, Kirsten looked round the cottage, "What is the difference? Why does," she gulped and continued muttering, "one die and another live?" She was moving now, first to Lennette lying in her bed, then to the children in their pile of blankets. "What is the difference!"

With difficulty, Kirsten concentrated on her starstone, gained rapport with each of the children and searched for some clue that would tell her why some could survive the plague and many would not. What was the difference? In Lennette's children, Kirsten found evidence the cleansing cells scoured their bodies, destroying crescents, carrying them to the collection points at neck and groin.

Kirsten moved on stiffening legs to Lennette's bed, sent her mind questing into blood and glands and bowels. The number of crescent-shaped invaders shocked her. Here the few cleansing cells groped past the crescents, never noticing them. Lennette's body labored to right itself, to fight an invader it did not even recognize.

Kirsten fell into a chair and leaned an elbow wearily on the rough-hewn logs of the table. The difference: Lennette's body did not recognize the invaders; the children's bodies did. Simple as that.

But what could she do about it? "If only I were a real *leronis!*" lamented Kirsten.

Lennette moaned, kicked off the coverlet. Kirsten sighed and heaved herself off the chair, bent to assist Lennette. Automatically, Kirsten made contact with her starstone, extended a tendril of her mind into Lennette's body. Her fever was up. Kirsten turned down the fire in Lennette's body, and brought the blood to the skin to cool. Even in the last few minutes, Lennette's attempts to fight the invaders seemed weaker.

The woman who was her friend, who had nursed her child, was failing fast. Death was already stealing the color from her face. Her eyes were unfocused; her breathing ragged. Urgently, Kirsten became one with the crystal at her throat, thrust her mind into the failing body. Everywhere, she saw carnage, tissues and cells breaking down. Everywhere the crescent invaders. Her friend was dying.

Abruptly, Kirsten withdrew. "Noooooo!" she screamed in misery and pain. "No!"

The children stared at her in fear.

"There must be something else I can do!"

Kirsten grabbed at the nearest child. He shrank back in terror, and Kirsten remembered herself. "No, child. I won't hurt you. Just let me look at you a minute. Child, hold still!" Trembling, the boy stood while Kirsten centered on her starstone, sent her mind into his body.

After several minutes she found the difference that allowed the children to destroy the invaders. She wondered that she had not seen it before. Yet, she had never used her *laran* so frequently and for such long periods. She had never entered rapport with others so easily. She had never sensed so much before. Clearly, Kirsten was growing into a use of her *laran* she had never guessed.

The child grew restless under her grip. Kirsten released him.

Gently entering Lennette's body, Kirsten scanned for the cleansing cells which destroyed crescents. In the children, the cells seemed to lock onto the invaders, the crescents fitting into the cells like a bolt into its socket. Kirsten searched, too, for an energy-net such as she had seen in the boy. To her it looked as if this shimmering net commanded the cleansing cells as a defending army.

Drawing on what she had seen in the child, Kirsten was able to discern a faint shadow of the energy-net. Summoning her courage and her reserves, she reached out, cleaned the clogged energy channels, watched the network begin to shimmer and pulsate with renewed life. Next, Kirsten searched through Lennette's body for cleansing cells that knew how to lock on to the crescents. When she had about given up hope, Kirsten found one cell, holding fast to a single invader. But her hope turned to fear when she realized the cell was sick itself. Gathering her wits about her, Kirsten set about healing the cell.

And was rewarded as the cleansing cell came alive. Kirsten was astounded to see the cell begin to divide rapidly, making an identical brother or sister cell. The two cells became four soon after. She could see the cells continue to divide even as they began to disperse throughout Lennette's body.

Kirsten followed them as best she could. She stopped to watch a cleansing cell sidle up to a crescent, saw the cell and the crescent lock together, sensed the life go out of the invader. In other areas, new cleansing cells began to confront more invaders. With hope, Kirsten carefully withdrew her senses from Lennette's body.

And saw her begin to rally.

"Domna, will she be all right?" asked the child she had terrified earlier.

"I hope so, child. I will be grateful to you if she does."

"Domna?"

"Pay no mind, child; I am overweary. Let me rest."

Hours later, Adonelle found *Domna* Kirsten at the table in Lennette's cottage, tears making tracks in the dirt on her cheeks. Donal knelt at his mother's bed carefully sponging her feverish face, arms, hands. *"Domna?"* Kirsten dropped her hand from her face, turned listlessly toward the door.

"Adonelle?" Kirsten's voice croaked with strain; she shook her head sadly. "I thought I had found our saving. Once I realized there was a defender in us, it seemed to be so easy—

"I felt so joyous . . . and now all is lost."

"Domna, I do not understand." Adonelle looked from Kirsten to Lennette and back.

"Her body is fighting the invaders, but . . . the fever . . . there is a roaring fever. . . ." Kirsten's voice faded and her trembling body betrayed the extent of her pain and grief.

Adonelle, filled with concern for Kirsten, crossed the room, gathered up her mistress, and guided her toward the door. Adonelle supported Kirsten as they walked through the gloom of the darkening village, the air heavy with the cold hand of death.

As they entered the manor, Adonelle said, "Can you make it to your rooms? I will bring you something to eat from the kitchens."

Kirsten squeezed Adonelle's arm, said, "Thank you," and started up the stairs, leaning heavily on the handrail.

After she had eaten some bread, fruit, and soup, Kirsten began to stir, pulling on a robe and looking for house shoes.

"Where are you going?" asked Adonelle.

"I must see to Thomme," responded Kirsten. Adonelle protested that she was not strong enough, that Suzonna cared for the young one, that Kirsten must rest and—

Suzonna burst into Kirsten's rooms without warning, face streaked with weeping, gasping from the plunge down the long hallway, and fell in her hurry to reach her mistress. Adonelle dropped the serving tray with its load of dirty dishes and Kirsten dropped to the floor beside the terrified girl. "What has happened? Suzonna! What has happened?"

The despair in Suzonna's uplifted eyes, her trembling lips, confirmed what had already forced open the door of Kirsten's unbelieving mind, even as she had started out of bed—Thomaste was dying . . . or even now dead.

In her sleeping gown and robe, Kirsten ran to her son's room. His frail body was limp as Kirsten reached out with her mind, touched her starstone, thrust out. Quickly, she cleaned the channels of his defending energy-net, urged it into action. She found a cleansing cell locked onto an invader, healed the weakened cell, rejoiced as it multiplied. Here and there, throughout Thomaste's body, Kirsten found damaged and dying tissues, touched them with healing. She could feel Thomaste fighting, trying to rally. Silently, she urged him on.

But it seemed too late. Soon, too soon, she felt his life force ebbing. *Thomaste, don't die!* Frantically, Kirsten tried everything she knew, to no avail. Thomaste was no longer in the body on the bed! Anguished, Kirsten propelled her mind into the astral planes. The gray featureless expanse stretched before her, empty. Then, in the far distance, enveloped in wisps of fog, she spied a small, frail figure walking purposefully away. Leaving her. Going. Dying.

In agony, Kirsten started toward him. Trembling, she forced an image outward, toward her son. He took a few more steps, then stopped. Encouraged, she reached out to him with heart and mind, hands outstretched before her. Hesitantly, he glanced back over his shoulder, looked at her, then turned back and resumed walking. Kirsten groaned in pain and fear, damned the destiny that had denied her the full use of *laran*. Again, Kirsten sent images of love and living, reached out with all her power, reached until she felt consciousness slipping from her grasp. In one final, desperate effort, Kirsten shouted, *"Thomaste,"* then collapsed, her mind slamming back into her still body.

The day dawned cloudy and with a hint of rain. It brought hope, for rain would stop the fires. And it brought fear, for the plague still claimed many. Adonelle, taking a cool cup of redfruit juice to Kirsten, heard wailing cries as family members carried loved ones to the graveyard. She grieved with them.

Upon entering the room, Adonelle sensed tension, disquiet. Nervously, she approached the bed, then dropped the cup from lifeless hands. For Kirsten lay in the throes of the fever, her linens sodden with the desperate efforts of her body to cool itself, her hair stuck in damp strings to her forehead. "Oh, my lady! What hope is there now?"

Dom Lennart arrived at Rockraven that afternoon in a clatter of hooves, followed by Rederick, the family *laranzu,* and other *leroni* from the surrounding districts who had been at the fire.

"Thank Avarra!" exclaimed Adonelle as she greeted Lennart.

"Where is *Domna* Kirsten?" Lennart's voice boomed against the stones in the entryway.

"Your lady-wife has taken the fever."

"And Thomaste?"

"Oh, *Dom.*" Adonelle seemed to crumple as tears sprung from her eyes, and she was unable to continue.

Lennart strode for the stairs, shouting back over his shoulder for Rederick and the white-haired *laranzu* Kirk to accompany him. Adonelle followed.

At the doorway to Kirsten's rooms, Lennart sent Kirk on to attend Thomaste while he and Rederick attended the *domna*. For a long moment, Lennart stood looking at his wife, lying pale in her great bed. "How long has she been like this?" he asked.

"Since morning. *Dom* Lennart, I fear for her life. So many have died. The entire village—"

Concern etched deep lines on *Dom* Lennart's face. For a moment, he closed his eyes, giving in to the weariness of days fighting the fires, to the pain of lost lives, and to the fear of losing his own loved ones. Lennart placed a hand on Rederick's shoulder, spoke in a voice thick with emotion, "You are the most skilled *laranzu* here. Take good care of her, Rederick. I must see Thomaste, and have the others see to the villagers."

Hours later, Rederick retreated to the dining hall. There he found the other *leroni* gathered over meat and brew, dejectedly comparing their failure to heal villagers afflicted with the plague. None had seen such a thing in his lifetime. Sadly, they told Lennart their best efforts did little more than ease the discomfort of the victims.

Lennart urged, "There must be something you can do!"

Then Kirk, who had gone to the village after attending the stricken Thomaste, spoke up, "It were a good thing to ask the mistress were she not so ill herself." Faces, blank with tiredness and bewilderment, turned to stare at him. Kirk continued, "The villagers kept saying *Domna* Kirsten healed a woman yest'day. Right sick *Mestra* Lennette was, too, near to dying, they said."

Startled, Lennart commanded the serving boy to fetch Adonelle to him immediately.

Adonelle arrived bleary-eyed from long-needed sleep ended too soon. *"Mestra* Lennette? Why *Domna* Kirsten tried so hard to heal her. Thought she had found a way, too, but the fevers returned." Adonelle shuddered.

"Knew you not that *Mestra* Lennette is free of the fever?" Adonelle shook her head, her eyes wide. *"Dom* Lennart, I'd swear *Domna* Kirsten brought Thomaste back from death last night!"

"What?" cried Lennart, "Tell me what happened."

After hearing Adonelle's story, Lennart sighed and said evenly, "Rederick, can you find out what Kirsten did?"

"She is so ill, *Dom,* she could die."

"Can you promise we won't lose her anyway?"

"No."

"Then you must do it. She may be our only hope."

Lennart and Kirk joined Rederick in Kirsten's rooms. First Rederick eased Kirsten's growing discomfort. Then the three men lightly linked minds. Rederick slowly reached out to link with Kirsten, searching for her memories of the past few days.

And met resistance, a barrier. Rederick hesitated, unwilling to enter another being through force, knowing it could bring the information they sought or could kill her.

Through their link, Lennart urged Rederick to press on. *"Already, I sense her fever rising. For all of us, you must."*

Rederick gathered his psychic forces, exerted them where there seemed a weakness in the armor covering the fabric of Kirsten's mind. She moaned softly, made small pushing away movements with her hands. Rederick continued to ease his way in.

Kirsten became aware of a strange presence within her and panicked, tried to pull up her barriers, but couldn't; she was too weak. She tried to fight off this other who had invaded her, to push it back, she would never give in.

Kirsten, let us in! We are here to help.

No! I will die rather than be ravaged—

Kirsten! bellowed a familiar voice. Kirsten gasped,

confused, knowing that Lennart was far away at the fires, that he would never come to her this way unbidden. Unless. . . .

Kirsten, dear one. Fear not. We must know the secret of Lennette's and Thomaste's healings.

A great sadness descended on Kirsten. *I tried so hard and failed. The fevers returned.*

You did not fail. Both Lennette and Thomaste live!

They sensed a swirl of confusion, of hope. Then Kirsten suddenly pulled away and strengthened her barriers. A moan of utter despair rose from her depths. *Avarra help me. All is lost. Why do I torture myself?*

In fear and pain, Lennart cried out, *Kirsten, do not go from us!* In response, Kirsten pulled more tightly into a deep corner of her being.

Rederick, what—?

I fear she has not the strength to face the possibility that Lennette and Thomaste live for fear she will have to experience their deaths a second time, responded Rederick. *The pain may be too much for her to bear.*

You're saying we may lose her because she thinks Thomaste and Lennette are dead. The fear and not the fact will kill her.

I have seen it before.

How do we reach her?

I do not know.

Damn it, we must do something! Lennart pushed toward the place where Kirsten had walled herself off from the offending presences. Lennart knew that her sanity, perhaps her life, depended on his reaching her somehow.

With a finger of his consciousness, Lennart reached out and touched the wall Kirsten had formed. It repelled him. In desperation, he allowed the barriers to the most personal part of himself to fall, revealing his innermost thoughts and feelings. His love for Kirsten and Thomaste were tangible things, his fear of losing them a glowing ember. From a reservoir almost empty, Lennart poured out the strength of his being, offered it to Kirsten. Even behind her protective wall, Kirsten sensed his gift. It triggered a release of memories—of her and Lennart together, of Thomaste, of Lennette.

Quivering, fearful, Kirsten reached toward his presence, allowed his strength to surround, infill her. Her walls thinned, but did not drop.

Kirsten, said Rederick, seeing the change. *Many are dying. We must know what you did to help Lennette and Thomaste, so others may live.*

Beloved, added Lennart, *I will be with you.* Heedless of his own needs, Lennart continued to pour out strength and love to Kirsten.

Feeling reassured, Kirsten began trying to lower her barriers, so they might see what she had learned.

Rederick withdrew from Kirsten with care, then healed the defender in her before leaving Kirsten in a deep, healing sleep.

Lennart knelt at the side of the bed, Kirsten's hand in his.

Rederick, standing behind Lennart, said, "I am amazed at what the *domna* has accomplished. When she recovers, Lennart, perhaps a journey to the Towers. Her gift deserves sharing and more training. She has a great strength." Lennart nodded, keeping his eyes on Kirsten.

Silently, Rederick bowed and left to tend the sick throughout the village.

The Tapestry

by Micole Sudberg

For a long time, Vera Nazarian was the youngest writer ever to sell to me; but that was a long time ago and now there is a younger writer in these anthologies. Micole Sudberg says she wrote this story when she was in ninth grade. Every few days I receive a story from some amateur hardly out of childhood, but their efforts are seldom professional enough to give a second reading; at most I write them a polite and hopefully encouraging note, telling them something about this business they want to get into (that it's more communication than self-expression, for one thing), and encouraging them to persevere. Micole's story, however, was—like most salable stories by beginners—good enough that it bore no marks of extreme youth. I didn't have any idea she was so young until her contract came back countersigned by her parents. She says that this story was more in imitation of my style than her own, asking me to "please consider it the sincerest form of flattery." I do. She adds that she is now a sophomore in high school, and is currently working on her second novel, which has the intriguing title of GODBRIDGE. Well, that's how I started; I've been writing literally since I could hold a pen; but I didn't sell till I was in my twenties. Which reminds me of a story attributed—among others—to Mozart. Someone asked him how to write a symphony; he replied, "Oh, you're too young." The presumably teenage querent said indignantly, "But you wrote your first symphony when you were only eight years old." and Mozart replied, "Yes; but I didn't have to ask anybody how to do it, either."

And the moral of this story is; if you can do it, you're obviously old enough. (MZB)

A raven soared like a black spear into the sky. Its mate hopped irritably on a window ledge, searching haughtily for crumbs—most common behavior for symbols of the Goddess Avarra, Fiona noted with a small, distant part of her mind that could still be amused. She forgot the thought immediately as she leaned dangerously far out the window. The wind was clean and cold on her face; she closed her eyes to luxuriate in the upsweep of air. She thought with longing, *To be a bird and free—*

"My lady!" a voice gasped—*my betrothed's voice*, she thought in disgust.

She turned to face him. "You need not worry, my lord," she said bitterly, "I have no intention of casting myself out the window." *Though you may drive me to it yet.*

"Yes, yes," *Dom* Marius stammered hurriedly, wiping his fat, perspiring face, "of course not, I had not thought so—" He didn't say what he *did* think. Instead he turned to a safer topic. "That is a fine tapestry, my lady. It is of Avarra and her handmaidens, is it not? Though near Syrtis we say she has but two, one to help her watch over birth and another to watch over death. . . ."

"In Neskaya," Fiona explained, with a wave toward the tapestry, "it was said that she had four, after whom the moons are named: Idriel, to watch over labor; Mormallor, to keep the souls of those stillborn; Liriel, to bless those liveborn; and Kyrrdis, to help gather the souls of the dead."

"Well," he said, jerking his eyes away from her breasts, "it is a lovely tapestry. A lovely tapestry."

Fiona stared at him, her stomach twisted with hate. He was a short man, fat and ugly, dressed in too-elaborate clothes; she always expected to see him drooling and was always surprised that he was not. And even in a cloistered Tower, she had heard stories of his depravities. She looked away. "If you please, my lord," she said in a low voice, "I would like to be alone."

When he had left, she sat down on her stool, carefully keeping her back straight and refusing to cry. She stared unblinking at the metallic glints in the tapestry so that her eyes could not tear. Those threads were truly metal;

she had only recently woven them in. Barely a month ago, Fiona had received the thin, ductile wires from Damon of Arilinn. She scooped up a handful and fingered copper threads on her palm with a distant wonder. As she had moved her hand, they had caught the sunlight and gleamed a bloody gold.

This is excellent work, she thought bitterly. *It was kind of Damon to send these to me when I was Keeper. We could not spin metal this thin in Neskaya, our work is too powerful; we have no subtlety, no fine control. —No,* she corrected herself, *I have no fine control. I must not blame the circle for my own shortcomings. Are not they why I was—was* sentenced *to this marriage?*

She turned from the threads of pure metal to her loom. It was a vertical loom, taller than she was, and longer than it was tall. The half-completed tapestry on it was a picture of Avarra, the goddess of birth and death, and her four handmaidens. Above their waists, the vertical warp threads were white and bare. When the tapestry was finished, they would be invisible, completely covered by the horizontal weft threads. Right now the tapestry was only half-done, the maidens still faceless and the Goddess' dress, which would be embroidered with copper, innocent of ornamentation. The raven, Her symbol, on Avarra's left shoulder still had white eyes; Fiona had not found a sufficiently gemlike shade of thread to use.

Fiona began weaving the threads over and under the warp, completing the embroidery on the handmaidens' dresses. It was delicate work. Fiona had always been pleased to notice that her heavyhandedness with a matrix meant nothing with a loom. *I would far rather,* she thought now, *that it was the other way around.*

A man knocked at her door. She called permission for him to enter.

"Domna?" The servant hovered respectfully. He wore the colors of the Alton Domain. His hands almost crumpled the package he held, then he restrained himself with a nervous start. At her glance, he said, "Lady Alanna of Neskaya sent this to you as a wedding gift. She said to tell you that as anything could be made into thread if one

could produce the right conditions, she thought you might like thread like this.'' He proffered the package he held.

Fiona was slow to move from the window and take it, surprised both that the woman who had been her over-Keeper was here and that she had brought Fiona a wedding gift. She felt strangely reluctant to take the package. Forcing her fingers to close on it, she felt hardness beneath the silken wrapping. ''Thank you,'' she murmured. ''Please tell the *vai leronis* that I appreciate her gift.''

The man bowed and left. Fiona hesitated internally for a moment, but her fingers were undoing the wrappings before he had left the room. She stared blankly at the threads revealed. She picked one up, but it slid out of her loose grasp and shattered on the floor.

On her lap, others glowed: ruby, emerald, diamond, amethyst . . . jewel-colors. Jewels.

This time she was more careful with the thread. She held it tightly and bent it carefully. It would bend a little; the threads would be easy to weave if she was careful with them.

''. . . *Anything can be made into thread . . .*'' It was her man who had said it, but Fiona heard the words in Alanna's cool, subtly taunting voice. Involuntarily, she remembered the last time she had seen Alanna. It had been in the over-Keeper's private rooms.

Alanna's rooms were blue and gray, strangely reminiscent of cool, unworldly overlight. The Keeper herself was dressed, like Fiona, in shimmering crimson; both tended to wear it even when not involved in matrix work. Fiona, oversensitive about her lacks, was afraid of being mistaken for a mere technician or mechanic. She did not know Alanna's reasons.

''Alanna,'' Fiona said, carefully calming herself—*Keep your voice down, keep it even, show you have a Keeper's control*—''They cannot take me away to marry—'' *Marry!* The word, the very thought, shocked her. ''—if you refuse them. You are the head Keeper here, no one will deny you.''

Alanna Cassandra Alton plucked a rose from a vase

and studied it with more concern than she gave Fiona. "But why should I refuse them?"

"*Why!*" Fiona was nearly incoherent. "I am a *Keeper*—Keepers don't marry!"

Alanna gave the rose one last searching look, then laid it in her lap. Clasping her hands, she looked at Fiona clinically. "Then you are no longer a Keeper, are you?" she said in her cool, husky voice. "Frankly, my dear, I am not unrelieved by this. There are many who refuse to accept that women have the strength necessary to be Keepers; therefore we must be twice as good as any male Keeper. You're not; you can't do delicate work, and many of our critics point to you and say, 'There. She can't do half what a man can, she proves women are incompetent.' You are a liability to me and to all female Keepers; if you can be of use to your father in forming this alliance, then he is welcome to you."

Fiona stared. "I had not—had not suspected you of such fanaticism," she stammered.

"Call it what you will. I mean to see women accepted as Keepers by the time I die and I will do what I can to achieve that goal." Her tone softened. "Go now, child. I *will* miss you. I wish you well in your marriage." Having dismissed her, Alanna rose and placed the flower back in the vase. After a moment's thought, she changed its position.

Neskaya . . . Fiona remembered it with bitter longing. Had anyone even been surprised that the failing Keeper had been sent away? Her hands closed convulsively on the jeweled threads. She rose and asked one of her servants how to get to the chapel. She had forgotten the way.

She bent her head before the mosaic and altar, trying to feel humble. For a *comynara* and a Keeper, it was a difficult task. The chapel was dark, though clean. She suspected its cleanliness was an unusual thing, due only to the preparations for the wedding that was to occur in six days. In her childhood, she remembered, it had been dirty and almost frightening. She had much preferred to pray at the chapel at Castle Hastur, which the Domain women kept clean for offerings of flowers for celebrations or new births. Sophisticated city-folk, the Comyn did not really worship the gods they descended from, unless they were truly desperate. Fiona certainly was.

Blessed Cassilda, she prayed to her ancestor, *I do not know what to do. If I avoid this marriage, do I bring dishonor on my house?—Or do I go to something worse? You I can believe in—but a Goddess? I have never been sure the Gods were real. . . .*

She looked up, but Cassilda's face was blank and unreal, bare of comfort. To one side of her, the mosaic showed Dark Avarra. Fiona breathed a little more easily, her heart settling back to its accustomed pace. The Goddess' eyes were kind.

She was weaving that night when her father and *Dom* Marius came to see her. She had nearly finished the handmaidens. Each stood in front of a tree with wide, sweeping branches. There was a fifth tree to one side, looking almost naked with no maiden in front of it.

She stood to greet them. For a moment, she wondered wildly, *If I ask my father to stop this—to marry me to someone else at least, if marry me he must—would he do so?*

Looking at King Mikhail, she knew what his answer would be. He had promised her to Marius and the word of a Hastur was proverbial. In any case, he would have little concern for a daughter's wishes, especially one he did not know. He had five daughters, and six sons, all past threshold sickness. He could be careless of her desires; he did not lack children and she was not one to whom he had ever been close.

"I was telling *Domna* Fiona before," *Dom* Marius commented politely, "how I admired her tapestry. It is beautiful . . ."

"Then," Mikhail said genially, "you shall have it as a bride-gift." He looked at Fiona perfunctorily, not bothering to really see her. "I am sure she would like to see it hung in her new home's hall . . ." His eyes glittered angrily for a moment as another thought occurred to him. Ignoring Fiona, he said, "About the bride-price you have promised . . ."

So that was it, Fiona thought later, after they had left. The advantage *Dom* Marius would achieve by wedding her and becoming kin to the Hasturs was obvious, but her father's gain was not. He must need money—perhaps he intended a war or some other expensive venture. She had heard *Dom* Marius owned lands far from Syrtis that contained iron deposits on them. Doubtless they were included in the bride-price. There was no chance of her father refusing this match.

Fiona began to pace. *Merciful Goddess, help me. What I plan will take fine control—and that I do not have. . . .*

She caught sight of the Goddess' dark eyes on her tapestry. From far off, she thought she heard a painfully beautiful voice say, *Fear not; you will be guided by Me.* She was not sure, after a moment, she did not imagine it.

She went over to a drawer and pulled out a silken envelope. Button-sized matrixes spilled out onto her hand. She stared at them and prayed.

The crystalline threads were the blue of starstones. They trapped light in themselves and let it out in twisted, alien forms. When she dropped one and broke it, the shards lay black and burnt, lifeless. The whole threads glowed internally, dark blue lights caged in paler blue gems. She wove them over the threads of the fifth tree, creating a double layer. They glowed the solid overlight blue of matrix screens, arrayed in the rectangular shape of a door.

"I cannot do this," Fiona whispered to herself, afraid. "I can't . . ."

Then, said a familiar voice—cool and husky—or too powerful to hear? It could have been either Alanna's or the Goddess'. She was not sure which. She was not even sure that she was sane.

Then, the voice said, *you will marry a man with wet lips and sweaty hands and an ugly heart. He will bed you, probably without gentleness, and you will die in childbirth, bearing him children that he will pervert into his own image.* Underneath the cool tones was a hint of cruelty. *And while you still live, what will you have?*

Nothing—*nothing, less even than you had in a Tower position you were not equipped to fill. At Syrtis, accustomed to Marius, they will not even humor you for what* laran *skills you have, let alone honor and obey you.*

Fiona moaned. She thought she heard, distantly, the cawing of ravens and the rustling of their wings.

Or, whispered the voice, *you could come to Me.*

Fiona stood hesitantly in front of the tapestry, trembling. Almost without her will, her hand touched it. Touched it and began to go through it . . .

"My lord," the Guardsman said pleadingly, "we've searched all over the Domains for the past two tendays and we still cannot find her . . ."

"It's all right, Gabriel." King Mikhail stared at the tapestry. "She seems to have disappeared into thin air. It's no fault of the Guard's. Recall your men."

"Will you tell *Dom* Marius to go?"

"No," the king said absently, "I have other daughters . . ."

He was still staring at the tapestry when the man left. It seemed—*changed,* somehow. But what could be different? Five placid-faced handmaidens with gold-embroidered dresses gathered around Avarra worshipfully as the Dark Lady stroked her glittery-eyed raven. *No, not placid,* he decided. The maiden farthest from the Goddess had a razor-edged smile. Matrix-fire gleamed behind her eyes. An interesting effect, he mused, wondering how his daughter had done it. It was an excellent tapestry, he decided, and religious in subject, too: most fitting. And he was no longer obligated to give it to *Dom* Marius as a bride-gift. *Perhaps,* he thought, his mouth quirking as he considered it, *I shall have it hung in the main hall.*

After a moment, he turned away. Somehow, through the thick stone walls, he heard a raven's harsh, cawing cries.

To Serve Kihar

by Judith Sampson

Judith Sampson is handicapped; when I bought "To Serve Kihar," she indicated that I could mention this or not as I chose. I chose to mention it, because I feel that every time a handicapped person accomplishes something, it's an inspiration for every other handicapped person who chooses not to go along with the tendency in this country to feel that the handicapped should only mention their disabilities and not their abilities.

And along with her biography, Judith submitted a quite impressive list of accomplishments; working as a teacher for the Fan Kane Research Fund for Brain-Injured children; lecturer and teacher/instructor in the University of Arizona Psychology Department; and a single-spaced page of similar credits. Her B.A. is in Creative Writing, at that university, and she has had a great deal of poetry published. She has also had fiction published in the shared-world anthology MAGIC IN ITHKAR (TOR, 1985) and has been the subject of an Emmy-nominated documentary—for Judy is severely brain-injured and suffers from cerebral palsy. Somehow I think this is a very special way to wind up this anthology with a story which—especially in light of its exceptional insight—certainly betrays no mental handicaps. (MZB)

Jerilynn Vedart: Cottman IV Archives #709643
Personal Data: Age: 30 Standard Terran, Height 168 cm.,
                          Weight: 57 kg. Hair; pepper & salt
                          brown Eyes: Hazel
                          STANDARD TERRAN EMPIRE
                          XENOBIOLOGIST, specializing in

                          primate species observation; Spe-
                          cial Abilities: Martial Arts, fenc-
                          ing, xeno-archaeology
Assignment: Gather pertinent data on the classification
            of auctothonic primates.
Equipment issued: Cottman IV History-Linguistics
                  learning cassette, Standard Terran
                  Science Pack, Standard Terran
                  Medical Pack, Cottman IV riding
                  horse, native knives
Guide assigned: Elhali n'ha Cathri, age: 25 Standard
                Terran, Height: 175 cm., Weight: 59
                kg., Hair: black Eyes: gray.

                  *** *** *** ***

Elhali n'ha Cathri had spotted a wink of metal that did
not belong in the remote, rugged section of the Hellers
they searched, and when she mentioned this, the Terran
was intrigued. "Let's have a look. Part of my job is to
report artifacts no one else has bothered to check."

The Free Amazon shrugged. "All right. We'll have to
watch for catmen."

"Why? We're no threat to them."

Elhali was surprised by her companion's lack of knowledge, but then, she *had* requested a guide. "They like to
take prisoners to torture to death. It's one way they gain
honor."

Jerilynn found that impossible to imagine but refrained
from comment.

Despite the bursts of wind that made their cloaks and
rein-ends stream briskly, the two women urged their
horses toward the spot of glitter at the base of a foothill.

As they drew closer, Elhali frowned and slowed her
horse to an almost soundless walk. Jerilynn tried to im-
itate. Just as they reached a horse-length near to their
goal, both their animals squealed, reared, and plunged
backward.

"An evil deed, even for cat-hags!" shouted Elhali, and
she reined her horse quiet, swung to the ground, and ran
to a steel cage set on a flat-topped boulder. Her own mare

calmed, Jerilynn caught up with her guide, then stared
and shivered at what the cage held.

Once a delicate and pollen-scented vision of silver-
maned, gray-eyed, slim-bodied loveliness, the *chieri* who
lay twisted within the bars now looked to be a withered
branch used as scratching post by great cats more brutal
than any carnivore of Terra. Dull streaks of silver blood
runneled the *chieri,* whose mane had been dry-shorn
from its gashed scalp, whose eye-sockets were two holes
full of clotted tarnished-silver lumps.

"Merciful Avarra," breathed Elhali, "this poor Child
of Grace still lives!"

Jerilynn's stomach clenched. "Can we help it somehow? Or has it gone too long without aid for us to do any
good?"

"I don't know. A *chieri* who can't heal itself alone is
usually too hurt to be saved. But we'd better try. We have
to help it." Elhali removed her cloak-brooch and used
its point to pick the cage door lock open.

Jerilynn returned to her horse and dug out her medical
kit from her saddlebags. She leaned against the mare for
a moment, sickened all over again when she recalled the
two blood-stoppered sockets where the *chieri's* gray eyes
should be.

She forced herself to go back, and saw that Elhali had
opened the cage. The Free Amazon eased the wounded
chieri onto the nearest mound of soft grasses.

Both women began the touchy process of triage: ster-
ilize open cuts, apply poultices, seal the covered wounds.

Jerilynn unscrewed the cap from her merthiolate applicator, and leaned over to use the soft foam tip daubed
bright orange with antiseptic, then hesitated.

"Go on," Elhali urged.

"I don't know where to start. I've never dealt with
such deep injuries before."

"Start with the eyes, then the scalp cuts. After that,
the chest, arms, and legs. Avarra be thanked, those catmen didn't tear through the *chieri's* spine, or it'd be useless."

Jerilynn shuddered inside, and aimed the applicator
toward the *chieri's* right eye. As she was about to paint

over the clot of blood there, she said, "I hope the *chieri's* not conscious. Merthiolate won't sting, but pressure on the wounds will hurt greatly."

Elhali's mouth tautened. "We'll know soon enough."

With slow, light strokes, Jerilynn swabbed the right eye-socket, then the left. Numbed cooperative, the *chieri* lay still.

But it woke and gave a child's whimper as Jerilynn reached for its scalp. She froze, tears ran down her face. Yet a moment later, she pulled herself together, and went on.

The *chieri's* six-fingered hands twitched, but it made no attempt to evade Jerilynn's efforts. Glad to be done at last, she let Elhali take over the task of applying packs of crushed herbs to the *chieri's* eyes.

"Must have a powerful anesthetic in those herbs," Jerilynn remarked. "Our patient's gone limp-asleep."

"Yes. I'll poultice the other wounds, you tape everything in place with your surgi-linen, and I'll pad all the injuries with vines."

Once the *chieri's* head had an extra layer of gauze and vines snugged about, Elhali pointed out their next problem. "Can't leave the Child of Grace here, where banshees or catmen can do it more harm. And we must track down the catfolk responsible for this maiming."

"How can we bring the *chieri* with us?"

"We'll make a litter of vines. One of our horses should be able to pull the litter."

"All right. Is either horse harness-broke?"

"Mine's not. Trained it myself for riding and warfare. Don't know about yours. Only way to find out is try a vine harness. . . ."

Cottman IV's red sun had started to slip below the topmost peaks of the Hellers before they had constructed the litter and harness of vines collected from the closest stand of trees.

Jerilynn removed all the gear and saddlebags from her horse, except for the girth to hold the harness in place. While she fastened the vines to either side of her beast, she spoke soothing nonsense, "Good girl, sweet brown mare, hope you are harness-broke, don't shy, vines won't hurt you.''

The mare's ears flicked a bit and she bobbed her head a few times, but otherwise she stood quietly. Jerilynn walked her about, let her get accustomed to the feel of all the extra strappings, and left to pile her belongings in the litter. Next, Jerilynn hitched the litter to the harness, and walked the mare around again.

"Well, she's not kicking at the drag of the weight behind her," said Elhali. "I think she'll behave with the *chieri* aboard."

"My saddle pad and blankets can act as cushion for that fragile body, and my saddle straps will hold all in place. Don't want our patient jounced when we cross rough ground."

As the two women guided the litter burdened with the sleeping, bandaged *chieri* back the way they had come, Jerilynn asked, "Where do you think those catmen are?"

"Could be anywhere. The cage holding the *chieri* was trade goods and new. That means a trader nearby, with catmen customers. Let's go back to the hut we passed earlier today, and investigate."

Elhali rode her horse and Jerilynn led hers along the rocky path, stopping at intervals to check the *chieri's* bandages for excess tightness or seepage. Red-tinged dusk found them at the trader's stone cabin, where a crude signboard limmed a man behind a counter piled with furs accepting a pelt from a second man.

Elhali dismounted and strode inside the hut, while Jerilynn waited by the litter. She surveyed the clearing that surrounded the hut: to one side, sunward, row on row of bare curing racks for furs, to the other, empty crates, some with Terran Empire labels.

But Jerilynn forgot all about possible contraband when she noticed large box-traps scattered among the other crates, just like the trap that the *chieri* had been imprisoned in to die. She went at once to the open door of the hut.

Elhali met her just inside, and said, "Trader's cleared out. But he left plenty behind. Let's move the Child of Grace into the sleeping furs on the bed."

After they had settled the *chieri* in the thick plush furs, they quickly fed and stabled their horses. Back in the hut, they hunted out the abandoned nut-grain supplies and cauldron, to prepare porridge.

Once the mushy cereal-nut mixture had cooked to the right consistency, Jerilynn spooned up a bowlful for the *chieri*. But she paused.

"Uh, Elhali? Is our food safe for a *chieri?* I don't have any data on what they eat."

"Our legends don't mention their diet. We see them so seldom."

"Hold the bowl for me. I'll have a look at the *chieri's* teeth. Dentition usually can tell what a given subject will eat."

Jerilynn walked from the hearth to the trader's bed, and knelt by the *chieri's* head. Bowl in hand, Elhali followed.

Fingers curved to part the wan gray lips, Jerilynn halted as the *chieri* quivered, rolled its head, and broken fragments of *casta* dribbled from its shaking mouth:

"Cat-hags, why hurt me? . . . Not *kihar* to harm me . . . No! Keep your claws away from my eyes!" Next, a groan, and the six-fingered hands strained to shield its face.

Jerilynn caught the *chieri's* wrists before it dislodged the bandages on its eyes. "Elhali, help me tie it down, quick!"

The Free Amazon brought a bolt-end of canvas, which she and Jerilynn tore into strips and lashed the *chieri* to the bedframe with the ripped fabric.

"What's wrong?" panted Elhali. "*Chieri* don't go mad!"

Jerilynn felt the sweaty gray forehead. "I'm afraid it's fever. Those wounds went untreated too long."

"Avarra forfend! I don't know what to do for a fevered *chieri!*"

"Nor do I." Jerilynn's hands drooped. "We'll just have to hope for the best. I got a look at its teeth. It should be able to eat porridge."

Elhali gave a wry look. "If we can force its mouth open."

Jerilynn rubbed the cracked gray mouth with a spoon-

ful of mush; after a moment, the *chieri's* lips parted, but
it could not summon the strength or coordination to chew
and swallow. Elhali had to assist by manipulation of the
chieri's jaws and throat muscles.

Two spoonfuls later, Jerilynn said, "That's all its
shrunken stomach can hold right now. Several small
meals will probably work best."

"Same way to feed horses," commented Elhali.

The two women ate their own bowls of porridge, each
quiet.

The unfamiliar term the *chieri* had used, *kihar,* prodded
at Jerilynn. Was *kihar* parallel to the ancient Japanese
concept of *on,* a strict code of moral obligation?

She mentioned her comparison to Elhali, who responded with a mirthless smile. "Catfolk condone cruelty to the helpless in their code of honor, and that cruel
streak shows up well in cat-hags especially. I don't see
any similarity to the Terran culture you described."

"Some of the primitive auctothon tribes of Terra did
use ritual torture of captives as a means of achieving
honor. Of course, no cultural parallel is exact, but as a
xenobiologist, I have to be aware that they exist."

Elhali looked thoughtful as she rose to wash her bowl
and spoon, but did not answer.

They prepared a fresh batch of porridge to cook
through the night, and took half-a-night watches, alter-
nating as each needed sleep.

Jerilynn rolled out of her bed-blanket at dawn as Elhali
curled up in hers, and asked, "How's our patient?"

"Not good, but no worse."

Jerilynn crossed the hut, drew back the sleeping furs,
and gazed down at the *chieri*. It appeared to be calmly
asleep in the canvas ties.

She loosened the outer bandages; no silver blood had
leaked past the herb-packs, the gray flesh no longer
looked raw and slick with pus.

As she tightened the linen and vine wrappings, Jerilynn thought, *I hope the anesthetic effect holds. Heavy
sleep, free of pain, is the best medicine. . . .*

As she started to turn away, Jerilynn noticed that the
chieri stirred and tried to speak.

"Cat-hags . . . Trapped, trapped by cat-hags . . . Why war with my people? . . . We war not with catfolk . . . Ohh, my eyes! . . ." Its muttered *casta* faded into dry sobs.

Jerilynn shook her head, and thought, *Poor Child of Grace, does it even want to live?*

"Elhali," she said, "the *chieri* must be made aware that it's not in cat-hag hands, or it won't thrive. How do we get past the fever and convince it we're friends?"

"That takes someone with highly trained *laran*. Mind-to-mind contact requires precise attunement."

"Who'd have that?"

"A trained healer with a matrix crystal, impossible to find this far out in the Hellers."

When Elhali took her next turn at feeding the *chieri*, Jerilynn watched the chieri lick six spoonfuls of mush from the bowl before it had enough.

That was a good sign. To replace herb-packs and bandages became more difficult; awake and over-sensitized by fever, the chieri trembled under the touch of both women.

But it lay as quiet as it could, and this prompted Jerilynn to say, "Maybe the fever has gone down enough to let the *chieri* think clearly again. We haven't had to tie it now."

"You're right. If we can help it heal itself, the war's half-won."

"What else can we do?"

"The *chieri* needs to describe those cat-hags for us, so we can hunt them down."

A sigh, then a thready whisper issued from the *chieri,* "Kaznir hears you, will help, when can . . ."

Elhali grinned. "Avarra be praised, you're sane again, Child of Grace!"

Kaznir's bandaged head cocked toward her. "Who breathes beside you, not of this land?"

The Free Amazon introduced Jerilynn and explained how they had rescued the *chieri*.

Kaznir's placid face made Jerilynn wonder, *Why isn't the* chieri *distressed by its lack of sight? Can it "see" telepathically?*

But the fever had closed down a part of Kaznir's memory; it could not tell the two women who of the cat-hags had attacked it.

"Catfolk come here, not know trader fled," assured the *chieri*. "Catfolk will want to help."

"But how soon will they be here?" Jerilynn said.

"After sun leave sky."

"We'll know when they arrive," added Elhali. "Our horses'll scream the moment they scent catfolk."

"Are you sure the catfolk will help us, Elhali?"

"It concerns their *kihar*," reminded the Free Amazon.

"Once told of wrong done to Kaznir," stated the *chieri*, "catfolk must assist, to save face . . ."

Shrill horse bleats sounded from the stable. Despite herself, Jerilynn winced. When she glanced at the hut door, she noticed that Elhali had gone outside.

Although it was not yet moons-rise, the night had grown dark enough for hundreds of pairs of greenly gleaming eyes, at different heights, to show in a ring about the Free Amazon.

She conversed with the catfolk in a series of yowls and coughed purrs. They replied in long modulated roars, and Jerilynn clenched her hands each time.

"Remove furs, sit Kaznir up," insisted the *chieri*. "Catman chief enters soon, must see harm done."

Grateful to be distracted, Jerilynn obeyed. She discovered that Kaznir still lacked the strength to sit alone, and she sat behind, to provide unobtrusive support for the lower back.

Meowed parley completed, Elhali returned, followed by a tall, supple catman who stalked across the hut floor, his black ear-tufts flicked forward, his auburn-brindled fur highlit from the hearthfire. A wide band of hammered copper encircled his upper right arm, and copper wires had been inlaid into his hand claws.

He snarled as he halted before Kaznir, and Jerilynn saw that the catman's more than tiger-sized fangs also had copper inlays. By the standards of Cottman IV, he was a proud, wealthy chief of his people, who might be hard to convince.

Kaznir responded with a similar challenge growl. His bandaged head focused on the catman chief as though no barrier existed, and the *chieri* purred and meowed in the catfolk cadences without accent or hesitation.

Now Kaznir asked the two women to unwrap its bandages. They removed the vines and linens from its head, to disclose its empty eyesockets and scarred, bare scalp.

An outraged hiss left the catman chief, his ears flattened, his mouth ricked back to display all his fangs. No translation was needed; Jerilynn knew his *kihar* had been smirched.

Kaznir and the catman talked on, and Elhali explained, "He offers to act as tracker for Kaznir."

"You mean, work with us? That's more than I expected."

"Looks like Kaznir told him we're warriors of a like rank to catfolk, so he'll cooperate."

Elhali addressed Kaznir. "Child of Grace, we well appreciate that the catman chief enhances our *kihar* and his own, because we will hunt together. What name shall we call him?"

"In his own speech, he is titled Bright As Copper, but in *casta* he is Copperfang."

Jerilynn had a question of her own. "Can he speak *casta* or *cahuenga*?"

"Copperfang speaks simple *casta*, but you may find his pronunciation complicated."

"Probably understands more *casta* than he can say," remarked Elhali. "Let's find out if he'll pick up ours, shall we?" She eyed Jerilynn.

"You first," the xenobiologist said. "My *casta* is rusty."

Elhali's wry smile lingered an instant, but her expression sobered as she breathed out the syllables.

His ears pricked up, and he raised one hand in salute, every copper-spiraled claw bright as his true name. *"Kihar* shall be served, warrior-females."

"Lend us the grace of using our names," Jerilynn added. "I am happy if you call me Jerilynn, and my guide-friend goes by Elhali."

His ears twitched in assent, then he spoke once more in miaows to Kaznir.

"Copperfang wishes to make a presentation," announced the *chieri.* "Because Kaznir cannot go with you on the hunt, Copperfang gifts us with three of his best *silblu* hides."

"The lightning-blue shimmerfur?" Elhali's eyebrows shot up.

"That's priceless!" gasped Jerilynn. "What can we possibly give in exchange?"

"Do not fret. As you work together, you will learn what he treasures."

Copperfang padded out the doorway and returned with three folded pelts, undersides up. He flipped the topmost fur open and laid it across Kaznir's lap.

"Most wonderous," purred the *chieri,* as its slim gray hands smoothed the long shafts of lightning-blue hair.

Jerilynn thought for a second that the blue fur shone enough to restore the *chieri's* eyes to sight. But she realized Kaznir's psychic vision must be at work.

"These *silblu* are lovely, Copperfang," sighed Elhali. "You add luster to our *kihar.*"

His green eyes glowed as though they were twin comets. "Some day you will burnish mine."

Copperfang detested daylight, as did most catfolk, and insisted that they start their hunt at the next dusk. Since their horses could not tolerate catman scent and must be left behind, Jerilynn and Elhali finished their night's sleep, then spent the rest of the day collecting fodder for their beasts, and selecting what to carry in their backpacks.

Now agile enough to look after its own wounds, Kaznir no longer needed herb poultices, but Jerilynn decided to gift the *chieri* with a reel of surgi-linen.

"I hope you heal swiftly and well," she said, as she set the spool on Kaznir's right palm.

Bandaged head tilted toward her, the *chieri* replied, "I hear worry in your words. You do not wish to leave me alone."

"I don't."

"Do not be troubled, Jerilynn." Kaznir patted her hand.

Such a simple gesture, she thought, *as a child might make to comfort an adult, yet it soothes like a sunbath.*

She went over the much reduced contents of her pack once more. Medical supplies, rations, essential recording tools were all she dared bring. She smiled grimly to herself. *I chose Cottman IV as a fairly high-risk tour of duty, but I never dreamed it would be this tough. I hope my skills are adequate. . . .*

Dusk thickened to night as Jerilynn met Elhali and Copperfang at the north edge of the hut clearing.

"I agree," said the Free Amazon, "a renegade cathag band would lair high in the Hellers. Must we search every cave?"

Copperfang flicked one ear in negation. "When I saw Kaznir's wounds, I recognized distinct claw-patterns, those of a she-cat who calls herself Sharra's Spear. I do not understand why she wants to maul the *chieri*. But once we catch her, we can learn from her why she stains our *kihar*."

"You are sure we will catch her?" Jerilynn queried.

Green eyes lofty, Copperfang regarded her. "Of course. *Kihar* must be served."

For two tendays Copperfang led them northward. Jerilynn did her best in the uncertain starlight between the thinning stands of conifers to videocord what few primate artifacts she could locate. But the results lacked promise, and she began to wonder if she should drop this facet of her job for now.

At dawn of the last tenday Copperfang brought them to a height where trees gave way to bare, sheer mountain walls. Red light stained the peaks, and Jerilynn asked, "How do we climb without ropes and pitons?"

"Copperfang will show us the best catfolk trails," assured Elhali.

"Don't we have more than banshees to watch out for this high?"

"Yes. Better put your videocord away. Its infrared is a

magnet to banshees now, and *kyorebni* home in on bright flickering surfaces like your videocord case.''

Jerilynn shut the videocord, slipped it into a side pocket of her backpack, and resolved to use manual transcording for the rest of the hunt.

Copperfang took them to a cave at the base of a cliff, and curled up to sleep away the day. While Elhali arranged their blanket-beds, Jerilynn retrieved a blank notebook and an electric inker from the bottom of her pack, to jot down details of the first catfolk home she had seen.

Reddening daylight revealed a set of niches clawed into the walls at eye-level, and a pit dug in the floor. A pile of gnawed, split bones had accumulated at the far end of the cave. Jerilynn felt relieved that these were just bush-jumper and rabbit-horn. But she soon had to stop; she had grown too accustomed to nights awake and days asleep.

At nightfall, Copperfang shook both women out of slumber. ''We need fresh meat. Let's find a *kyorebni* nest. That's where it'll bring game for its young.''

''We won't waste time stalking or chasing our meal through the rocks,'' agreed Elhali.

Although Jerilynn thought such a venture might easily bring banshees on them, she did not voice her fear; she sharpened her native shortsword and dagger, and wished for more skill with weapons.

Four moons made a silver bonfire of the peaks. The three hunters walked without concealment among the scarps and boulders, eyes alert for the untidy heap of large branches that was a *kyorebni* nest.

Jerilynn stayed close to her guide. If the giant gore-crows or banshees or Sharra's Spear and her renegades spotted them and attacked, she stood a better chance of remaining alive at Elhali's side.

Two of the moons had set before they located a *kyorebni* nest, where a pair of fledglings shrieked, amid rabbit-horn antlers and bush-jumper hoof-shells.

Copperfang crouched behind a projecting rock, and signed with his hands they were to wait for the mother bird to fly in with a new kill. Both women dropped down in lee of a second boulder.

A heighted clamor cawed from the *kyorebni* fledglings. Jerilynn glanced up, and grabbed her sword pommel.

Huge and black, the red-eyed crow clutched a brace of rabbit-horns in its talons, while a bush-jumper fawn dangled between its jaws, the prey's tan fur contrasted with the *kyorebni*'s massive yellow beak.

As it glided in to land on the rim of the nest, Copperfang darted from his rock and snatched the bush-jumper fawn from the great bird's mouth. With a booming screech, the *kyorebnin* let go of the rabbit-horns, and launched herself after Copperfang. Dodging into crevices and crannies the oversized crow could not thrust beak and claws into, the catman soon disappeared from view.

"Grab those rabbit-horns before the fledglings get 'em," whispered Elhali. Each woman caught up a carcass, then scrambled down the moonlit mountainside back to the catfolk cave.

"Where's Copperfang?" exclaimed Jerilynn. "I thought he'd be here first!"

Elhali frowned. "He should be, he was well ahead of us. I hope he hasn't run into a banshee or Sharra's Spear. That *kyorebnin* made enough noise to bring Zandru from His ninth hell."

Silent and tense, they started to stew the rabbit-horns. Jerilynn thought she had herself under control, until she noticed that her hands shook as she sprinkled the cut-up meat with crumbled protein chips.

Don't blurt! she admonished herself. *Say what's bothering you in a calm tone, and Elhali can help you much more than if you go to pieces on her.*

"What if Copperfang doesn't come back?"

"I can sniff out catfolk scent well enough to go on with our search. But we'll have to poke through every cave in these mountains, and there are more caves in the Hellers than sands around the Dry Towns."

"Shh! I hear something outside!" Jerilynn plopped the last protein chip in the stewpot, and went into a crouched fighting stance.

In the same instant, Elhali whipped out shortsword and dagger.

As they watched the cave mouth, they saw a single gleam of green catfolk eyes, they heard one click of claws on stone, and Copperfang's arm-ring, dented and blood-smeared, bounced into the cave.

"Is Copperfang dead?" Jerilynn tried not to let her gaze fix on all that they appeared to have of the Catman chief.

"Not yet. Sharra's Spear and her band are torturing him, as they would any captive. They taunt us, as his warrior-females, to rescue him if we dare. We'll have to show them we mean to get him back." Elhali sheathed her weapons, and seized the rabbit-horn heads, each by an ear.

With a deliberate, exaggerated swagger, she hefted the skulls to the cave entrance and flung them from her. Jerilynn heard the rabbit-horn heads shatter on the rocks below. A moment later, both women picked up the sound of a high-pitched snarl.

Braced for a leap, hands on hips, Elhali replied with a long, harsh laugh. Then she turned her back on the watching cat-hags who must be there, and strolled back to the stewpot.

"Why did you do that?" fretted Jerilynn. "To make them mad enough to try something stupid?"

"Just threw their insolence back in their faces." El-hali's eyes had gone from mist-gray to blade-bleak. "As a Free Amazon, I can't let them get away with the capture of my comrades."

"What next?"

"They won't move without sending a message to Sharra's Spear. While they wait, we can ready ourselves for whatever they decide. First, we eat."

They finished the stew, then cleaned and repacked their eating gear.

"Hide your things in a safe place," instructed Elhali. "Then practice whatever combat you do best. We must be as battle fit as possible."

Jerilynn removed her swordbelt and its weapons, bundled them into her backpack, and hid all behind the discarded bones at the back of the cave. She studied the Free Amazon for a moment, as Elhali combined blade-play with explosive kicks, jumps, and sideleaps.

I can't fight with swords, thought Jerilynn, *but I do know tai chi-kenjupo. I can make my whole body into a weapon.* She began the routines, her arms, head, body, and legs following from one defense-offense position to the next. Calm in the certainty that she was honed and poised, and she had no doubts that she could handle anyone sent to combat her; why and how no longer mattered.

Her senses, at fighting pitch, revealed to her how she and the Free Amazon complemented each other. Elhali, taller, heavier, cap of black curls a contrast to her steely eyes, was the dominant warrior. But Jerilynn knew her own slight frame, cropped salt-and-pepper brown hair, and hazel eyes hid other strengths.

Side by side they waited, wordless and alert. Beyond the cave, winds whipped and keened, plant stalks crackled, rocks grated.

Pad-pad-pad, and a young cat-hag stood before them, tufted ears forward, eyes fixed on them, her gray fur dappled with yellow stars. She carried no weapons, and her claws were retracted.

"Sharra's Spear bids you to see the truth of our claim," she said. "You are to follow me to our lair. You will do battle for the male we have taken. Sharra's Spear has spoken." She turned to lead the way.

"Copperfang's bad luck's a good break for us," Elhali whispered to Jerilynn. "We won't have to hunt all over the Hellers."

"Is it possible he planned this to happen?"

"Perhaps. But he's no gallant fool, he'd avoid capture if he could. I'm sure it's just bad luck."

Their gray-yellow guide took them higher in the peaks, by the dim light of the last moon. At moonset, she halted, and pointed out, "Our lair."

A squat bush-jumper tallow candle burned in a single niche, in a much larger cave than where the two women had lodged. Jerilynn counted at least eighty cat-hags, young, older, gaunt, gross, seated in circles around a trap-cage, green eyes locked on their prisoner.

Copperfang's flesh and fur hung on him in bloody strips, and he sprawled limp as a fresh-skinned pelt, eyes closed. But he had not been blinded.

Elhali nudged her. "Keep a calm face. We're being assessed."

Jerilynn's mouth threatened to spasm into a tic, but she managed to hold a remote expression.

Eighty pairs of eyes probed them, then swung to focus on the cat-hag who had just sauntered in.

Her green eyes contrasted with her orange-striped, smoke-blue fur; on her right arm gleamed a hammered copper band; both her ear-tufts had been braided with copper wires. A necklace of catfolk claws, some copper-inlaid, others plain, dangled from against her firm teats.

"Sharra's Spear!" her females roared, and bounded to their feet.

She did not acknowledge their devoted cries, but continued her easy walk to where the cage and the two women stood. As Sharra's Spear drew closer, her eyes held a strange, sulphuric glint that did not reassure Jerilynn.

The Free Amazon nudged again. "Be ready for battle. A challenge could come at any moment."

Toes pressed hard into the soil of the cave floor, Jerilynn filled herself with the power of this world with its red sun, chill climate, peoples like divinities or nightmares. . . .

Soft and disarming as a Terran housecat, Sharra's Spear purred, "We are honored that the Bright As Copper clan sends fearless females to maintain *kihar*. You will battle my two best warriors."

Elhali's eyes went dagger-sharp. "You and your females destroy *kihar*. We are here to serve *kihar*, as best we can."

"We do not?" Sharra's Spear mocked.

"You captured and maimed a Child of Grace. You want us to combat for our guide's life, when one of us is not a blade-user. With the odds bent in your favor, you pretend to maintain *kihar*!"

Elhali's scornful words cued Jerilynn; hands and feet

ready to lash out in the blossom-attacks of tai chi-kenjupo, she awaited the signal to fight.

Sharra's Spear twitched both ears, black-tufted copper-twined tips flashing like spearheads. "*Kihar* shall be served. Which of you is no bladeswoman?"

Jerilynn stepped forward two paces. "I fight in other ways."

A smallish cat-hag with mottled white fur moved from the waiting clan to face Jerilynn. They circled, prowled each other, limbs tensed to strike or feint.

Must get past her claws and fangs, thought Jerilynn. *Can't let her wear me down. . . .*

She led the bout with a series of in-and-out blows designed to test her opponent's speed. Eyes talon-bright, the young cat-hag parried; Jerilynn dodged her every slash and bite with micrometers to spare. Neither had reached the point where breaths grew ragged, when Jerilynn saw an opening.

She darted her right heel under the cat-hag's chin, and could have ruptured the young female's soft throat with precise pressure. But Jerilynn eased off just enough that she only folded into a stunned heap of smeary white fur.

After a glance at her defeated foe, Jerilynn relaxed from fight-crouch, and eyed Sharra's Spear.

Her orange-barred gray-blue tail stiff, her eyes hard to read as raw emeralds, Sharra's Spear spoke in an unruffled voice, "*Kihar* is well-served. Now, you, bladeswoman."

A tall rangy cat-hag with auburn-tipped black fur twirled two curved swords of equal size before she attacked Elhali.

As Elhali sidestepped the cat-hag's steel swipes, Jerilynn ducked into a spot close to Copperfang in the trapcage. His eyes opened, and he rose on knees and elbows, then sat on his haunches, less harmed than Jerilynn feared.

She remained in place, ready to back up Elhali if the fight turned against her. Copperfang's breaths altered as he watched the combat.

The cat-hag maintained a continuous cartwheel with her twin sabers, from which she lunged at Elhali. Shortsword and dagger stabbing under and above these thrusts, Elhali coaxed her out of her tight-spun defense, and, at the right moment, jerked away the cat-hag's right-hand sword with a hook of the dagger-hilt quillions.

Auburn-black neckfur bristled, the cat-hag hissed and sprang forward to the skewer. Elhali appeared to flatten against Copperfang's cage, but instead she vaulted over the cat-hag, landed behind her, threw her off balance with a nick at her tail-tip.

Copperfang yowled, then hurtled himself and the cage toward the falling cat-hag. A flurry of bars, blades, dark red fur, green eyes, claws, and fangs spiraled faster and faster.

Jerilynn tried to grab Copperfang's neck scruff and pull him away, but Elhali shouted, "Stand clear! It's their fight now!"

As she obeyed, Jerilynn noticed Sharra's Spear smile. Since this bared most of her fangs, Jerilynn tensed.

"Ver-r-ry nice," purred Sharra's Spear. *"Kihar* is fulfilled to perfection."

Copperfang and the auburn-black cat-hag gripped in killing embrace, teeth in each other's throats, claws snagged in each other's ribs. Too blood-slicked to remain this way long, they slid apart, tottered a few steps and collapsed, the cat-hag beneath Copperfang.

He heaved himself to his knees, waved the piece of cage-bar he had used as a club, and crashed facedown, dead as the cat-hag under him. All the other followers of Sharra's Spear rose as one, spat, drew their swords, exposed every fang and claw.

Jerilynn dropped at once in her tai chi-kenjupo crouch. Odd, how calm she felt . . . Elhali poised her blades to meet an onslaught of enraged cat-hags.

"No-o-o, my dear sisters-in-blood," Sharra's Spear crooned, green eyes glassy, tail switched lazily back and forth. "Why are you angered? We have to thank Copperfang's warrior-females for a most sublime achievement in *kihar.* Sheathe your swords, sleek your fur . . ."

As the mob of cat-hags sank back on their haunches, Elhali whispered to Jerilynn, "Avarra help us! Sharra's Spear liked our crazy duels!"

"She's too sweet. I don't know much about the insane, but I bet she'll swing to violent hatred of us any second."

"Sprint out of here before she shifts!"

Both of them leaped in the same instant, huge high jumps between the circled rows of cat-hags, and they reached the trail beyond the cave-lair before Sharra's Spear stopped lulling her females and began to rant orders. The two women raced down the mountainside, but the red dazzle of dawn prevented a chase by Sharra's Spear and her band.

Elhali skidded to a boulder, sat on it, and panted. Jerilynn dropped to her knees where she was. She ventured,

"Did we finish what we came to do?"

"No. Must get back to Kaznir, have it alert the other *chieri*. They know how to turn off mob insanity."

"Sharra's Spear and her crazies will follow us!"

"Not if we march by day. Make false trails for 'em, too."

Back at the cave where their backpacks lay hidden, the Free Amazon created a scent-path to the *kyorebni* nest with the remains of the bush-jumper and rabbit-horn carcasses. Jerilynn made final entries in her notebook and buried all traces of their camp in the bonepile.

Elhali returned with two skinned rabbit-horns on her belt.

"Gift from the *kyorebni* fledglings," she said. "We'll cook and eat 'em later."

Jerilynn dusted off her hands and stood up. "I'm ready if you are."

At a hard lope, they headed down the Hellers.

Jerilynn wiped back sweaty strands of salt-and-pepper bangs from her forehead, and blinked as she stumbled toward the stone hut they had left two tendays before. Elhali exerted one last burst of speed and raced to the cabin door, shortsword out.

"Do not fear for Kaznir," said the eyeless *chieri*, stepping to meet them as though it could see. "Healing is complete."

Too weary to speak, Jerilynn tried to form words of warning.

Kaznir must have caught some message from her mind, and from Elhali's as well, for the chieri had a sudden resemblance to a coiled spring. "Kaznir knows Sharra's Spear and her females now. We shall face them together. *Kihar* demands this meeting."

"Can you summon your people to assist us, Child of Grace?" asked Elhali.

Kaznir tilted its head as though it heard what was beyond human ears. "Not needed."

"But we're up against a charge of mad cat-hags!" blurted Jerilynn.

Kaznir's blind face swung to her. "Trust Kaznir."

Elhali shrugged. "Might as well face those crazies here." She braced herself on the cabin wall, to the *chieri's* right, shortsword and dagger out.

Jerilynn forced her overtired muscles to a semblance of calm, pressed her feet into the soil, and started the measured breaths that would make her once again a rod of flowering blows and thrusts. A part of her that she had no words for projected like a slow lightning bolt toward a similar surge from Kaznir and from Elhali.

Their three lightning bolts merged, expanded to a sphere about them; it hummed, crackled, spurted flares of energy like a sun, a great red sun. . . .

Caught up in this play of mind-forces, Jerilynn almost did not hear Kaznir say, "Sharra's Spear is here, alone. Her females dared not brave daylight, but she has."

Jerilynn peered at the lone cat-hag, whose smoke-blue, orange-striped fur had gone dull from sweat and dust, whose copper ornaments now bore a green tinge, whose eyes' raw emerald glare wavered. She lurched closer, her frame gaunt, her teats thirst-shriveled under her necklace of claws.

"*Kihar* is all!" she croaked.

Sunstroke, thought Jerilynn, *that's what she has. She can't fight all worn out, but she wants to anyway.*

"T'cha!" snorted Elhali, and sheathed her blades. "I won't fight her, she's already defeated herself!"

Gray lips curved in a luminous smile, Kaznir walked from the hut side, arms extended, hands palm out.

As the *chieri* moved to within a finger's length of Sharra's Spear, she stiffened, raised her arms to slash.

Voice soft as a breeze rustling through leaves, Kaznir murmured, *"Kihar* is all, indeed. But *kihar* is better served if you and I exchange healing. I shall mend your mind. If you then wish to, you shall be my eyes."

Arms slack at her sides, Sharra's Spear did not resist as Kaznir placed its fingertips on her brow. The *chieri's* face and empty eye-sockets grew lustrous, while it smoothed her forehead fur.

"No longer will Sharra's Fires bemaze your mind," Kaznir said. "Gaze on life, and the clear goddesses of your own people."

Jerilynn discovered that she held her breath as she watched. Elhali stared, too.

Sharra's Spear made a faint mewl, threw off her necklace, crouched for a backward leap.

Hands outstretched, face almost as bright as the red sun above, Kaznir spoke again, "Your name is not Sharra's Spear, but Day Spear. Lead well in leading me."

She shook her head as though to clear it, rose, and set her hand in the *chieri's,* her claws retracted.

"Avarra be blessed!" Elhali whispered. "Kaznir's done it!"

Day Spear looped her tail about Kaznir's waist, and the *chieri* draped an arm across her shoulders, as they paced from the clearing into the Hellers foothills.

Jerilynn released her breath in a gape. "They'll never believe *this* when I report back to Thendara. I almost don't believe it myself."

DAW

BESTSELLERS BY MARION ZIMMER BRADLEY

THE DARKOVER NOVELS

The Founding

☐ DARKOVER LANDFALL — UE2234—$3.95

The Ages of Chaos

☐ HAWKMISTRESS! — UE2239—$3.95
☐ STORMQUEEN! — UE2310—$4.50

The Hundred Kingdoms

☐ TWO TO CONQUER — UE2174—$3.50
☐ THE HEIRS OF HAMMERFELL (hardcover) — UE2395—$18.95

The Renunciates (Free Amazons)

☐ THE SHATTERED CHAIN — UE2308—$3.95
☐ THENDARA HOUSE — UE2240—$3.95
☐ CITY OF SORCERY — UE2332—$3.95

Against the Terrans: The First Age

☐ THE SPELL SWORD — UE2237—$3.95
☐ THE FORBIDDEN TOWER — UE2373—$4.95

Against the Terrans: The Second Age

☐ THE HERITAGE OF HASTUR — UE2413—$4.50
☐ SHARRA'S EXILE — UE2309—$3.95

THE DARKOVER ANTHOLOGIES
with The Friends of Darkover

☐ DOMAINS OF DARKOVER — UE2407—$3.95
☐ FOUR MOONS OF DARKOVER — UE2305—$3.95
☐ FREE AMAZONS OF DARKOVER — UE2430—$3.95
☐ THE KEEPER'S PRICE — UE2236—$3.95
☐ THE OTHER SIDE OF THE MIRROR — UE2185—$3.50
☐ RED SUN OF DARKOVER — UE2230—$3.95
☐ SWORD OF CHAOS — UE2172—$3.50

DAW

The first new DARKOVER novel in five years!

THE HEIRS OF HAMMERFELL

Darkover: The Age of the Hundred Kingdoms
by MARION ZIMMER BRADLEY

Set in the age of The Hundred Kingdoms, *The Heirs of Hammerfell* takes place in a time of war and strife when Darkover was divided by border conflicts into numerous small, antagonistic kingdoms. It focuses on a devastating clan feud between two of these realms—Hammerfell and Storn—a feud which has seen the land soaked red with blood for countless generations. But now Storn has struck what may prove to be Hammerfell's death stroke, setting the ancestral castle ablaze, slaying its lord, and sending its lady fleeing into the night with her twin infant sons, Alastair and Conn.

Conn is separated from his mother and lost to her on that fateful night, but she and Alastair find sanctuary in Thendara City, among the wealthy and the *laran*-gifted, keeping the memory of Hammerfell alive with them in exile. Yet Conn, too, survives, rescued by a loyal servant and raised in secret among those who would see the might of Storn overthrown and the banner of Hammerfell flying proudly high once again.

But it is not until Conn's *laran* manifests that the fates of the twins are finally, inextricably linked in a pattern which could bring a new beginning or total ruin to Hammerfell and its heirs. . . .

☐ **Hardcover Edition** (UE2395—$18.95)
